"No, I will hold on

"You still do not trust me.

"The Cross contains hidden powers that could be harmful to your kind. I have already proven I can carry it."

He met her gaze. "As you wish." His words were evenly spaced, and he lowered his hand.

"What next?"

"We meet Ohma and the others in Jahl."

"Can you ride?" she asked, looking at his bandaged leg and chest.

"What? These few scratches? I have had worse in the training ring." He smiled down into her eyes and raised his hand to tuck a lock of white-gold hair behind her ear. "Were you afraid for me?"

"I still need your help."

His hand dropped to his side. "Of course, how foolish of me." He stepped back. "I should have remembered." He made to turn away, but she grasped his arm.

"I am glad you are alive."

He expelled a short, dry laugh and pulled from her grip. "Sure, you are." His tone was hard, dry. "I suggest you saddle the horse while I dress." He raised a brow. "If I still have clothes, that is."

Tannith turned away as visions of sculpted, bronze muscle flittered through her consciousness. She had never seen a man naked before, never realized a man could be so artistically beautiful, albeit covered in blood. "I mended your clothes the best I could," she said quietly, her head bowed, her hair falling forward to hide the flush heating her cheeks. He would know it was she who had undressed him. "Your tunic and breeches are in your pack." She swung away and fled...

Praise for Julie A. D'Arcy

Cross of Tarlis: The Reckoning

by

Julie A. D'Arcy

The Tarlisian Sagas, Book Two

Cross of Tarlis: The Reckoning

Cover Art by *Kristian Norris*

The Wild Rose Press, Inc.
PO Box 708
Adams Basin, NY 14410-0708
Visit us at www.thewildrosepress.com

Publishing History
First Edition, 2022
Trade Paperback ISBN 978-1-5092-4305-1
Digital ISBN 978-1-5092-4306-8

The Tarlisian Sagas, Book Two
Published in the United States of America

Dedication

This book is dedicated to my beautiful daughters, Errin and Tegan, for all the times we missed together while I was lost in the world of Tarlis.
And to my two lovely grandchildren, Oliver and Lyla.

Acknowledgments

To my writing group friends: Susan Graham, Sandra Alan, Anne Smith, Ruth Ross, Heather Williams, and Ian Deakin who were always there with a helpful word or suggestion. And my dear friends in faraway places: Mary Brehe, Steve Westcott, Kathryn Bryan, Deborah Nemeth, Sherri Good, and Frank D'Arcy.

Also, a big thank you to my publisher, The Wild Rose Press, my extraordinary editor, Lill Farrell and my excellent proof readers, Malcolm Barber, and Cheyenne Chambers.

Dorrachian War Song

We Dorrachians stand and fight,
Great courage fills our heart.
Ever for us, the sun will shine,
Ever the night depart.
Our faith is in the power of right,
No truth, no shame can cheat.
Ten thousand times we'd rather die,
Than sound a base retreat.
So, come to me, oh enemy mine,
Lift your swords up high,
And death to you this day will come,
And with your Gods ye'll dine.

~Julie A. D'Arcy

Chapter One

Five hundred years have passed since the great Mage War.
The Necromancer, Sernon of Asamos, has risen from the dead.
His insidious presence now dominates the world of Tarlis.

An orange sun spread its last golden rays across the jagged tops of the Wolfstag Mountains, bringing with it a chill wind portending to the night ahead. The white moon had already begun its slow ascent into the ever-changing hues of the night sky. The smaller mauve moon trailed lazily in its wake.

Tannith of Ellenroh, Elisian Princess descended from the legendary King of Dragonbane, dragged her fur-lined cloak closer about her shoulders. Although she shared Phoenix with Kaden, the Warrior Prince of Glen-Dorrach, and her chest was pressed tightly against the warmth of his back, the biting wind still infiltrated her body.

She turned her head to the side, peering into the trees as they wound their way through the gnarled forest of large ornamental fig and miniature Macohann trees. She gave an inward laugh. Why that name, she wondered, as most of the trees were at least thirty feet tall. But then again, the other variety stood around sixty feet tall with trunks close to ten feet in circumference, making them perfect dwellings for the Elves to build their homes. She broke from her thoughts as something caught the corner of her eye. A Dryad. A woodland sprite. A fabled creature of Fae. Although it held female form, it had taken the appearance of the fig tree's flaky white bark like a chameleon blending perfectly with its surrounding.

She thought they only existed in Faerie tales.

Yet, why not? She had seen a myriad of strange creatures over the long days of her quest for the Cross; talking trees, griffins, a Druid Mage, an ice tiger, and now they rode toward a vampire water sprite who drank the blood of the living.

And should they survive that, they were to seek a race of dwarves who had not been seen for several hundred years. She gave a short laugh.

"Did you say something? Are you all right?" Kaden asked over his shoulder.

She murmured an affirmative, realizing the warrior prince had allowed Phoenix his head to pick the truest path through the thick piles of dried leaves and white flaky bark strewn across the forest floor with its loose sticks and jutting rocks.

The beast of an animal. She knew had she been riding him he would have bolted by now.

She laid her cheek against Kaden's heavy fur cloak and peered into the surrounding forest hoping to catch sight of another Dryad. The more she looked, the more of them appeared. Almost every ornamental fig, she noted, had a Dryad clutching and writhing in its naked glory against the trunks. Several had partially detached themselves, turned their heads, and raised their hands in greeting. She had no idea whether to reciprocate or not.

She pushed a stray lock of hair from her face as the wind caught it. When she glanced back, they had once more blended into the silvery-white trunks and could only be seen if she really focused. Or was it all her imagination? But no. As they rode close to another large fig, it moved and raised its hand in greeting or, she shrugged, was it goodbye? She leaned closer to Kaden's ear. "Did you see…?"

"Yes," he cut in quietly. "They are known to be gentle folk."

"You have seen them before?"

"Yes." He did not elaborate. "However, to be certain they do not see us as a threat we must not draw too much attention to ourselves."

She nodded against his broad back and turned her thoughts from the Dryad. She had other matters plaguing her, and she allowed her memory to flow back to earlier that evening when she and Kaden had bid farewell to their comrades, the wily old mage, Ohma; a small red-haired Faerie, Skylah; and an enchanted ice tiger, Erik.

Etan, her bodyguard, and best friend, had been captured by the Urakians and the evil priest leading them. Ohma had released his spirit to the air, attempting to seek the young captain. On locating him, the Druid grasped the Urakians were headed toward the old military fort in Kerbac.

Ohma and the others planned to attempt a rescue while she and the Wolfhead Prince began their separate journey. They were to snatch the second part of the Cross from beneath the nose of a blood-drinking Nymph.

She had begun this quest to locate the remaining three pieces of the legendary Cross which had once belonged to the god Magus.

She laughed inwardly. If someone had told her the story in which they were cast, she would have been hard-pressed to believe it. A castle besieged daily by blue-skinned Urakians, a newly risen evil sorcerer, and his henchman Dannock-Shae, a former priest of the Origen. And still, she was certain there would be more trials to face should they survive the night.

She snapped from her reverie as Kaden drew Phoenix to a halt. "There," he said, pointing up at the sky.

She glanced up to see the white and mauve moons beginning to merge.

"That is the sign for which Ohma told us to watch."

As he spoke, a brilliant flash of silver light spread a burnished cloak across the tops of the tall spruce forest up ahead. Then, as quickly as it appeared, it disappeared.

"Did Ohma say anything to you about a silver light?"

"No." He shook his head and dismounted. "But should it lead us to our destination, I would be most grateful." He helped her slide down from Phoenix's back, not that she needed any help. But it was easier than getting into a squabble over something so trivial. She released a hefty sigh of relief to have her feet set firmly on flat ground again. Riding all day perched on a blanket behind Kaden, she found she was aching in places she had no idea could ache.

****

The two moons separated and hung in the sky like lanterns. Their light filtered down through the trees that surrounded the far side of the lake. Frogs croaked among the reeds and an occasional ripple could be seen where a fish skimmed too close to the surface. Night closed in, and the stars shone like pinpoints of diamonds scattered across a cloak of black velvet. In the center of the lake, the water churned. A vortex appeared, and from that vortex a flat-topped rock bearing a shining object emerged.

Moonlight bathed the rock, and for several heartbeats, the two moons merged as one. Then the moons parted. But all was not as it had been…

A shadow of a tree fell across the lake, and from that shadow, she emerged.

Sleek, black hair rippled over pale shoulders. A form-fitting, pale green gown hid nothing of her slender curves. To many, she would appear beautiful, but like an apple with a worm at its core, corruption lay within. She was a creature of the night, her sole purpose to guard her treasure. She was *Lan-awn-Shee*, Glaisling of the Lake.

She stepped from the water, taking in her surroundings—the lake and trees—always the same. How often had she tried to leave but was drawn back by the mystical shackles with which the sorcerer had bound her? A bright image flashed before her eyes. She groaned and shook her head, but the vision persisted—a shining gold object on a black rock. Ah, yes…

Turning, she stared out across the lake, possessiveness overwhelming her. It was there. She could see its soft glow highlighted by the darkness. She smiled serenely and stepped down into the water, losing herself in its cold depths, making her way toward her coveted prize.

****

Several hundred paces to the north, Kilain of the Elisi, a middle-aged hunter from the House of Dorian, shook his head in puzzlement. Not an hour ago he had witnessed a silver flash lighting up the treetops and two moons merge into one. Despite the stories of strange disappearances near the lake, he was led by curiosity. He had to know why the sky turned silver. It would make a fine tale for the telling at the Hunters Feast.

Cutting north through the forest, he made his way toward the shore of the lake and stopped to lean on his wooden staff peering out over the water.

His curiosity met with disappointment. The water lay still, bathed in glittering moonlight. Except for the occasional ripple caused by a fish or a Night Eagle diving for its supper, he could see nothing out of the ordinary.

He shrugged, about to turn away when something caught his eye—a small pinpoint of gold in the center of the lake. As he watched, the light turned green and grew brighter. It emanated from a large, flat rock barely visible from the shore. However, he prided himself on his eyesight.

Could the light have something to do with that which lit up the trees? He shrugged. He would not know until he swam out there in the morning, though as he thought it, he moved closer to the edge, failing in the moonlight to notice the mushy earth beneath his feet, too late.

The muddy bank, caused by the receding water level, gave way, and he fell headlong down the steep bank, through high Soap Reeds into the night-black water below.

Gasping for breath, he struggled to break the surface and find his feet. Wading through the water and gaining the bank, he spat out a mouthful of rank lake water and silt. It tasted of uncooked turtle, turning his stomach, and he began to shake from the water's icy temperature. His teeth chattered and shivers lanced his body, prickling his arms and legs. He had to get out of the water, or he would end up with a fever.

He scrambled and clawed his way up the muddy bank, missing the soft hiss behind him and the long-taloned fingers reaching for his leg.

Gaining the bank and solid ground, he stopped to wring the water from his shirt and tunic and push his sodden hair from his face. He gave the lake a last cursory look, then turned and wended his way into the forest toward the camp he had set before his attention had been drawn by the light. Come morning, he would swim out and see what lay on the rock ledge.

Being an experienced huntsman, he soon had a blaze burning and hung his shirt and breeches over a large leafy bush to dry. He pulled a spare pair of leggings and a jerkin from his pack, which he had collected with his horse from within the trees.

After donning the dry clothes, he set about preparing a fat cony he had brought down with his bow earlier that eve. As the meat browned slowly on the spit, he munched on dried fruit and hazelnuts and partook of a draught of his wife's fine mead from the flask she had packed. It rid the chill from his bones.

A twig snapped, and he tensed. He reached for his bow, notched, and aimed at the dense stance of fir trees to his left. Instinct told him there was something or someone in the shadows, watching.

"Show yourself. I know you're there." Confident in his ability to hit whatever it was should there be trouble, he was not overly worried. He had once belonged to the King's archers but had left that life after wedding a lass from the House of Minalta in Lemma. He smiled, feeling

7

well satisfied with his life. A fine woman, three strapping boys, and a full stomach…what more could a man ask for?

A woman stepped from the trees, and all thought of his good wife dissolved. Ebony hair coiled about her alabaster shoulders like a living thing, drawing attention to the low-cut linen gown clinging to the slender curves of her body. The gown hid nothing from his sight.

Her large, slanted eyes glowed like black jewels in her pale oval face, bright, cold, and seductive. Her red lips, full and wide, held a smile that was sensually inviting.

For several heartbeats, he stared, motionless, then he dropped his bow and closed the gap between them. "Lose your way, lass? Or did you slip in the lake as I did? You are soaked. The lake can be treacherous at night."

The woman did not respond or move a muscle.

"Come, warm yourself by my fire." Kilain took her cold hand in his.

Still, she did not react but continued to watch him in the same heavy-lidded, seductive manner. It unnerved him. Why did she not speak? "Now lass, do not be shy." He attempted to draw her toward the fire. "There is plenty of heat for all, and I have food, a plump roasted cony."

She hung back, and he turned to face her. The woman took the step separating their bodies and laid her free hand against his thigh. His first instinct was to pull away, having always been faithful to his wife. Then he smiled and relaxed, musing it would only be this once and no one would know. Drawing her closer within the circle of his arms, he lowered his lips to her neck, licking, sucking, and tasting her skin. She countered by sliding her cool palm over the bulge in his mole-skin leggings.

He swallowed, his mouth suddenly dry, his breath coming harsh, pluming in the misty air. His blood ran hot. "So that's the way of it," he murmured, his eyes feeling heavy in his head as his gaze slid down to the swell of her breasts. "I do not know where you came from, but you are a welcome addition on a chilly night." He raised his palms to cup and knead her breasts.

She remained passive beneath his touch, emboldening him further. He dragged her gown down and squeezed and plucked at her nipples with callused fingers.

The woman raised her arms, encouraging his mouth to her breast.

"Anything to please a lady." He smiled, his anticipation growing. Lowering his thick lips to do her bidding, he drew one pale globe into his mouth, sucking and nipping at its taut peak. When he felt her soft lips nibbling at his neck, he thought he had finally reached Elysium. He hardened and swelled against the woman's pliant body. He thought he would surely burst if he did not take her soon.

Then all changed. Rigid arms fastened about his waist like steel bands, locking him tight to her chest. Sharp, pointed teeth punctured his neck. Agony, deep and penetrating, ripped through him. A cry tore from his throat, echoing into the night. He wrenched free from her mouth, stumbled, and fell. With arrow speed, she was on him, holding fast, feasting on his blood, drawing all strength from his limbs.

Soon there was no fight left.

He lay staring up at the sky as she hovered above him, and the last of his life's blood flowed onto the soft grass beneath.

A sad smile formed on his lips as he envisioned his wife's serene face wavering before his eyes. "It was only once," he whispered. Then the pain was gone. Release and relief came as one when all life faded, and his soul slipped free.

****

Her long-taloned fingers tore into the man's flesh. Lan-awn-Shee drank swiftly, lifting her shaggy mane of dank, dark hair often, peering into the trees for more prey. She had now reverted to the nightmarish creature she truly was. The blood burned sweet upon her tongue. 'Twas a long time since she had tasted the blood of Man, and this meager offering far from satisfied the insatiable hunger gnawing at her vitals.

Slowly, methodically, she fed. When the man's body was drained and shriveled, nothing more than a husk, the vampiress kicked it aside and turned for the lake. Her hunger briefly satisfied, she sank back into the water to wait. However, before she submerged, she lifted her nose and sniffed the air.

It would not be long before she fed again.

****

The moons had risen high and separated when Tannith and Kaden arrived at the campfire they had spotted from a distance, drawn by the stench of something burning. They found the charcoaled cony well-roasted over the spit, and not long after, Kaden made the gruesome discovery of what once was a man.

Tannith stood staring down at the body as her night vision cut in. "He is barely recognizable. However, there is enough to know this is Kilain, the Hunt Lord of Drue Forest. I spoke to this man not three days ago."

"You knew him?"

"He was once in my father's service—a fine archer." She frowned. "A bear?" She queried.

Kaden, who had dropped to his knees beside the body, said, "No. I don't think so. Let me get a better look." He rose and plucked a piece of gorse from a large gorse-bush, wrapped it around a stick, held it to the glowing campfire, and the small branch flared to life, lighting up the dry, pinched face of the dead man. "This reminds me of a body I once saw as a child when my father took me to the Glen-Dorrach Museum of Rare Artifacts. The body had dated back to the time before the world toppled."

All the man's blood had been drained from his body, reducing him to a dry, empty husk. He swallowed as if there were a lump in his throat and dropped the branch to stamp it out. Even to a hardened warrior, the sight was a little too much. "No animal did this. A bear does not drink the blood of its prey."

He met her eyes across the body.

"Then it was her?"

He nodded. "I fear so."

Kaden grasped Tannith's arm, leading her back to the horse. "The Glaisling has claimed her first victim. Now she has tasted blood, she will be doubly dangerous. I will track her and see where her trail leads. Unsaddle the horse and wait by the fire."

"No," she replied emphatically. "I am no child to be shielded from danger. We should stay together."

She stood tall and proud before him, and he thought he had never seen her looking more lovely, her chin raised defiantly, her fair hair scraped back from her face, and her alabaster skin a pale glow in the moonlight. He wanted no more than to take her in his arms and sear his brand onto her body.

"Kaden." She waved a hand in front of his face. "Are you all right?"

He snapped from his reverie as she touched his arm. He frowned. "What did you say?"

"I said, it would be safer to stay together."

"You are not afraid?"

"Of course not. I am a shield maiden of Ellenroh. I fought on the battlements of Dragonbane Castle against the Urakians. And for the God's sake, I have fought Griffins."

He studied her for several moments, then as if making up his mind, nodded. "Fine, but be quiet and careful."

"Have no fear, Dorrachian, I want the Cross as much as you do."

****

His lips compressed and Tannith thought he was about to say something more, but instead he took her hand and led her through the underbrush the rest of the way to the shore. He had no trouble locating Lan-awn-Shee's small, delicate tracks, and the water sprite made no attempt to hide them. The trail brought them to the edge of the water below a high, muddy bank, and Kaden crouched to examine the footprints.

"What is it?" She asked quietly.

"The Glaisling entered here," he whispered back.

Tannith shuddered and peered across the dark water. "Perhaps we should approach from the other side."

He shook his head. "No, her gaze is probably fixed on us right now."

A ripple ran across the surface of the lake causing a

tremor to prick Tannith's neck and trail down her spine. The water seemed tranquil enough. Yet, somewhere out there, in the darkness below the surface or above, evil lurked. Watching. Waiting for them to make a mistake.

"Have you the dagger Ohma enchanted?" Kaden extended his hand.

She drew a silver blade from the scabbard strapped to her waist and handed it to him. He plucked a reed from the bank, tested the blade, then gave it back. "If anything should happen to me, do not attempt to be brave. I want you to run. Understand?"

She held her tongue, refusing to answer. Of course, she would not run. She was no child to flee at the sign of danger.

"You will do as I say, and no arguing. I cannot do what I must without knowing you are safe." He took her two hands in his own and brought them to his lips.

She remained silent for several long heartbeats, then softened. She liked him like this. Caring. "I will do as you say, but only if it is the last choice I can make."

Kaden regarded her solemnly, holding her gaze in the dim light. Then he raised one of her hands to his lips and kissed it. "Very well," he said, and released her. He stepped back with a thoughtful look on his face, then seemed to make a decision. He reached into his cloak pocket, withdrew a small wooden object, and placed it on the grass at his feet.

"What is it?"

"Ohma said it would see us safely across the lake."

"It measures no larger than my small finger."

He shrugged. "I must cover it with this powder." He brought out another small leather pouch, from around his neck this time, and yanked, breaking the cord. Opening

13

the pouch, he shook out a fine, red powder and coated the object on the ground. "Now I chant the spell," he said, grinning.

"You. A spell?" A gurgle of laughter escaped Tannith's lips. "You cannot be serious." She paused, sobering. "Are you?"

"I admit to feeling a tad foolish. At first, I refused, but Ohma insisted it was the only way to cross the water. I am not one to believe in magickle incantations, and the Druid's magick thus far has not proved good."

"Still, you must try."

He nodded and glared at the piece of wood, wishing he were somewhere else. Taking a deep breath, he pronounced the words the Druid entrusted to him.

"Kinnanah, Hammen, Barhem de Danan."

The tiny object swelled and grew, spreading, stretching, expanding, until it reached the length of two spears and was wide enough to seat him and Tannith comfortably. The ends tapered into points. Inside the craft lay a paddle the length of a broadsword. Tannith glanced down at the contraption. "A canoe?"

"It seems Ohma's magick is improving." Kaden laid his sword on the bank. "I will leave this. I will take my four knives." By the light of the moons, he pushed the canoe down the bank into the dark, murky waters of Tirfo Thuinn and stepped into the boat.

Tannith followed, leaving her sword on the bank, and climbed hesitantly into the narrow craft. Soon they were gliding toward the pale green luminescence at the center of the lake. They had noted earlier that the piece changed color, alternating from green to gold then back again.

****

Kaden grew more anxious with each stroke of the paddle. The rock shelf was wider than he anticipated. He would need to step from the canoe to reach the Cross. It was something he had not contemplated doing.

"Let *me* fetch the piece," said Tannith, drawing the same conclusion. "You can stand guard."

"No. I am stronger and more capable of fighting off the Glaisling should she attack."

"I am nimbler," she bounced back.

"No, you stay with the boat. If it drifts, we will have to swim. That is something I do not relish in the dead of night with a female vampire lurking."

They drew in alongside the rock, and Kaden steadied the canoe. "Do you see anything?" he whispered, glancing back at Tannith.

She shook her head. "Perhaps she is sleeping."

"I doubt it. This is a very special time for her. Ohma made the Glaisling to guard the Cross. I doubt she would waste her time sleeping. Mark my words, she will not be far."

He stepped from the canoe onto the rock shelf. The water reached to his ankles and was icy cold. A shiver prickled down his spine, but whether it was from the cold or the thought that she watched him, he had no time to ponder. He would grab the piece of the Cross and run.

He waded silently through the water toward the center of the rock shelf where the icon lay several inches below the surface.

Three steps. Kaden counted them out softly beneath his breath. "One, two…" He said a quick prayer to the gods-who-were, snatched his prize, and stared straight up into the sensual dark eyes of Lan-awn-Shee.

Beautiful, her eyes sparkled with hungry

anticipation.

He could not move. Rendered immovable by the sight of her pale, gleaming breasts fully exposed to his view. Intense sexual awareness slashed through his loins, igniting them to a fever pitch. His heart pounded and blood pumped, burning through his veins. The woman was exquisite in every detail—black silken hair, milky skin, sensual red mouth. She held him mesmerized, frozen like a cony in firelight, barely able to breathe even as she drifted closer. Her hands outstretched toward his throat.

Tannith screamed. High pitched and shrill, it cut through the air.

The Glaisling's enthralling spell unraveled.

He turned to flee, but Lan-awn-Shee pounced. Knocked off balance, he stumbled and fell, and cold water overwhelmed him. She was on him in an instant, arms closing like metal bands, her needle-sharp teeth sinking into his neck.

He thrust his knee into her stomach, and her arms slackened. He kicked out for the surface, but taloned fingers tore into his back, spreading fire through his flesh. Her hand clamped onto his leg, and he floundered, dragged deeper beneath the night-dark water. The pressure in his ears gave him the sensation of being crushed. His tortured lungs burned like fire and screamed for air.

Fear lent him strength.

He kicked, striking the creature in the head.

She released him, and he shot upwards, his lungs to the point of explosion, his vision distorted. He focused on the dim light above. His body sprang from the water like a cork, and he gasped for air.

****

Tannith watched him break the surface, Lan-awn-Shee at his side. She grasped Ohma's silver dagger and dived, coming up to see the Glaisling lock her arms about Kaden's shoulders, holding him immobile. Then the Vampire Sprite bared her fangs, and a gush of Kaden's blood stained the water.

"No!" Without hesitation to her own plight, she pulled back, steadied, and punched the dagger between the Glaisling's shoulder blades. The vampire screamed and released Kaden with a snarl, pushing him aside. She caught Tannith's wrist and held it away as she struggled to stab again. This time Lan-awn-Shee's mouth bore down on *her* neck. It did not connect. Kaden's hands closed around the Glaisling's throat from behind.

Lan-awn-Shee rounded with inhuman strength and elbowed him in the head. He fell away, unmoving. The vampiress swung back to Tannith, but she was ready. She brought the dagger down straight into the creature's heart.

The Glaisling's dark eyes widened. She opened her mouth, and her canines glowed in the moonlight, but she uttered no sound. Slowly, Lan-awn-Shee, vampire spirit of the lake, slid beneath the dark surface of the water for the last time.

Tannith abandoned the dagger and struck out for Kaden, who floated unnaturally, still face down in the water.

****

On the far side of the lake, well back in the shadows, two Urakian soldiers awoke to a demonic cry.

"What was that?" asked the first man, his pale blue eyes bulging as he came awake.

17

"A wolf. Go back to sleep."

His companion yawned, but as the first man slipped into slumber and his snores diffused the air, Captain Kraal of the Imperial Urakian Army leaned over and placed another log on the fire, then lay back and pulled his field blanket to his chin. The red-bearded man frowned into the darkness, not quite able to dismiss the unholy scream from his thoughts.

For many hours, Kraal stared into the night, his sight never wavering from the lake.

Chapter Two

Etan awoke to the stink of stale sweat and urine, his head at an awkward angle, and his cheek pressed into a ragged, moth-eaten blanket separating him from the moldy straw covering the floor. He forced down the bile in his throat trying not to gag and turned his head. Rope cut painfully into his wrists. Every inch of his body screamed in pain.

The soldiers had not been kind, resorting to fists and feet in the end to subdue him for capture, and the long walk through the mud flats and desert had not helped his injuries. At least he had dispatched two of the devil's whelps to their dark gods before they took him.

He gave a small grin through cut and swollen lips, then grimaced again as pain struck his ankle. He struggled to roll onto his side and spied a dim light seeping through a small, barred window in the iron door. He was in a dungeon, deep in the bowels of the Old Fort. A short laugh escaped his lips. Of all the ways he had imagined his death, he had never thought it would be starving to death in a rat-infested dungeon. He could see no way out of his predicament.

He lay back and stared at the ceiling, trying to remember what little he knew of the Old Fort. The fort was a remnant of the past, built decades earlier when the Hill Tribes of the Wolfstag Mountains and the Wild Men of Pantheon had banded together in a futile attempt to conquer the Kingdom of Glen-Dorrach.

Fearful of attack by the great number of natives, and with Wolveryne Castle unable to accommodate more men, Radin of the Wolfhead, King Farramon's great-grandfather, had ordered the fort to be enlarged at all costs. Because of the rapid rate of construction, the structure had been unstable. Its gray-green walls, squat purposeful towers, and massive water defenses occupied a thirty-acre site on the outskirts of Kerbac. Concentric in design, it had a seemingly impregnable series of moats and battlements, radiating in a succession of larger and larger circles from its inner ward. It was the main training center for new recruits as well as a backup should Wolveryne Castle fall.

The Hill Tribesmen were eventually beaten back into the desert after eight summers of fierce, bloody fighting, their casualties heavy, their hatred for the round-eyes running deep.

An uneasy peace had settled across the land over the summers, with only an occasional flare-up of trouble from the closer Lowland tribes. The Glen-Dorrach force, most being conscripts, had been sent on their way with five gold deemahs to return home, or others went on to become mercenaries, seeking service elsewhere.

The fort, of no more use, was abandoned and left to fall into disrepair. The keep now held a slanted lean, threatening at any moment to topple backward into the dry moat.

A scratching in the corner of the room brought him back to reality. Where, he wondered, was Tannith? Would his friends come for him? Or would they continue on with the quest? Knowing Tannith as he did, she would be torn between duty to her people and loyalty to him as a friend. He hoped Kaden insisted she continue with their mission.

A pulling on the bindings at his back had him tensing. He shook his hands vigorously to ward off what he considered could be a rat. He inched forward several paces across the floor, only to have the tugging persist. He wrenched against his bonds. Hemp cut deep into his raw flesh, rekindling old agony. He felt the warm stickiness of blood oozing from the wound and stifled the nightmarish images of emaciated rats feasting on his flesh.

"Stop struggling."

"Skylah! What are you doing here?"

"Hush!" The Faerie appeared before him. "I have come to get you out."

"Where are the others?" he whispered.

Her lips tightened. "You mean, Tannith?" She paused. "The princess has traveled to the lake with Prince Kaden. We are to meet them at Jahl, or Antibba if they do not arrive in time—I will explain later. Ohma and Erik are dealing with the guards. All I have to do is cut you lose and find a way out of here."

"Why are you doing this—risking your life for me?" When she did not answer, he spoke again. "Will you not give me an answer?" he prompted gently. "You have saved me not once, but twice now. Why?"

Skylah shook her head. "Do you not know, Etan? Can you not guess?"

Unable to face the truth gleaming in her emerald eyes, he turned away. Of course, he knew. He felt it too—the strong attraction, however impossible it was. The feelings so plainly written across her tiny face matched his precisely. Sadness and a longing for a love doomed to failure. Better he told her a lie than to have her live in false hope for something that could never be. "The reason eludes me, Faerie, but I am grateful anyway for your help." He glanced toward the door, unable to bear the condemnation in her eyes.

She lifted into the air. "Then let it be so." She blinked back her tears.

Etan groaned inwardly. Filled with self-loathing, he refrained from speaking while she worked on his bonds. Little by little, the hemp strands parted under Skylah's tiny knife.

"Erik should have dispatched the guards in the hall by now. Ohma was to manage the gatekeeper. All we have to do is find a way past the sentry at the door and we will be out of here."

"I have a plan," he said quietly.

"As I knew you would."

Etan was about to explain, when he was interrupted by a harsh grunt followed by a muffled thud and a rattle of keys. The cell door creaked back on its hinges to reveal a figure dressed in indigo robes. In his hand, he clutched a rosewood staff.

"Ohma." Skylah flew up to greet him.

"Well met, little one. I see you have accomplished your task."

"And you, yours."

"Indeed." The Druid's face dissolved into a thousand fine lines as he turned to Etan. "Still on the floor I see, boy. You seem to have a penchant for them."

"Is that your notion of a jest, old man? I am not amused. Hurry and cut me free."

"All through!" called Skylah, swooping down, and severing the last strand of rope.

Etan tried to stand but stumbled and dropped to his hands and knees. Ohma bent to help him to his feet.

"I can manage," the captain grumbled, shaking free and stepping back. "I am just weak. I have not eaten for two days, and they allowed me just enough water to keep me from death. I appear worse than I am."

"And you smell twice as bad," Skylah called, shooting toward the door.

Ohma chuckled, and Etan stared after her. "What did you say?"

"The sentry is waking," she threw back. "Ohma, your staff!"

The old mage scurried past her and struck the man to the skull. "There, that should settle him." He turned as Etan came up beside him. "Give me a hand to gag him. We can lock him in your cell. That way no one will hear if he cries out."

"It would be easier to slit the vermin's throat."

Ohma picked up the guard's legs and began dragging him toward the prison door. "I have taken an oath. I cannot spill blood."

"But I can." Etan's voice was cold and edged with steel. He bent and slipped the guard's dagger from his baldric. "If you have no stomach for the deed, leave."

Ohma dropped the man's legs, and Etan rested his gaze on Skylah hovering nearby. "You too." He motioned with his head. "Go! Get out of here."

She turned and fled after Ohma as he strode down the dimly lit corridor.

Etan watched them, a determined slant to his hard jaw. Then he knelt, and with ease born of necessity, drew the dagger across the man's jugular and straightened. He wiped the knife on the guard's crimson cloak and slipped the blade into his own belt.

"He and I had a debt to settle," he told Ohma, catching him up in the corridor.

He was the guard who dragged him behind his horse on the way to the fort.

An Elisian always paid their debts.

Chapter Three

In the chill light of dawn, Dannock-Shae, high priest of the Urakians, stood in the courtyard of the Old Fort. A premonition of danger held him uneasy.

He had no idea what was going on, Sernon had not deigned to enlighten him. A hush fell across the courtyard as he watched the sorcerer dismount the steps of the main entrance and stride toward him. Yet, could it be called striding? He floated more than walked.

He stopped at Dannock's side.

Dressed in rich robes of purple and gold, he fronted at least a thousand warriors. On the wave of his hand, they dropped to their knees onto the red dirt of the courtyard. With another command, they rose again.

However, five Urakian soldiers in the front line separate from their comrades did not.

The soldiers were dressed in full battle regalia—steel-ringed chainmail extending from neck to knee with sleeves to the elbows. The skirts were split front and back for ease in the saddle, and leather leggings protected their legs. Laced behind and attached to the coat was a coif covering the head, protecting the throat. Over this was worn silver helmets, visors open.

"Do you know why you are here?" Dannock-Shae heard Sernon ask Captain Bracus, a veteran soldier of twenty summers.

"No, my liege."

"You let a highly valuable prisoner escape. Have you nothing to say in your defense?"

"The man was aided by magick, Sire."

"That is no excuse for incompetence. I expect my men to lay down their lives in my service. Is that clear?" His voice rang out over the ocean of faces.

The captain bowed his head. "Yes, Sire."

"I should have you drawn and quartered," Sernon intoned softly, staring impassively at the five men.

Bracus's face paled.

"Yet, I have decided to be merciful." A cold light appeared in the sorcerer's death-like eyes.

The soldier relaxed his shoulders. "You are most gracious, Sire." He began to rise.

"Did I say you could stand?"

Instantly, he dropped to his knees.

Sernon smiled coldly. "Remove your helmets and coifs and place them at your feet."

The five soldiers complied, glancing down.

"Look at me!"

Their heads shot up to stare at their liege.

"That's better." A grim smile curved his lips as he raised a slender hand and extended it. As he pointed, a red light shot from his second finger, lancing toward the soldier on the end of the line to rest just above his shoulder, level with his throat. "As I promised, I shall be merciful. You will die without pain."

Before the horror of Sernon's words could register in the man's mind, the sorcerer directed the beam of light across the throat of the soldier at the end of the line and continued through the other men's necks in quick succession, and their world slipped away.

****

Dannock could barely believe what he was seeing. Blood ran, and heads toppled one by one to the red dirt, to rest beside their silver helms glinting in the newly risen sun.

Although their lives had been extinguished, the bodies remained kneeling, straight and unmoving, in the same position as if frozen by time.

"Let this be a lesson to those who fail me!" Sernon's voice rang out, deep and resonant, his eyes burning with an inner fervor.

A hush settled over the crowded courtyard. No one dared to whisper. Not even the wind dared to stir.

The sorcerer closed his eyes, raised his hands to the sky. and began to chant. *"Neela, Balah, Norendoch!"* Deep concentration marred his pallid face. Black clouds gathered overhead, billowing out to blanket the formerly clear sky, swallowing the sun. A chill blew in from the north, whipping at their cloaks, churning up red dust from every corner, and soft rain fell.

With the first drop of moisture to touch his face, Sernon lowered his hands and opened his eyes. When he signaled to the six Urakian priests standing to his left, they rushed forward carrying a flat altar stone to set upon a raised dais of bronze. Made of solid onyx, the altar measured six feet in length, three feet across. and two inches thick.

With a snap of his fingers, two sentries appeared dragging a flaxen-haired girl of no more than sixteen summers. Dressed in a gown of transparent white silk that molded to the slight contours of her body, she struggled. Her terrified violet eyes peered up at the sorcerer as she beseeched him, but he ignored her. She was merely a means to an end. He gestured to his men, and they tossed her down on the altar stone and secured her flailing arms and legs.

Only then did the sorcerer look down at her.

"Help me!" the girl cried, turning from him. She fought her bonds, but her struggles were of little worth. "In the name of Magus, release me. I will do anything you ask."

"Be still! I do not recognize your gods, especially that one."

Tears flowed from the girl's eyes, trickling down her pale cheeks. She opened her mouth to scream, but Sernon placed a finger to her lips. "You are vital to my plans," he whispered, a cold smile curving his full lips. "But perhaps I will leave it to my men to decide your fate?"

She nodded, terror marring her small, delicate face.

Sernon straightened and stared at the soldiers standing in rough formation before him. "This girl seeks mercy. I ask of you as representatives of the Urakian people, would you grant mercy to one of those who seek to destroy you? One who stands in the way of the Urakians becoming the greatest power in all Tarlis, the greatest power in the Universe?" He pointed at the crowd with one hand while the other rent the girl's flimsy gown from neck to navel, exposing white breasts and stomach.

The girl screamed, and the men roared their approval.

Sernon raised the sacrificial dagger high above the girl, and his voice boomed out across the courtyard. "Life or death?"

"Death!" a young Urakian called out from the front row.

"Death!" The crowd took up the chant.

The girl screamed once more, and Sernon plunged the dagger into her chest. With a vicious downward slash, he opened her from breastbone to belly.

Her screams fell silent, and a mighty roar like crashing waves against rocks filled the courtyard.

Sernon waited, allowing the crowd to vent their frenzied pleasure, then gestured with his free hand for quiet. The cheering ceased, and his lips curved in icy disdain, realizing he had the whole garrison under his dominance. They were his—or almost. Decisively, he reached down into the girl's gaping body, grasped her liver, and wrenched it free, holding it high in the air as warm blood dripped down his arm.

An ancient and almost forgotten bloodlust whipped through the crowd, stirring it once more into a wild frenzy. Feet stamped, fists punched the air, and shouts rang out across the courtyard, bouncing from the cliffs to the left of the fort.

Dannock watched in numb silence. Sernon had only to command the Urakians, and they would follow blindly. However, the dark sorcerer was not finished. Stepping toward the kneeling bodies of the Urakian soldiers, Sernon took his dagger and sliced the liver into six pieces. Dropping a piece onto each of the severed necks, he raised his arms and called upon Arahmin, God of Blood. In an ancient language, older than the mountains and the histories of Tarlis, he raised his arms and spat three words of power in rapid succession, *"Blah Nostran Nevah!"*

Lightning splintered, thunder roared, and five demons surged from the ground near his feet and merged with the five corpses. With a theatrical flair, Sernon raised the last piece of liver to his lips and bit down with relish, chewed, and swallowed.

The mob went berserk, and Dannock blanched, as the eyes of *The Five* heads still on the ground, slowly opened. With each bite the sorcerer took, the heads rose into the air. They floated upon the air currents, hovered above the bodies, and gradually descended. When the heads were sitting in perfect formation on the bodies from whence they came, *The Five* picked up their helmets and donned them. They stood as one and spoke as one. "What is your bidding, Master? What is your command?"

"There is only one command," thundered Sernon. He turned to the garrison and punched the air. "Death to the Prince of the Wolfhead! Death to the Elisian Princess!"

The crowd erupted.

****

Kaden awoke with a start, rolled onto his side, and groaned as stitches, shoulder to hip, pulled at tender flesh. The Cross! Was it safe? Had Tannith survived? How could she have defeated the Glaisling? His mind raced.

Purple shadows of dawn surrounded the campsite as he eased himself to a sitting position. He was lying on a crudely fashioned bed made of pine needles and covered by a woolen blanket. Over his body another blanket had been thrown and so had his fur-lined cloak. Underneath he was naked.

He probed at his wounds, realizing Tannith must have stitched them. There was pain, but not acute. More a throbbing reminder of the intense agony he felt when the Glaisling's taloned fingers had ripped into his flesh. He groaned and rose, knotted a blanket around his hips, and limped toward the lake. There, he found a fallen log and lowered himself to sit, contemplating the waters of Tirfo Thuinn. There was no sign of the rock shelf, no reminder of the night before. He put his hands to his temples. They throbbed. Had it been the night before?

****

Tannith watched from the shadows as Kaden crawled from his makeshift bed, knotted the field blanket around his waist, and limped toward the lake. The sheer magnificence of his body literally sucked the air from her lungs. She cringed to think he had almost perished in the same lake he now viewed so pensively. It was a blur now, how she had pulled him ashore—dragged him through the icy water in the way her father had taught her as a child. The same way she saved Etan, her childhood friend and now bodyguard, from drowning many summers before.

She had heaved Kaden up the muddy bank onto the grass, sheer determination having played a vital part, for his body was twice as large as hers. After rolling him slowly onto his stomach, she gently peeled his shredded shirt from his back. Holding the garment up to the moonlight, it appeared more like a rag, and his flesh was not much better. She remembered stifling her tears as she inspected his wounds. Eight gaping scratches ran shoulder to hip, seeping crimson blood. The way she had dragged him up the bank had compounded the problem. Mud had been smeared into the wounds.

On closer inspection, another five gashes cut through the leather of his breeches and ran down the lower part of his left leg. All had to be stitched. She ran into the forest to collect Phoenix where he'd been tethered well back among the trees. On returning, she built a fire, boiled clean water to bathe the wounds, and set about painstakingly rebuilding Kaden's body.

Long hours she had toiled into the night and the early morn, working over torn flesh, drawing ragged edges together, and sewing fine neat stitches so the scars would not be too unsightly. The thing that worried her most was that he had not regained consciousness. She had followed every procedure her father taught her—clearing his air passage, pushing his head back, and breathing air into his mouth every few heartbeats. When this failed to bring about the desired response, she pushed on his chest several times.

Finally, he had rallied and rolled his head to the side, coughing up a copious amount of water. Then without waking completely, he slumped back into unconsciousness. His color was good despite having lost so much blood, but his breath was labored.

He drifted into a fitful sleep from which he had not awoken until now. Perhaps just as well, for the sleep numbed the pain of the needle she had used to gather his flesh and join the ragged edges of his skin. Maybe the blackout was his body's way of telling him he had experienced enough pain for one day.

She took a step and cursed softly as a twig snapped underfoot.

He sensed her presence and turned. "How long have you been there?"

"Not long. I was scouting." She stepped through the bushes and walked toward him.

"How long have I been out?"

"Three days," she said, coming to a stop and leaning her back against the slim red trunk of an Umbrella tree.

A frown creased his forehead. "That long?" He

answered thoughtfully. "What of the Glaisling? I gather you killed her, or we would not be standing here now."

Visions of the nightmarish creature ran through Tannith's mind, bringing with it images of midnight, blood-stained water, and the worst fear she had ever experienced. Even now, her voice wavered as she answered him. "I would prefer…not to speak of it. The deed still haunts me."

"Did you get the piece?"

She straightened away from the Red Umbrella tree and moved toward him. As she did, she upended the pouch from around her neck and poured the contents into her palm. Kaden rose and tried to make his way toward her.

"You should not be walking. You will undo all my good work."

"Stop fussing, woman. I am not a baby." He held out his hand, but she shook her head and replaced the pieces of Cross back into the pouch.

"No, I will hold on to these."

"You still do not trust me?"

"The Cross contains hidden powers that could be harmful to your kind. I have already proven I can carry it."

He met her gaze. "As you wish." His words were evenly spaced, and he lowered his hand.

"What next?"

"We meet Ohma and the others in Jahl."

"Can you ride?" She looked pointedly at his bandaged leg and chest.

"What? These few scratches? I have had worse in the training ring." He smiled down into her eyes and raised his hand to tuck a lock of white gold hair behind her ear. "Were you afraid for me?"

"I still need your help."

His hand fell to his side. "Of course, how foolish of me." He stepped back. "I should have remembered." He made to turn away, but she grasped his arm.

"I am glad you are alive."

He expelled a short, dry laugh and pulled from her grip. "Sure, you are." His tone was hard, dry. "I suggest you saddle the horse while I dress." He raised a brow. "If I still have clothes, that is."

Tannith turned away as visions of sculpted, bronze muscle flittered through her consciousness. She had never seen a man naked before, never realized a man could be so artistically beautiful, albeit covered in blood. "I mended your clothes the best I could," she said quietly, her head bowed, her hair falling forward to hide the flush heating her cheeks. *He would know it was she who had undressed him.* "Your tunic and breeches are in your pack." She swung away and fled…

****

On his arrival at the fortress in Kerbac, Sernon ordered the northern tower restored and refurbished with furniture looted from wealthy merchants and the clergy. It was to this conical-spired tower Dannock-Shae was summoned.

Entering Sernon's quarters by way of a white stone staircase and answering the sorcerer's demand to close the door behind him, Dannock scanned the room with distaste.

Lead-light sashes decorated the deep bay windows, filtering the rays of the sun. Gold leaf had been applied to the legs of chairs and tables. Inlays of ivory and other precious materials were employed on desks, mantles, and wooden chests. The room was excessively ornate for his taste, which ran to more formal and functional pieces.

The necromancer rose leisurely from his chair and placed a leather-bound tome on a small table. He greeted Dannock with a solemn smile, yet his eyes remained impassive.

Dannock studied him uneasily. Once again, due to the incompetence of fools under his command, he had failed in his mission to secure the prison and capture the other members of the prince's party. It was with some apprehension, he now awaited Sernon's words.

"Well, Dannock, it seems your gods have conspired against you once again."

Dannock's tone was dry. "Indeed, it does, my lord."

Sernon strode to an open window and stared out. " 'Tis a pity matters have gone this way, for I will be eternally grateful to you for my resurrection."

Dannock's hand inched closer to the dagger hidden in a pocket in his voluminous robe.

"To that account, I have spared you your life," said Sernon, keeping a level tone.

He released the breath he was holding, but still he eyed his master's back with caution. He had witnessed the punishment earlier that day of the five men who had failed the sorcerer, and he had no desire to meet the same fate.

Sernon turned and pinned Dannock with his pale gaze. "However, I cannot allow failure to go unpunished, for mercy can be mistaken as softness. Softness, you understand, is a weakness. I must be portrayed as a strong leader with no leniency for those who fail me. I must make them fear me. For with fear comes power. And with power comes total acquisition."

Dannock frowned, noting the glow of fervor in the Dark Lord's eyes.

"Therefore, I have little choice…"

Dannock palmed the poniard in the folds of his black robes, ready for an assault.

"I would not, if I were you," the sorcerer said, keeping to a bored tone. "You would be dead before you drew your next breath. Did you think I did not know about the little knife you carry in the hidden pocket in your robes? I can walk the pathways of any man's mind. I know all."

Dannock's fingers uncurled from the dagger, and he allowed his hand to slowly return to his side. His fist clenched as he rested back nonchalantly against a heavy table in the center of the room. Rain pounded the roof of the keep. The weather suited his mood—foul. How could things have gotten so out of hand? His plans had been so well laid. Now he would probably die without them ever reaching fruition.

If only he had not been surrounded by imbeciles! He sighed wearily and ran a hand over his eyes. "What is it you wish, my lord?"

Sernon eyed him steadily for several heartbeats, then spoke. "You will ride with *The Five* on their mission and not return until Princess Tannith and the Wolfhead Prince are dead." The sorcerer paused, then quietly spoke again. "You will *not* fail me."

Dannock's lips pulled tight, and his jaw hardened. He stood away from the table. He could barely speak from suppressed anger. "No, my lord. I will not fail." He turned to leave, not waiting for the order to do so, then swung back. "Perhaps one matter."

Sernon raised a pale brow.

"A warding spell or troops. What is to stop those demons from turning on me while we search?"

The sorcerer waved his hand as if pushing away Dannock's words. "The creatures search by scent. You are safe if you do not touch anything belonging to their prey. And you have all the protection you will need from outside danger."

Dannock frowned.

Sernon's lips twisted into a smile which did not reach his ice-cold eyes. "You now command *The Five.*"

****

Etan dragged the hood of his stolen woolen cloak up over his hair and lowered his face as two Urakian soldiers entered the tavern. He leaned forward and poured a mug of frothing Trevilian Ale from the earthen jug in the center of the table, lifted it to his lips, and regarded the man across from him.

"So, where are they?" Etan released an exasperated sigh. "It is five days passed the specified meeting time. We should tarry no longer. The fact is, the longer we stay, the more likely we are to be recognized."

"I know that," Ohma agreed, his face appearing more like weathered parchment than usual. He gestured to four Urakian soldiers pushing their way through the door to seat themselves across the room from them. "Those same soldiers were in here yesterday and the previous day. I fear they may be watching us."

He nodded. "I doubt it is coincidence. And this is not like Tannith. I cannot shake the feeling there is something wrong. Perhaps, you could work a spell to see what stays them?"

Ohma shook his head. "Just like that." The old mage snapped his gnarled fingers. "Next you will have me pulling a dragon from my hat to harass those Urakians across the room." He released a sigh of exasperation. "These things take time, boy."

Etan drained his tankard and, in a low voice, called for another jug. Never once did his gaze waver from the storm-colored eyes of the Druid Mage.

Ohma sighed in resignation. "I suppose I could try, if you keep watch." He reached for the jug and poured a frothing pot of ale."

He leaned over and peered into the brew. "What is that for?"

"You wanted me to search, did you not?"

"Aye, I did."

"Then hush!" snapped Ohma. "Do you want to bring every Urakian in this tavern down on our heads? You do your job and let me do mine."

Etan crossed his arms and leaned back in his chair, allowing Ohma to stare into the slowly disappearing froth on his ale. The old man began to chant softly in another language. His eyes appeared vacant, then rolled back to reveal only the whites. His breathing slowed, almost stopped, and his carriage stiffened. Long moments passed.

The time-candle on the table burned low, and Etan began to wonder if Ohma had inadvertently gone too far and passed over to the *Otherside.* Then, without warning, the old man uttered a strangled cry and jolted upright. He stretched his arms and quaffed a mouthful of ale. "I know where they are," he pronounced.

"Where?" he asked softly. "And lower your voice." He gestured toward the Urakians sitting six tables away.

"Your princess and the Wolfhead are in a lot of trouble," he whispered and finished his drink.

****

Tannith and Kaden traveled on doggedly through the rain toward Jahl and their rendezvous with Ohma. Leaving the lake, they cut inland, through once fertile fields that now lay burnt or trampled by enemy horses. Continuing into forested hills, they followed a track, which hopefully would lead them to a back road and the village.

After ten days, Kaden could no longer hold himself upright in the saddle. Pain radiated through every fiber of his body. Pus oozed from ugly wounds on his left calf muscle. Unbearable pain stabbed at him with every step of Phoenix's great hooves. Sweat drenched his forehead, and his body burned with enough heat to rival an ice mountain volcano. As the sun dropped low over the amethyst horizon that afternoon, he slumped backward into Tannith's arms.

Trying not to panic, she held him tight and drew the stallion to a halt. With a strength she did not know she had, she slipped him carefully from the horse. She used her cloak and his and laid him upon them, then she set camp and waited.

By the fifteenth day of leaving the lake, Kaden's condition had worsened. Tannith knew he was dying, yet her heart would not accept it, although she had borne witness to his rapid deterioration.

She could not, would not, believe the gods had abandoned them in such a harsh manner. Were they not on a quest for Magus, the most powerful of all gods? How could their God allow this to happen? There must be a reason. She had to believe that, or all they had been through was for naught! There had to be something she could do. But what? She had lanced and re-stitched the wounds, searched the forest for herbs, formed a poultice, and strapped it to his leg. She even knelt and prayed to Magus for divine intervention, but her God left her plea unanswered.

Tannith crouched beside Kaden, poured water over a cloth, and sponged his damp brow. A groan rose to his lips as he labored for breath. Sorrow touched her then, so deep it was like a knife in her soul. Had she found this man only to lose him? She ran a knuckle down his cold cheek. His skin was pale as newly fallen snow. One moment he was ice cold, only to morph to skin so hot it rivalled a blazing inferno. He would thrash about and mumble unintelligible words. Maybe Dorrachian? Languages had never been her strong point.

This was her fault. She should have seen to his injuries along the trail, but he had been so obstinate. And knowing how proud and headstrong he could be, she had allowed him his way. He had said she had enough work and did not need to cater to him as well. So, she had shrugged and let him be. He was, after all, a grown man.

If only she had insisted.

Tears filled her eyes and trickled unbidden down her cheeks. She was a fool not to have taken what he offered, lingering over past grievances, being too proud and too afraid. Her values were steeped in the *Old World Lore*. Several hundred years of belief were ingrained into the Elisian people. But, by the Gods, had they not given her this strong, courageous man as her equal?

Was the prophecy doomed to fail?

Yes, he was hard on her at times and cruel with his words. Yet, deep down, she had come to realize he used this hardness to cover up his insecurities. He was not nearly as tough as he wanted her to believe.

Sorry—such a small word when faced with the grim reality of death. Why had she been so proud? Could she not have spoken those few small words to make her his? Days ago, she realized she had deliberately used the law of her people as an excuse to keep them apart, distancing herself from him until their quest was at an end. What had caused her fear? For deep down, it *was* a fear.

She had lost her mother when a child, and now her father could not be found. Was it this very thing she feared—losing Kaden? If she never had him, she could never lose him, but now she had to face reality. She loved him. Truly loved him, and now he would never hear her say those words.

Kaden's arm lashed out, just missing her jaw. His head thrashed from side to side, and in his delirium, he threw off his blankets. Her name splintered from his lips. "Tannith! Come back!"

"I am here, my love. I am not going anywhere," she whispered close to his ear, then reached over and retrieved his blankets from where he had thrown them, tucking them back around his body as he began to tremble.

With a damp cloth, she bathed his forehead, whispering soft words of comfort, but she knew they would be lost in the dream world in which he now resided.

Over the last five days, he had called out many names—that of his mother, father, sister, and others she had never heard before. There was one he called insistently—a woman's name—Zoreena-Rah. Who was *she*? A former lover? A family member? If so, it was one of whom she was not aware. Yet, she surmised, she had not known him overly long. She just knew she loved him and did not want to lose him.

The names came less frequently now. His breathing irregular and soft, a mere whisper. He had lost weight. The flesh having fallen from his bones—his complexion taking on a pallor akin to wax. His leg wound had turned to a sickly shade of green with streaks of bright red and purple spidering out in various directions. She had seen wounds like this after the battle at Dragonbane Castle. They usually led to amputations.

She pulled the blanket up to Kaden's chin and stood up to stoke the fire. The night had grown crisp, and there would be a frost by morning. She would have to gather more wood. She peered into the darkness at the edge of the campsite. The fire was the only thing protecting them from the timber wolves crying in the not so far distance.

She skirted the camp, gathering small logs and sticks, and returned to feed the fire. Flames licked at the new wood as she tossed on several more offerings, staring unseeing at the dancing flames flaring to life.

Pain throbbed at her temples, weariness threatened to engulf her, and her eyes ached with unshed tears. Unless help came and quickly, Kaden would die, and she would be forced to go on alone.

She swallowed hard, holding back a sob, and returned to his side to pull aside the blanket. Kneeling, she laid her cheek against his chest, allowing her tears to fall for the first time. She wept for the love they would never experience, the moments they would never share, the children she would never conceive.

When her tears were spent and she could shed no more, she lifted her head to dry her face. Ohma sat across from her, warming his hands by the fire.

She rubbed her eyes. Then rubbed them again.

"How...How did you get here?"

His lips curved into a grim smile, highlighting every crease in his weather-beaten face. " 'Tis my spirit body you see, lass. My physical body dwells in a forest near Jahl with the rest of our company. When you did not arrive, Etan insisted I seek you out." The Druid's voice carried softly on the wind.

"Etan escaped. Is he well?"

"Aye." The old man nodded. "The lad is fine. A few scratches, nothing more." His gaze shifted to Kaden. "Not so for your young prince, I see."

She swallowed the lump in her throat. "He is dying. I have tried every herb I know. I can do no more." She dabbed at her eyes with her sleeve.

"You have not tried everything. There is still the Cross. It has power. What sort of power, I am not quite certain, but we can only try."

Tannith removed the bag from around her neck and loosened the cord. A green light flashed from the opening, lighting up the heavy branches above their heads. "We have only two pieces. Do you think they will be enough?"

"We have nothing to lose."

Tipping the bag, the two sections spilled onto Tannith's palm. She tightened her fist over them, surprised to find they contained an inner warmth.

"Place the half-cross over Kaden's heart and then your hand over the icon." He waited until she fitted the pieces together and followed his instructions. "Now, close your eyes and concentrate. Focus with all your mind and all your heart. Feel the power of the Cross. Draw upon it, feed on it, and allow it to flow through you. Now send it out. Pour the power into his body. Fill him. Heal him."

Perspiration trickled down Tannith's back. "How?"

"Just do it. The power flows from the mind and the heart. Heart…hands, power…Heart, hands…power. Say the words!"

"Heart, hands…power. Heart, hands, power."

"Say the words like you *mean* them!"

Drawing a deep breath, Tannith mustered all the love she felt for the warrior prince into three simple words and shouted them out, filling the night with her vibrant voice. "Heart, hands…power. Heart, hands…power!"

The icon grew hot in her palm, but not once did she falter in her words or pull away. She repeated the chant into the still darkness.

Almost childlike, Kaden blinked and yawned. She ceased her chant as his eyes focused on hers. "You are beautiful." He raised his hand and stroked a loose tendril of hair back from her face. "Have I been somewhere? It feels like I have been somewhere."

She captured his hand and brought it to her lips. "Welcome back." With her other hand, she tenderly cupped his cheek. "I missed you. You have been gone from this world for some time."

He ran a hand over his eyes. "What happened?" He pushed his night-dark hair back from his face and rose onto his elbow. "What did I miss?"

She leaned forward, cupped his face between her hands, and kissed him hard on the lips.

His eyes widened in surprise. "I *have* missed something." He gave her a heavy-lidded look, which virtually took her breath away.

"You were dying."

He broke contact with her gaze, and she released her breath.

"I remember feeling ill." He ran his hand down his leg and frowned. "My thigh burned like hellfire from the Abyss. I must have blacked out." He drew her into his embrace and rolled her over, his mouth coming down and his tongue battling hungrily with hers while his hands skimmed her back.

A cough sounded at their side.

Remembering Ohma's presence, Tannith pulled away and straightened her tunic.

****

Kaden raised his head and twisted around, registering two things. Ohma sat across the fire, grinning at them, and his wounded leg no longer pained him. "How did you get here?" He rose to sit, bringing Tannith to his side, his arm resting comfortably around her waist.

Ohma smiled and threaded a gnarled hand through his beard. " 'Tis a long story, lad."

"Did *you* heal me?"

Ohma shook his head and gestured to Tannith. "For that feat of magick you must thank the princess, and her gift from Magus."

"The Cross?"

Ohma nodded. "Yes, you will find you are completely recovered." The old Mage's mist-colored eyes twinkled in the firelight.

"I…" Feeling a slight tingling, he touched his hand to his chest and glanced down. The half-cross had burned its imprint into his flesh. "How did she do this?" he asked of Ohma but looked at Tannith.

The old man shrugged. "The Cross has magick even I do not understand. Be thankful it worked. I was not sure it would."

Kaden took Tannith's hand and brought it to his lips, dropped a small kiss on her open palm then turned his attention to Ohma. "And you. How did you find us?"

"I am here in spirit form only, and unfortunately have no time to explain. I saw you were in need."

"And the others? Where are they?"

"Camped in the forest near Jahl."

"Etan?"

"Well, but you were the one we worried for. I saw in a vision you were injured. How do you feel now?"

"Fine, but I am starving. I could eat a dragon's haunch."

Tannith gave a chuckle as she rose and disappeared into the shadows. Several moments later she returned. " 'Tis no Dragon," she said with a smile in her voice. "But it might do until we find one." She handed him a small loaf of grain bread, dried fruit, and a flask of red wine, which they had taken from the pack beside the body of the Hunt Lord.

Kaden accepted the food and laid it on the grass beside him, then took Tannith's hand. "I am sorry I put you through this ordeal."

She settled down beside him. "I am only glad you are with me now."

Kaden was about to respond, but the Druid cleared his throat, breaking the moment.

"You must leave this place," he cautioned. "Great danger approaches. Five of the walking dead stalk you."

"Zombies?" Kaden, bit off a chunk of bread and chewed it with gusto, then washed it down with a mouthful of mulled wine. He rolled the wine over his tongue, savoring the tart freshness of the raspberries and sunberries. It was good wine. His stomach growled, and he grinned. "It feels like I have not eaten in days." He finished chewing. "Keep going." He made a gesture with his hand. "I thought Zombies were made up stories told to frighten youngsters if they refused to go to bed."

A half laugh escaped Ohma. "No. These are quite real. Sernon created the living dead from five guards he executed."

"He killed his own men?" Tannith stared incredulously.

"They were the guards we overpowered when we rescued Etan. Etan killed one. He apparently was the lucky one, to have died so quickly."

"Their punishment was to be transformed to demons?"

Ohma nodded. "Demons from the Hell Pit. They were given orders to track you down and kill you."

"Lucky us." Kaden scooped up a handful of dried fruit from the bowl Tannith had put beside him and picked out the raisins. He hated the dried-up little black things. He tossed the raisins aside then tipped back his head and devoured the rest of the fruit from his hand. "How do you know this?"

"I had a vision of the ritual. He sacrificed a young Elisian girl to bring forth five demons from the Hell Pit to inhabit the corpses."

****

Tannith wrapped protective arms about her body as if to ward off Ohma's words. Kaden saw her shiver and laid an arm around her shoulders, pulling her close to his side to bathe in the delicious heat from his body.

"How can we defeat what is already dead?" she asked in a small voice.

"I will not lie and say it will be easy, but I can do one thing to help. Place your weapons on the ground before me." The prince rose to collect his weapons from where Tannith had stashed them, then laid out his sword and five knives. Tannith followed suit and slipped her short sword and dagger from their scabbards and the slender blade from the special sheaf sewn into her boot. Two slim poniards from her wrist sheaves joined her pile of weapons on the grass at the old man's feet. A variety of emotions knotted her insides. What could Ohma possibly do to protect them? She had seen him perform small feats of magick since their meeting, but had he the skill to ward off demons?

While she was thinking, Ohma had begun to chant the words of an ancient ritual.

"Azdomo, Nikoidon, Alrosso, Ballindoh!"

The Druid mage cupped his hands, and a blue light appeared, balled, and swelled. Mage fire spewed from his fingertips, searing each weapon in turn. The blades grew bright to flash silver in the moonlight, then gradually dimmed to a metallic blue.

"I have instilled into your weapons an old and deadly magick. This will enable you to fight Sernon's Demon Warriors as you would any other. If struck by your blades, they will die as any mortal man would die."

Kaden reached for his sword, sheathed it, and began to dress. Tannith averted her gaze from his naked chest. In the moonlight, his torso resembled that of a bronze god, conjuring a warmth in the pit of her belly. To think she had almost lost him. She had been terrified. She pushed the thought away and bent to retrieve their small store of belongings.

"Go north toward the Poniard Ranges," Ohma

advised. "Use the cliffs to your advantage. That way the creatures can attack only from the south. We will meet again in Antibba."

Kaden nodded and kicked dirt over the embers of the dying fire.

"Your enemies are but a day away. And know this, Dannock-Shae rides with them."

When he looked around, the old man was gone. Not even the dust where he'd settled was disturbed.

Chapter Four

Three leagues from the village of Jahl, Kaden called a halt. He shaded his eyes and surveyed the surrounding land. At the edge of his vision, he saw the rugged pinnacles of the Poniards in the north. "If we force-march, we could reach the far side of Lake Tarlis by late afternoon tomorrow."

Tannith sighed wearily. "I was hoping we would make it by dusk."

Kaden dismounted and ran a hand over Phoenix's heaving flanks. There were small bubbles of froth around the stallion's muzzle. "The horse is tired. We dare not push him further today. Besides, it will soon be evening. There is a cave on the hill." He pointed. "We will shelter there tonight and leave before dawn."

Slipping from the saddle, Tannith followed Kaden as he began to climb. The hill was not steep, but it was mostly shale, and it slid beneath their feet with each footfall, making the climb more laborious than it should have been.

Finally reaching the cave entrance, Kaden bid her to wait with the horse, while he checked for danger.

She settled onto a nearby boulder.

In the distance, the tips of the Poniard Ranges jutted up to dominate the vast stretches of the parched lowlands before them. In the approaching evening, the ancient mountains seemed like sculptured fire, deep orange, flaming yellow, with a tinge of blue. To the south, there was no sign of pursuit. So desolate it was hard to imagine that somewhere out there deadly creatures of Sernon's making hunted them. She wondered if it was possible to escape such evil, even with the magick Ohma provided.

Kaden joined her and passed her Phoenix's reins. "The cave is dry and large enough. It harbors naught but a few spiders, no more."

"I hate spiders."

"Everyone hates spiders," He returned with a short laugh. "Though, I do remember you telling me once that you feared nothing. Have you not battled Griffins and fought a Vampire Water Fae?" He laughed, striding past her. "I am sure the spiders will eat very little." He glanced over his shoulder. "There is not much *to* eat."

Tannith huffed and watched him pick his way down the slope to cover their tracks, then with some trepidation, she turned to lead the horse into the cave.

****

The cavern musty and shrouded in shadows, appeared dry and warm. She tethered the horse inside the entrance and took a taper from her pack. Striking a flint, she set the taper alight and moved further into the interior to explore. As she did so, she allowed her thoughts to flow back to the past several days...

They had pushed themselves and the thoroughbred hard to put as many leagues as possible between them and the creatures that dogged their footsteps. Late yesterday they caught a glimpse of dust over the horizon and spurred Phoenix to even greater speed. Although the big stallion had tried his best, the burden of carrying two had taken its toll. They walked him throughout the night and had not ridden again until daylight. Over the last half a league, the horse stumbled several times and his pace slowed. It was good Kaden discovered the cave as they were all in need of rest.

The cavern floor had a natural incline toward the back. Loose shale lay scattered about the ground. She picked her way toward the rear, collecting small sticks, making certain to steer clear of the thick mat of cobwebs adhering to the walls.

She stumbled and almost fell, then righted herself and peered down at a stack of kindling lying neatly beside the remnants of an expired fire. She crouched to clear away the loose scree to make the area habitable but turned as she heard Kaden enter the cave. He called out a greeting and moved to unsaddle and feed the horse. Then filled his hands with water from a small pool fed by an underground spring just inside the entrance, allowing the stallion to drink. Tannith smiled contentedly and turned back to her task, positioning a small pot of broth to simmer. Then she set out to explore more of the cave.

She had not gone far when her foot struck what she thought was a rock. She glanced down and gave a small shrill scream. Nausea pooled in her stomach. It was not a rock but a body she had stumbled upon. The woman lay in the shadow of an over-hanging ledge, half buried by rubble. She swallowed the bile in her throat and took a quick step back.

"Kaden, I think…you better come here. Quickly…"

Kaden dropped what he was doing and closed the gap between them. He knelt beside the badly decomposed body. Beside it, lay a garment partially covered in dirt. Tannith leaned down and picked up the cloak. Giving it a hard, shake, she flicked the debris from its folds, then held the garment up to the firelight. "The woman was of noble birth. The cloak is of good cloth and look…there is a crest."

Kaden snatched the garment from her hand. "What trick is this?"

Tannith frowned. "I see no trick only a ragged cloak, filthy at that."

"This was my sister's cloak." He pointed to the crest. "This is the Wolfhead crest. A golden wolf on a black pennant."

"You must be mistaken."

"No. I gave this cloak to my sister on her fifteenth birthday. I had it made specially in Antibba."

He pushed aside the dirt and debris to reveal the rest of the body.

Myriad thoughts raced through Tannith's mind. Had Asleena escaped Dannock-Shae wounded and then died here in this forlorn place? She touched Kaden's shoulder, feeling his muscles tense beneath her palm. "Are you sure it is her?"

"No," he answered sitting back, "it is not her. This woman was taller with fair hair. My sister's hair was blue-black like mine."

"Then who is she?"

"Moreover, why was the woman wearing Asleena's cloak?" He bunched the garment in his fists. "My sister would never have parted with it. She loved it."

Tannith touched his arm. He was visibly shaken. "We may never know what happened here and dwelling on it will not bring your sister back," she said gently.

"No. But revenge exacted upon her murderers will release my sister's soul to walk freely in Elysium and allow me to feel like a man again." He came to his feet and gave the cloak several hard shakes before draping it around Tannith's shoulders. "The garment is musty. Still, the velvet is rich, and it is dry and warm. I am sure my sister would have liked you to have it."

Tannith covered his hand with hers as he made to help her with the fastening. "Are you sure?"

He remained silent, concentrating on the clasp and her hand dropped to her side as she studied his face, all harsh lines, and shadows in the dim light. She wondered what thoughts occupied his mind right now. Had he fastened this same cloak, in another time, in a place more to his liking? She stroked his cheek, and he looked into her eyes. His were the color of a deep jungle pool and mirrored his pain.

"I am sorry, I spoke so harshly," he said, stepping away. "I will bury the woman while you finish supper."

She forced a smile and watched him go, knowing he needed time alone. She gathered their limited supplies and fashioned a light meal. When he returned, they dined on a broth made of dried beef, herbs and wild onions, and a portion of cheese and bread washed down with spring water and the last of the mulled wine.

Every so often she would cast a furtive glance across the fire, wishing she could lighten his mood, hoping he would speak about something, anything. However, she sensed his thoughts were on his sister, and her death was not a subject he had chosen to discuss.

When he finished his meal, he washed and stowed the cooking utensils in the saddlebags, then took her bedroll and spread it close to the fire. "Get some rest," he said, picking up his sword and heading for the exit.

"What of you?" she called.

"I had enough sleep while I was injured. Besides, I

hate those little snatches of death." He stepped into the night and was gone.

****

Outside, Kaden stared down the hill in the direction of the road. Both moons were hidden by clouds. All was dark. The night suited his mood—a dark night, for dark thoughts.

Dragging his fur-lined cloak more securely about his shoulders, he sank to the ground and laid his sword on a small patch of grass at his side. Tannith's bow, he propped against a boulder to his right. Then he punched four green-feathered shafts into the earth beside the bow. It was best to be prepared—the night had all the markings of being a long one.

A breeze sprang up, and in the distance a Wolveryne cried. A mournful, solitary sound, riding the wind. It brought back to him the fragility of his own mortality.

He missed his father. A wise, strong man, his advice always so freely given, and his mother's gentle smile and soft words of wisdom. What would have been their thoughts about Tannith? He smiled knowingly into the darkness. His mother would have approved, no doubt, if it had meant a wife. She had always been at her sons to provide her with a bounty of grandchildren.

Settling with his back against a large boulder, his musings reverted to the woman's body in the cave. Fear had flowed over him with the discovery of the cloak— horrified to think Asleena had died alone in this dismal place. Relief had been welcomed when he realized the woman's body was not hers. However, it was short-lived when he thought back to the terrible circumstances under which his sister had died.

He turned his head at the sound of a snapping twig

and slipped his dagger from his boot.

" 'Tis only I," Tannith whispered, dropping down beside him. "I could not sleep. Would it help if you spoke of what haunts you?"

Kaden raised his head and threaded his fingers through his long hair, pushing it back from his face.

Tannith took his hand, placed it around her shoulders, and laid her head against his heart. He drew her close. "Do you know how she died?" he asked.

She shook her head, saying nothing. She knew he needed to talk.

"They took her from the castle in the early hours of the morn. You know, at that time when it is neither night nor day? They hid her in a cave in the Carrum-Bahl Mountains. When evening came, they rode with her up to Dalen-Gae and weighted her body with chains. They stabbed her and tossed her into the icy depths as a sacrifice." Kaden's voice broke. "Dannock-Shae sacrificed *my* beautiful little sister to his dark gods, using her innocence in his ritual to bring Sernon, that spawn of all evil, back from the dead. May the Hounds of Death feast upon his black heart." He smashed his fist into the ground beside him. "Asleena, who never hurt a soul, had to die for that depraved fiend to live."

Tannith pulled away and twisted to look at his face. "Her death shall not go unavenged. When we find the Cross, he and Dannock-Shae will pay for what they have done to you, to me, and thousands of others. Until then, you cannot allow the hate to win, or it will eat away at your insides, your heart, and destroy you."

He gave a short derisive laugh but remained silent, searching her midnight eyes.

"How long before Dannock finds us do you think?"

"If the gods are kind, never. If they are not—two—maybe three days."

She put a hand to his cheek and ran her fingers over his three-day-old stubble. She reached for the clasp of his cloak in the darkness, but he placed his hand over hers. "What are you doing?"

"Let me." Her lips were close.

He could almost taste the sweetness of her tongue. The white moon stretched forth from beyond the clouds, and he watched her lips thin into a small bow, concentrating on releasing the looped clasp on his cloak. His breath hissed in his throat, and he looked straight up into her eyes as the laces of his shirt melted beneath her fingers.

She pushed both garments aside and put her warm hands against his thundering heart, holding his gaze. "If you still want me, warrior. I am yours."

His heart went from a gallop to a dead stop. "I do not want your pity, woman."

"I offer you none," she said, moving to kneel before him, resting her hands on his shoulders. She pushed him back onto the grass and followed him down. Taking his mouth in a kiss more savage than gentle.

He groaned and his hands threaded through her curtain of white-blonde hair. Their bodies straining as one, wanting, asking, and seeking that which only the other could give. They broke apart panting, their breath frosting the cool air. He raised his hands to her hair allowing it to trail through his fingers. Wild silk, clouding about her beautiful pale face in the moonlight.

He leaned forward and touched his lips to her ear nibbling softly on its delicate point. "Perhaps we should go inside."

She nodded and made to stand.

"No. Stay as you are." He rose, scooped her into his arms, grabbed up his sword and strode into the cavern. Reaching the fire, he dropped his sword, and lowered her gently to her feet. Then he spread his cloak over her bedroll by the fire and lay her atop of it. Coming down over her, he stared deep into her eyes.

Smiling in reassurance, he loosened the ties of her tunic and pushed the cloth aside to reveal her breasts. They were perfect. Firm yet soft, they fit the size of his hand to perfection. He ran his fingertip around one rose-pink aureole and drew the other hardened tip into his mouth, grazing her nipple with his teeth, nipping delicately until she could stand no more and pushed him away.

He laughed, and reluctantly raised his head, bringing his lips down swiftly to taste her mouth. His tongue entered, seeking, and finding warm sweetness, while his hands slid down her thighs to her small, rounded derriere.

****

A groan escaped her lips as she ran her hands up under his shirt. Her fingertips scraping lightly over the puckered flesh of his many scars. Each one, if it could speak, could tell its own tale. She trailed her fingers further around to his chest and shoulders, his muscles hard beneath her hands, then back to the naked expanse of his back. She trembled as he snagged his hands in her hair and arched her neck to the side, his lips touching the small pulse beneath her ear. Their legs entwined, and he crushed his body against the junction of her thighs. Boldly, she lowered her hand to just above his belt to lay flat on his stomach.

"Touch me," he urged, his breath a whisper in her ear.

"I cannot." She slid her hand back up to his chest.

"Trust me." He loosened his belt, took her hand, and placed it against the lower part of his stomach where the soft, dark hair trailed to his navel. Ever so slowly, her fingers slid downward. He was hot, ever so hot, pulsating, and her hand trailed lower and curled around him.

****

Her fingers were like a velvet sheath. He groaned but dared not move, or he knew he would explode. She leaned back, and he searched her eyes. They were filled with everything he had ever wanted to see, trust, love, longing and more. His loins grew heavy and ached with need. He wanted her beneath him, to meld her body against his, plunge into her depths and never come up for air. Instead, he took her mouth in another drug-inducing kiss.

Again, a groan escaped from deep in his throat as he savored her touch, knowing it could be for only a moment. He had been too long without a woman, and he would not rush her. As he took the hand holding him and slid it from his pants, she breathed harshly against his throat.

"Please Kaden. I need you."

His lips found hers again and all he could think of was slipping into the warm soft junction of her thighs, but with as much willpower as he could muster, he wrenched away.

"What—"

"Not here, not like this." The words ground hoarse from his throat. He leaned over to place a callused finger against her lips as she tried to speak. "When I make love to you for the first time, it will be special. Not on the rough floor of a dank cave on a soiled cloak." He dropped a small kiss to the tip of her nose and rose to his feet. "Sleep now, my lady. We will rise before the sun."

****

Tannith sighed, her body aching with unfulfilled need as she watched him walk away.

She sighed and resolved herself to the fact that she would not be losing her virginity this eve. She rolled onto her elbow and squealed as something hard and sharp jabbed into her arm.

Kaden hastened back and dropped to his knees beside her. "What happened? Are you hurt?"

Pulling the cloak that once belonged to Asleena from beneath her, Tannith ran her hands over the folds of the fabric. "There is something in the lining." She squeezed two fingers into a small gap, ripped the hem and upended Asleena's cloak. Pieces of gold, silver, and copper deemahs spilled out in a rich, bright pool. She dug into the lining again, this time retrieving a piece of old parchment she straightened and tried to read.

"The words are scratched in what appears to be blood. I cannot make out the lettering."

Kaden took the parchment from Tannith's hand and brought it into the firelight. His heart beat frantically as he scanned the document. "It is written in Dorrachian."

"What does it say?" she asked, taking a moment to lace up her shirt.

He watched her, allowing time to take in the bounty of her beauty, then he bent to study the words. "The writing is smeared in several places, and you are right, it is in blood. From what I can see, the woman's name was

Nadiya. She was Asleena's lady in waiting. I should have known from her fair coloring."

"What else?" She peered over his shoulder.

"Apparently it was she who betrayed the people of Glen-Dorrach to Dannock-Shae, by showing him the entrance into the castle through a secret passage. He in turn betrayed her. He set his men to hunt her. She was wounded and managed to escape to this cave. Knowing she was dying, she wanted to clear her conscience, hence the letter of confession."

"It must have been terrible, knowing she was going to die all alone in this dark hole."

Kaden scowled. "I feel no sorrow for the woman. She deserved to die. She destroyed many lives for her thirty pieces of silver." He stood and donned his cloak and pushed the treasure into his satchel. "I hope she took some silver to pay the Ferryman to cross the River of Chaos. The Gods of Creation would never grant entry into Elysium to one such as her."

Tannith shivered. What would it be like, she wondered, to be locked out of Elysium to roam aimlessly in the Void? Worse, to be condemned for all eternity to the Fiery Abyss?

Seeing her grim expression, Kaden ran a knuckle down her cold cheek. "Sleep now, Princess. The rest of the night should be uneventful, but to be sure, I will stand guard for a time."

She patted the place beside her. "Are you certain you will not join me?"

He gave a small laugh. "Tempting as your offer might be, our time will be more memorable for the waiting. Besides, I would see you my wife first. That is what your father would have wished. Is it not?"

"Well, yes, I suppose..." Her words trailed off as she watched him walk away. Wife. Wife indeed! He had not even asked her formally, but the thought did lend her comfort as she settled down with her back to the fire.

As much as she tried to find sleep, it eluded her. Looking toward the mouth of the cave she could see the moons had long risen, and the clouds had cleared. She heard Kaden return and feigned sleep. He removed his cloak and lay beside her, pulling her into the warmth of his arms. She wriggled, snuggling back into his body spoon-fashion. She knew he would lie awake, watching, waiting, and listening for danger, like countless other nights. Secure in the knowledge she was now safe, she drifted into sleep. But, deep in the recesses of her mind, the insidious presence of a thin, tall man in a black cloak and robes, loomed.

Dannock-Shae and his five demon warriors were gaining every day, and with one wrong move, the creatures would be upon them.

Chapter Five

Rysha-Taan's roar ripped through the frosty air. She whipped back her tail and slammed it into the chest of the charging Urakian. It spun him around and carried his mail-plated body into the raging swell of the river.

A second warrior hurled a brass-tipped spear. It pierced the great Draig through her outstretched wing, slicing cleanly into her leathery hide to lodge deep within the bulk of muscle beneath. Her agonizing cry rent the air like a sharp dagger.

Rysha-Taan knew she was faltering. Over a hundred leagues she had traveled this morn, searching for a safe haven to migrate her herd. Somewhere, where the man-beasts with their shining beetle chests could not rain down death like they had to her mate and ten-score others of her kind.

Blood ran from huge gashes in her scaled chest and dripped down her front legs. Her tail hung askew where a battle-axe had sliced its tip—and now her wing…

With spirit low, the dragon wept for the little ones she was sure she would never see again, a high-pitched wail of insurmountable pain.

The wound to her wing rendered Rysha-Taan earthbound. She knew fifty leagues would be impossible for an injured dragon to travel afoot. Deep abiding anger replaced the sorrow in her breast, and in that instant an axe-man attacked. Leaping high, the Urakian swung his battle-axe in a vicious blow toward her neck, but with one swipe from her mighty clawed arm, she sent him sprawling to the riverbank.

Let these man-creatures see that Rysha-Taan is not yet done. With outstretched talons, she slashed at the warrior and continued down his body, shredding him neck to groin. His cries died on his lips long before his life's blood departed. Nevertheless, seeing their comrade annihilated only increased the anger of the other warriors. They regrouped and charged, their war cries filling the air.

****

Erik, who had doubled back to check behind his party, stopped. *"Did you hear that?"*

Skylah ceased flying and hovered around his face. "What was it?"

"Not sure, but I am going to find out. Coming?" Erik twisted and bounded in the direction of the river.

Quick as a wink, Skylah flew past him. "Race you."

It was not long before they found their quarry. Skylah watched from the shadows as three Urakians charged a wounded dragon but were stopped by the reverberating roar of a large cat.

The three froze, and slowly turned as one. The breath of the ice tiger fanned their cheeks as the animal bared his teeth, enormous fangs gleaming in the sunlight.

A lone wounded dragon may have been good sport but faced with the threat of both dragon and tiger, the Urakians' courage fled. Weapons dropped from fear-paralyzed fingers and guttural cries split the air. The warriors raced for the nearby forest with Erik in close pursuit, and the immediate danger over, the dragon *heaved* a mighty sigh and slumped onto the blood-colored riverbank.

Skylah rounded at a cry to see Erik bring down a Urakian straggler.

Winded, the warrior rounded to fight, but with one swipe of razor-sharp claws, and one snap of his powerful jaws, the tiger staunched his escape. Fear lending speed to their legs, the remaining Urakians disappeared into the forest with the tiger on their heels.

Skylah swooped down beside the huge beast. Since a toddler, she had heard tales of the mythical creatures but never had she seen one. The dragon was amazing and larger than expected and so much more beautiful. Silver-green scales the size of a large saucer covered its back and tail. Multicolored scales glowing like precious gems encrusted the under part of its extended neck and breast. A short horn jutted from the dragon's elongated snout and a smallish beard bloomed from its chin.

"Is it dead?" Erik called out, returning to rip aside the first Urakian's armor, his large teeth sinking into the man's barreled chest.

She shot the tiger a quick glance then looked back at the dragon, not wishing to watch Erik feed. At times like this, she realized how much of a creature of the wild he really was.

Sometimes it was hard to remember when she rode his back and he related to her the philosophies of the world and told her stories of the great bards of old. However, deep down, she had to acknowledge, as much as she respected Erik, his instincts were still those of the Wild.

She sighed and concentrated on the dragon, steering her thoughts from the tiger. The draig's eye flicked open; a yellow-gold pupil glared out in resignation.

"I am dying, leave me be."

"I will get help. Do not despair, *Great One.*"

"Do not waste your time, child. There is no mortal cure for me…tonight I will dine with my ancestors." The eyelid drooped. *"Be gone."* The Dragon sighed and her head rolled to the side.

"Erik! Leave that carcass! Come and stand guard whilst I fetch Ohma. We cannot let the creature die. There are very few of these magnificent creatures left in this world."

The tiger bounded across the stretch of grass separating them and looked at the enormous beast lying in the red river mud. The dragon's breathing slowed to barely a whisper. *"You best hasten quickly then, for she is not long for this world."*

Skylah nodded and called on her light-travel.

Light-travel, although unpredictable, was the fastest way for a Faerie to transport oneself from one point to another. One had merely to memorize a certain landmark, visualize it, concentrate hard and blink. Sometimes luck was with her, other times it was not. She landed awkwardly upon Etan's head.

"What the…" He swiped at her, but she dodged and hopped clear.

Since leaving the Old Fort, Etan had resorted to his moody, unpredictable behavior. Never could she please him. "Where is Ohma?" she snapped.

Hearing his name, the Druid hurried from the trees in a flurry of indigo robes. "Here, lass. What is it? Where is Erik? He cannot be hurt?" The Faerie pivoted at the sound of the old man's voice. He stood behind her, breathing heavily. "I was searching for juniper leaves. They ward off demons, you know?"

Skylah nodded impatiently. "Yes, but you must hasten; there is a dragon, and she is dying."

"Why did you not say?" He hooked his satchel over his shoulder and hoisted his navy robes to his knees, taking off at a run. "Which way?"

Skylah fixed Ohma with a long-suffering look but refrained from answering and set flight toward the river, Etan and Ohma keeping pace the best they could.

****

Blood contrasted vividly with the metallic silver-green and bejeweled dragon scales as it seeped slowly from the deep gash in the draig's upper chest. It pooled with the scarlet mud beneath her underbelly. The dragon's head lay at an awkward angle. Small plumes of sulfur steam burst in short agonizing breaths, blending with the frigid mist beginning to form around the riverbank.

With one look from his aging eyes, Ohma knew there was little time before the draig's mighty spirit departed. He squatted before the dragon, his hand going to a cracked leather pouch at his waist. He spilled four large gems into his palm. An emerald, a diamond, a ruby, and a large rose crystal. He chose the latter, setting it on the mud between him and the dragon, then returned the rest of the gems to his pouch.

He faced his companions. "No matter what happens, you are not to interrupt me."

The old Master, deep in concentration, bent, placed his hand over the stone and closed his eyes. He focused all the power that he was and ever would be into the rose-colored gem. The stone glowed, radiating a pale pink aura that grew to encompass the whole of the Dragon in its magical sphere.

****

The sun dimmed, drifting behind a cloud. The air grew frigid. A cold wind sprang up from the north, whistling about all before dispersing the mist.

Skylah felt icicles forming on her nose. She leapt high in the air, flying hard against the wind toward the safety of Erik's back. She reached her destination, grasped hold with both hands to the tiger's fur and burrowed deep within his warmth. From the safety of her vantage point, she watched the strange events unfurl.

After several long heartbeats, the dragon flicked open one yellow-flecked eye, then another, stretched, and climbed to her feet. Suddenly, the wind dropped. The sun burst through the clouds, bouncing off the Draig's shining scales, sending rainbows of color scattering in a milliard of directions.

****

Rysha-Taan shook her head to clear her vision and peered down her long snout at the assortment of creatures before her. Neither fear nor animosity could she detect.

In low guttural words of a nearly forgotten dialect, she spoke to the mage through her mind. *"I am in your debt, human. What is your wish?"*

The old man took a step back and peered up at her. "There is nothing you owe me, *Old One.* You were wounded, I healed you. It is part of who and what I am."

Rysha-Taan lowered her scaly head to glare into his face. *" 'Tis told in Dragon Lore that should a dragon's life be saved by any other than its own kind, the Dragon must in turn grant a wish to that savior."*

Ohma frowned and scratched his mane of snowy hair. What was he to do? He needed no wish he could not grant himself, yet he was a wiser man than to cross a dragon. He scrounged through his mind for a plan, then smiled up at her. "That may be so, but it was not I who in truth saved you. The tiger harried off the Urakians, while the Faerie fetched me to your aid. Would they not be more deserving of your gift?"

The shimmering beast moved, her look encompassing the tiger and the diminutive creature hiding among his fur.

"Aye, the tiger who is not a tiger at all. Why do you wear this guise young man if it displeases you so?"

Erik rose to all fours and padded toward the dragon. *"I was transformed by a man who used a dark book of conjure."* His long tail churned up the dust. *"I have found no spell able to rescind the curse."*

Rysha-Taan snorted, curled one paw, and contemplated her claws. Skylah could have sworn she was smiling. *"Dragon magick is strong—indeed stronger than all others. There is no spell a dragon cannot counter if she so wishes."*

"Then you know my want." Erik inclined his head.

The dragon released a puff of steam into the frigid air, arched her neck and craned low to see Skylah sitting upon the tiger's back.

"Do not be afraid, small one." Rysha-Taan spoke in the ancient language of the dragon. *"Long have the Fey been friends of the Dragon. What is this wish that fills your heart with longing but of which you are too afraid to speak?"*

Skylah remained silent. Now that her chance had finally come, she was afraid, in fact terrified. What if she chose the wrong wish? Should she choose to find her people or become an Elisian maiden? What if she chose to find her people and found they had all been slain? What if she was transformed to a real woman and never found true happiness? She was resigned to the fact Etan would never love her. What if she abandoned her heritage for naught?

The dragon sensed her dilemma. Her voice filled Skylah's head. *"Be brave my friend, follow your heart. It will not lead you wrong."*

She straightened and dug deep to find her courage. "You are right, and perhaps I may live to rue my decision. Still, I would not be true to myself if I did not take the chance. Do it. Take my wings and make me an Elisian maiden."

The dragon bent low to peer into the Faerie's eyes. *"Elisians are not quite as long-lived as Faeries, you know this?"*

Skylah nodded. "I do."

"Then perhaps I shall leave you with one reminder of your Faerie heritage. The power of light transportation can be most useful."

She swallowed the lump in her throat. "Do what you will but do it now before I lose all courage." She leapt from the safety of Erik's back to land beside one of his furry feet. Although she was not certain if Erik had heard her wish, she was sure he would be supportive of her. She gave him a tremulous smile, and in his feline way he smiled back.

Rysha-Taan drew herself up to her full height and peered down the length of her scaled snout at the creatures who had chosen to be recipients of her magick. Slowly at first, then faster, she began to chant an ancient dialect, words dredged from the beginning of time.

"Niah slowen beh, tri sleannah kiaelah dah, tri

sleannah riania rah, tri sleannah triangah slah."

The she repeated the words in a language they could all understand. *"There will be fire, but it will not burn. There will be ice, but it will not freeze. There will be din, but it will not deafen."*

She threw one last apprehensive glance at Ohma who smiled his reassurance, then turned to Erik and met the gold glitter of his eyes. "May the gods grant that I see you on the other side, Erik."

He reached out a large paw and touched her gently on the head. *"And may the gods be with you, little one."*

She squeezed her eyes closed, heard the dragon take an enormous breath to fill her lungs, and felt warmth as the beast exhaled. Yellow-blue fire flared from bright red nostrils to engulf them both, and she screamed.

Etan grabbed his bow. With deft precision, he notched and aimed, but Ohma knocked it from his hand.

"You old goat. They will burn alive."

"If I am a goat, then you are a fool. It is as the beast said, the fire does not burn." He pointed. "Look."

Skylah stood unyielding beneath the flames—orange, red, blue through to green. She felt a dreadful sucking, a dragging at her bones as if they were being torn from their sockets. Excruciating pain ripped through her body. She dropped to the ground, bent, and curled into a fetal position. Words began to form but were gone before spoken. Time was inconsequential and numbing cold penetrated her bones. Darkness, then the clanging of a thousand temple bells. She crawled to her knees, hands over her ears, bowing low as the intolerable ringing filled her mind—her head. She tried to stand. Pain tore at her insides—then light—scorching, burning blue. Violent waves reared like foaming beasts, threatening, consuming, engulfing her. Then she fell, headlong into darkness.

Skylah awoke to strong hands lifting her. She opened her eyes to a face she thought she would never see again—golden, strong, and ruggedly beautiful. His lips came down over hers, and she was crushed in his embrace, safe, secure. After long moments, she pulled back, and he released her.

"I beg your forgiveness, little one, but I promised myself I would do that should this miracle occur."

She stood on her toes and touched her lips to his once more. "And that is something I have wanted to do since I first saw you at Ohma's cottage. Now we are even."

"We will never be even as long as I have breath in my body to kiss you," Erik said, drawing her back into his arms.

"Is that a threat?"

He smiled. "No woman. That is a promise."

****

Rysha-Taan swung from the scene and lumbered toward Ohma to drop down beside him on the grass. *"Funny creatures…man."*

"Why so?" The mage asked.

"I could have sworn the Faerie's aura was entangled with the snow-haired Elisian who now stands in the forest with a face like thunder."

Ohma laughed shortly. Etan. How knowledgeable the Dragon was. The captain uttered an expletive to rival the dark gods when Erik took Skylah in his arms, then he charged into the woods. "Who can read the heart of a mortal woman? Or most women for that matter." Ohma's eyes sparkled.

The Dragon grunted an affirmative. *"You are a man of much wisdom, Mage. What name do you go by?"*

"I am Ohma, Mystic Druid of Merrum Island."

"Well met, Druid. You may call me Gahna-Tah. That is my Elvish name."

Ohma gave a slight bow and a knowing smile. "Of course," he said, solemnly, playing the game. For he knew to name a dragon by her *true* name was to forever enslave her. And a dragon would rather be dead than enslaved.

Erik stepped forward, having overheard the last part of their conversation, his hand entwined in Skylah's.

"When the ballads are sung by the bards of my kingdom about the dragon who broke the Tiger spell, *Gahna-Tah's* name shall be spoken in reverence." The young king stared directly into the dragon's golden eyes, much the same color as his own. "Know this, *Gahna-Tah,* when I have driven this demon spawn now inhabiting my kingdom from our shores, you and your herd may dwell in the mountains near Wolveryne Castle without fear for all eternity. This I swear on the blood of my parents' graves."

"You are a king to honor, and your words shall be long remembered. I will look forward to such a time. For now, I must gather my herd and travel east to safer ground." Rysha-Taan swung to face Ohma. *"Yet first I would bestow a small gift on you."*

The old sorcerer raised his hands in surprise. "You owe me nothing."

Rysha-Taan pawed the ground and took a pace forward so her large snout overshadowed the Druid's face. *"A Dragon does not leave a debt unsettled."*

Ohma groaned in weary resignation. "Then if you

must, I would be honored to accept your gift."

Rysha-Taan curled her neck around to reach her long, spiked tail, then tore a flat saucer-like scale from her hide and dropped it at Ohma's feet. She repeated the process once more. *"If you ever need me, tap these scales together three times and I shall appear."*

Ohma, stunned by the magnitude of the gift, bowed his head. To have a Dragon at one's call was most wondrous indeed. "Your gift is truly generous, *Gahna-Tah.*"

"Without your healing, the crows would now be feasting on my eyes. You are deserving of the gift, otherwise I would not have bestowed it. Now farewell and may your gods be with you."

"And yours." He stood with Erik and Skylah and watched the great beast of legend ascend into the air.

Rysha-Taan gave a piercing cry, circled once, then pointed her snout northwards to soar with the speed of a shooting star, toward the mountains and those who whispered her name.

****

As evening blanketed the land, Etanandril Jarrisendel, Captain of the Elisian Elite, sat well back in the shadows, burrowed in his heavy cloak. The rough bark of a tall pine dug into his back, but the hurt was inconsequential compared to the pain in his heart.

Over and over in his mind, Tannith's words kept returning to haunt him. *"One day you will rue the way you treat that girl."*

Jealousy ate at his gut as he watched. She had always been beautiful, but now that she was a woman—a full-sized Elisian maiden—she was magnificent.

Copper-red curls hung in a tangle to her tiny waist.

Her lips were as red as berries, her eyes like deep pools of forest green. And her body—ah! He cursed into the night and fought to control his aching loins. He breathed deeply, ran his hand through his hair, and pushed the fringe from his eyes, then took another swig from his flask of Vagarian Red. The spirits only heated his belly more, increasing his agony. Lowering his forehead to rest on his knees, a harsh sigh fell from his lips. How would he get through this? It should have been him sitting beside her, holding her, touching her, making her his.

A strangled sound rose in his throat when he caught sight of her lovely face touched by firelight. Her laugh, like the pure notes of music, wrenched at his gut as he watched her throw back her head at some jest of Ohma or Erik's making. His hand rested on his dagger. Why did he feel like killing the man, cutting his dark gold eyes from his too-handsome face?

Tannith would have teased and said he deserved to wallow in self-misery after the way he had treated Skylah. But he did what he did with the purest intentions. What sort of life could an Elisian have made with a Faerie? He had been forced to be practical, save her from the pain of loving him…a pain he now suffered tenfold.

How was he to know she would save the life of a dragon and in turn be granted a wish, and that she would wish to be a full-sized Elisian woman? How was he to know she would turn to Erik believing *he* did not care?

Skylah rose from beside the fire and sauntered toward him. Her short leather battle skirt hugged her firm, rounded hips. Her long, shapely legs stretched on forever, her breasts jutted against her leather vest.

He pushed to his feet and leaned lazily against a

pine, his gaze hooded, lingering over her flawless features as she walked. "Milady." He made to bow.

"Do not call me that. And do not bow to me." She searched his face. "You never did before."

He looked over her shoulder into the dark forest.

"Will you not join us by the fire?" She moved a pace closer to stand directly in front of him. "Ohma has been regaling us with tales of his youth."

Etan swallowed. Did this woman know not what she was doing to him? Just a step closer and her body would rest perfectly against his. Her hair smelled like heady roses in spring. He could almost taste her lips, feel her soft palms sliding up over his heated flesh. He closed the distance between them and rested his hand on her nape beneath her heavy curtain of hair, drawing her toward him.

"Etan?" Her eyes widened in confusion.

For a moment he stayed as he was, gazing into her questioning green eyes, then he slid his hand to her shoulder and touched a tender, almost brotherly kiss to her brow. He could not do it. She had made her decision. She had chosen Erik. He would not spoil her happiness.

"Go back to the fire, Skylah. The air is damp here by the river; you might catch a fever. Besides, those Urakians who escaped earlier could still be lurking."

Skylah stood for a moment watching his face. "I am sorry," she murmured.

"No." He shook his head and lowered his hand to his side. " 'Tis I who should be sorry. Is it not said that a knight should always tell the truth?"

Skylah frowned and gave a small shake of her head. "I do not understand."

"No." He smiled sadly. "Of course not."

****

Skylah tried to read his expression, but as always it was inscrutable. With another searching look from his midnight eyes, he rounded and strode into the darkness. She stared after him, desperately wanting to follow, wanting to call him back to ask him what he meant, but knowing she would not. Had she made a mistake? Was it possible Etan cared for her after all? She thought now that she was Elisian, she could at least face him on the same level—that they might be friends. However, as usual, Etan was anything but predictable and the tension between them still prevailed.

Would he always be an enigma to her? With a sigh, she turned and ambled back across the clearing to Erik and Ohma. The young king took her hand and kissed her palm, and she snuggled down with her head pressed against his heart, but her thoughts kept wandering to a certain Elisian Captain standing his lone vigil in the forest. Try as she might, she could not unravel his cryptic words. What lie had he told?

Chapter Six

The sky was thick with Vagarian Vultures and Scarlet Crows as Tannith and Kaden crested the ridge and stared down into the shallow valley. Corpses lay strewn across the vale floor like windrows of harvested death. On the periphery of the carnage, small wild desert dogs tore into rotting flesh whilst they fought for the choicest portions.

"May the gods have pity," murmured Kaden.

"Do you think the Urakians did this?"

"I cannot say for certain. These wild tribes are known to war amongst themselves. Stay here. I will check if anyone is alive."

Tannith was about to challenge his authority, but something must have changed her mind because he watched her bite back her retort. He could not blame her. He did not really want to go down amongst the dead either.

He slid from the horse and picked his way down the slope on foot.

Vultures, overstuffed with carrion, flapped their wings in frantic alarm and scuttled away at his approach. The stench of death was heavy in the air. He gagged, resisted the bile in his throat, and forged on through the bodies.

It was not hard to see what happened. The killers attacked at pre-dawn, before the tribesmen rose from their beds. The tribesmen tried to rally, but the attackers cut them down with ruthless efficiency. It appeared the murderous attack had turned into a ritual bloodletting as many were beheaded, mutilated, and disemboweled.

He heard a low moan. Wading through an ocean of dark bodies, he finally came across the source of the sound. The black-skinned man was of middle age, yet even in his distressed state he was obviously a royal; swirling crimson tattoos, the symbol of royalty marked his face.

He remembered when he was a lad that one of the Chieftains from the Vagarian Desert fostered his son at Wolveryne Castle. The boy's face had held similar markings to the man who now lay crucified to the ground at his feet.

The tribesman stared up at him, but his eyes appeared feverish, and his mouth hung slack. Blood stained his massive chest where an axe blade had struck a glancing blow, leaving a gaping wound to his upper torso. A rawhide thong lay across his throat. The thong had most likely been wet when it was tied, however, with the sun beating down drying it out, he was slowly strangling to death.

Kaden drew the knife from his boot and the man's eyes bulged. Weakly, he began to struggle.

"Hold, friend," he assured. "Do not waste your strength."

The tribesman relaxed, and with infinite care, Kaden slipped the point of his knife under the leather thong and sliced cleanly through the hide. The man gulped mouthfuls of sweet fresh air while Kaden cut the rest of his bindings.

The prince released the waterskin hooked to his belt

and dribbled a small amount of water between the man's parched lips. The stranger rallied and tried to snatch the bag from his grip. He drew back. By experience, he knew if an injured man gulped the water after deprived for so long, it could cause severe cramping. He placed his hand under the stranger's shoulders, raised his head, and held the waterskin to his lips. The tribesman managed to swallow a few small mouthfuls.

"Can you walk?"

The big man nodded, crawled to his knees, and attempted to stand, then slumped back down. Although Kaden could see he had been a strong man, the heat, the wounds, and lack of food and water had all contributed to diminish his strength.

"Wait here." He took off at a fast lope through the battleground and up the hill toward Tannith. When he was halfway to the top, he gave a shrill whistle.

Phoenix pricked up his ears and galloped down the slope to meet him. He caught hold of the stallion's bridle, swung into the saddle, and guided the horse at a slow pace through the killing field. The stink of death caused the horse to flatten his ears and roll his eyes as he tried to shy away, but Kaden gentled him with soft words, forcing him on until they reached the tribesman.

"Can you ride?" He asked the man as he slipped from the horse's back.

The tribesman nodded and stretched out his hand. "I will need help."

Kaden grasped his hand and helped him to his feet, then cupped his hands beneath the man's bare foot and boosted him into the saddle. Swinging up behind him, he leaned forward, took the reins, and brought the horse about, turning his head toward the ridge.

****

Tannith watched as they approached. "Who is he?" she asked as Kaden drew level.

He slid from the horse ignoring her words. "Help me get him down. He blacked out on the way up, and I swear he weighs more than a mountain bear."

Between them, they managed to drag the giant from the horse's back and carry him into the shade of an over-hanging cliff. They lowered him onto a blanket Tannith made ready.

"He is suffering from dehydration and blood loss. You better stitch him up."

Tannith raised a brow. "Why me?"

"You did such a pretty job of stitching me, perhaps you can work the same miracle on him." He gave her a handsome smile. "Besides, I want to see what sort of supplies I can find. Our food is running low."

"Could you fetch me some water before you go?"

Kaden retrieved the water skin from their pack and placed it in her hands then took off at a lope down the hill.

She turned back to her patient and poured a small amount of the water onto a cloth, cleaned around the man's largest wound, then probed the cut with her fingers. The axe had torn into the flesh and deflected off a rib. Other than producing a severe amount of bleeding, the tribesman was otherwise unharmed. A small flask at his waist held rum, she released it and splashed a good amount of the alcohol onto the long cut to sterilize the wound. The tribesman jerked at the touch of the spirits but remained unconscious. Drawing the edges of the torn flesh together she stitched the cut, then sat back to await the outcome.

She was biting into a piece of dried venison when Kaden returned. "So, who do you think he is?"

Kaden unloaded water skins and two pair of moccasins he'd found in the camp onto the blanket. A flask of rum followed a round of moldy cheese and several sticks of dried goat meat. "The pair of the boots are for him. He will need them. He is probably a chief from one of the Vagarian hill tribes. The tattoos are a symbol of royalty. I will take the horse down later and gather more food and maybe a couple of blankets before we leave."

She was about to agree when their guest bolted upright and shouted. "Yasmin!"

He dropped beside the man and eased him back. "Careful, friend, you will split your wound." Using the chief's own language, he gestured down the slope. "What happened here?"

Tannith stared at Kaden and frowned.

"It is a hill tribe tongue," he assured her, noting her look of curiosity. "A lad fostered at my father's court taught me the language."

"Ask him who he is."

The stranger peered up at Kaden, blinking. "Who are you?" the man asked, in the same language, before Kaden could speak.

"Kaden of Glen-Dorrach, Son of Farramon, Prince of the Wolfhead."

The chief stilled as if taking in Kaden's words and eyed him slowly from his long hair and three day's growth of beard to his bare feet. He had lost his boots at the lake. At last, he spoke. "The prince with the cursed eyes. I have heard of you. They say you fight like a demon unleashed." He nodded solemnly. "I am Phalae,

Chief of the Blue Panther. You are well met, Prince of the Wolfhead."

Kaden offered the chief water and a strip of dried meat. He had not known his exploits had reached so far.

Phalae groaned, and with help, rose to sit. "You are a long way from home, young prince." He tore at the goat meat with whiter teeth than Kaden would have expected. "And it looks as if you have weathered much."

"That I have, tribesman, but you are also a long way from your village." He settled across from the chief and pulled on the other pair of boots. "What brings you this far north?"

"Urakians raided our village while I and my men were attending a feast with the Gray Bear. The dogs stole our children and raped our women. They took my wife and three daughters."

"Slaves." He cursed. "They are taking captives of every race and using them to work the mines. They harvest the precious golden metal in the Carrum-Bahl Mountains. I was able to get close enough while trying to rescue some of my men. The Urakians are using the stronger ones like pack animals to shift dirt and the weaker to dig."

"Then we must free them." Phalae gritted his teeth and pushed gingerly to his feet.

"No." He stood and placed a hand on Phalae's arm. "Now is not the time. You are weakened by your wound, and first we must recover Magus's Cross."

The Black man's brow furrowed. "What is this Cross of which you speak?"

"A powerful talisman, which is told, can resurrect the God Magus. He alone can vanquish the sorcerer who is behind all this evil in our land. Sernon of Asomos wishes to enslave us all, rob the land of its treasures and take Tarlis for his own."

"Then our prophecies are true. The Dark One has risen from his grave? Our Shaman foretold it. In a dream, he saw Tarlis covered in darkness. He said it would stay this way until the Ancient Cross of the Round-Eyes was found, and the One of Light returned to the land. Do you think this God you speak of was the one foreseen?"

"I believe so. Magus was a great sorcerer who once ruled on Tarlis. He was transformed to a God by the Gods of Creation when he died."

"His magick must be magnificent indeed if he hopes to destroy the Dark One. They say the sorcerer has an army of demons and converses with Arahmin, Prince of the Abyss."

"Sernon is mortal, and as far as I know, the only army he rules is the two-legged kind. However, I have heard he converses with demons. Five demons track my companion and I even as we speak."

The swarthy warrior ran a look down Tannith's body then turned back to Kaden. "I must not keep you long." He fingered the stitches in his wound and inclined his head toward Tannith. "You have done well, woman."

Tannith gave the chief a hesitant smile. He knew she could not understand the man's words. "He said thank you for stitching his wound."

She smiled at the chief again, this time brighter.

Phalae gave her a more concentrated look, then once more spoke to Kaden. "Although my grief for my family is deep, I must think of the continuance of my tribe. As Chief of the Blue Panther, I must have sons, and my wife was stolen. In my village, I have many fine ponies. I would buy the woman from you."

Kaden bent and drew his ten-inch dagger from the sand and ran his thumb lightly over the edge of the blade. The look he gave the other man was deadly. "The woman is mine. She is not for sale."

Phalae grinned, showing a full set of yellow teeth in a black face. "I meant no offense. He turned from Tannith dismissively. "She is too skinny anyway. Her hips are too slim; she will not birth well." He stared into the blue distance. "My woman was strong." He gestured the width of her hips with his hands. "Already she has given me three daughters." His eyes grew sad. "She was to have my son in the Time of the Winds."

"Fear not, we will get her back. The time is coming when the Urakians and those who lead them will pay for the suffering they have caused. I ask you, Chief of the Blue Panther, will you stand with me on that day?"

"The Gods of Sand and Water know I have no love for the round-eyes. Yet you are truly a man of honor, Prince of the Dorrachians. For the service you have rendered this day, I would deem it a privilege for the Blue Panther to stand beside the Son of Farramon and see the blood of our enemies stain the earth."

Kaden reversed his black-hilted dagger and passed it to Phalae. "Take this blade. You will need a weapon on the journey back to your village. I shall send the dagger's twin when I have need of you."

"Your gift is much honored. And may the Panther always be a friend to the Wolfhead."

Kaden passed the chief the pair of goatskin moccasins and waterskin he took from a corpse in the valley. "Also, for your journey."

Phalae inspected the tool work in the leather waterskin, his features darkening even more. "This was

Greko's water bag. He was a fine warrior. The Urakians killed his wife. They had been wed for only seven days." Phalae stared into the distance, a faraway look in his brilliant turquoise eyes. "Perhaps now they stand together in the land where the sun always shines, and water and game are plentiful."

Kaden nodded, unable to think of anything to say to lessen the man's grief.

Tannith rose and laid a hand on Kaden's arm. "Is something wrong?"

He ran a gentle knuckle down her cheek. "No. What could be wrong? The chief promised to join us in our fight against Sernon when the time is right."

"And?"

"He offered to buy you." He grinned.

"I see." She raised a brow. "And what was the knife for, a bonus?"

"No. However, he did offer me eight ponies."

"Only eight?"

"They are fine ponies."

"Indeed?" Her comeback was dry. "And what did you reply?"

"I told him you were disagreeable. That you would make a terrible wife."

Tannith snatched up a waterskin and tossed it at his head, then bent to gather their belongings.

"Thank you." He grinned, taking a swig of water from the bag as he caught it. "All that bargaining left me dry."

She turned to look over her shoulder. "What bargaining?"

"Phalae then offered me ten ponies and a goat."

"Could you not do better?" She straightened. Her

tone dangerous.

"Precisely. I told him it was not enough." He gave a rakish smile as he watched her face. He loved the way her violet eyes sparkled when she fought to hold her emotions in check. He turned back to Phalae. "He said you were too skinny anyway." He smiled without looking at her.

"Too skinny?" He said I was too skinny?" She scooped up another waterskin and tossed it, and he caught it without thought and dropped it to the rug.

Tannith's hands went to her hips. "You best watch your back Dorrachian. One night you will find your other dagger lodged between those manly shoulder blades of yours." She stomped over to the horse to stow the supplies, and Kaden's laughter followed her.

The chief, having watched the scene, laughed with him. "I see your woman has much fire. I prefer my women more docile. I fear that one will cause you much trouble. Perhaps you should keep her after all."

"She has already caused me much trouble," Kaden replied gently. "But it was a pleasure I would not have forgone."

"I see your love for her runs deep. Nonetheless, there is a saying among my people. A woman is a lot like a good horse. First, you must show it who is master. Next, gentle it to your hand. Only then can the filly be ridden."

Kaden grinned. "Good advice, Chief. Perhaps one day I will take it." He glanced at the sky. Already the moons were beginning to rise in the east and the sun setting over the ranges. "It is time we took our leave. We dare not linger too long in one place."

Phalae fingered the knife at his waist. "I fear I have

slowed you down."

"Not at all, we needed to rest. Nevertheless, I worry for your safety. You are certain you are well enough to travel?"

The Chief straightened and winced. "I have suffered worse. A blow from a puny Urakian axe will not see the end of me. I name my own time to die." He stared into the distance. "At the river I will find Blackroot and make a poultice for the wound. It has many healing properties and will ward off a poisoning of the blood. Do not fear. My hate for those blue dogs will keep me strong. When the time comes to fight, I will be there."

He raised a hand in a sign of farewell and Tannith returned his wave. However, Kaden reached out and stopped him before he turned. "I would know one thing. If our roles were reversed. If *you* had found me down, there." He gestured to the valley. "What would you have done?"

The tribesman looked him in the eye. "I would have left you there." The tribesman grinned.

Kaden laid his head back and laughed and Phalae joined him. Then he watched as the big man walked away, his sure stride eating up the sand. He climbed to the next ridge and disappeared. Phalae headed southeast, the opposite direction from which he and Tannith would take. By nightfall, the chief would be at Tarlis Lake, then he would cut west toward the Vagarian Desert.

Tannith touched his elbow. "Will he make it, do you think?"

He bent to wipe the signs of their stay from the sand. "Phalae is a tribesman. They are born to survive. Besides, he has much to live for."

"His family?"

Kaden stilled his movements and looked up. "No, to see his enemy's blood run red on his hands."

Chapter Seven

Dannock dabbed the sweat from his brow with a lace-edged handkerchief and observed the scene spread across the valley floor. His black destrier shifted restlessly beneath him, the stallion's nostrils quivering at the stink of death.

The priest dragged on the horse's reins to regain control and watched with impatience as five silver-helmed warriors climbed the rise and approached him.

"So, what did you find?"

"They helped someone." *The Five* answered as one. "He journeyed southeast."

"I do not want to know where *he* went, fools! I want to know where *they* went. The princess and the Dorrachian. Cannot you do better?"

The demon warriors moved away, sniffed the air, and searched the ground.

Dannock despised the creatures. Having to speak with them, travel with them, eat with them, though they ate little. The decaying stench of their rotting flesh was foul enough, but they never tired. All day they sprinted beside his horse, never requiring food or water, never raising a sweat. He felt inferior each time he needed to sup or attend his bodily functions.

In his eyes it made him appear weak, and weakness was something he truly detested. It reminded him of those insipid priests he had been forced to live with in his early days, years he had used to study the ancient chronicles of the Old World and discover the location of Sernon's book of incantations. The monk Arkahis had been his only friend then, and always he had thought Arkahis would come over to his side.

Unfortunately, he was wrong. It was the first time he had experienced remorse in an age. He sighed and shrugged his bony shoulders. The Abbot had preferred to be a fool, and he had been forced to take his life. Dannock pushed the morbid thoughts from his mind and stared around the campsite. Dismounting, he called to the demon warriors. "Surely you imbeciles have searched enough. 'Tis only one man and a woman. How hard can it be to read a few signs?"

"We track by scent, Master."

"Then get your noses to the ground and start sniffing!" He began to empty his bladder over a corpse of a young tribesman at his feet. As he did so, he stared down into the man's face—a youth of no more than sixteen summers.

"Scum of the earth," he muttered. "You are not even worth pissing on." He shook himself, dropped his robes into place and kicked at the corpse.

The Five stood at attention as he mounted his horse. "We have the scent, Sire."

"Well?"

"They turned south last sundown."

Dannock's lips pulled tight. "South again." He cursed. "Where on the blood of demons are they heading? There is nothing south except desolate peaks, dry gullies, and more desert. Surely the Cross cannot be hidden in the mountains?"

He grasped the reins of his warhorse and pulled it

around. If Prince Kaden and the princess were heading toward the mountains, they would never live to collect their prize. He would see to it. They were only a day and a half ahead. "We will soon be upon them. Then the sport will begin." The priest pointed. "Go!"

The Five set off at a steady pace.

Dannock replaced the stopper on his waterskin, peered out over the vast stretch of red sand merging with the crimson mountains on the horizon, and smiled. Soon, he promised. Soon he would make the Prince of Glen-Dorrach pay for the humiliation he suffered at the Dorrachians' hands.

Perhaps before he ended the prince's life, he would tell him of the pleasure he gained from his mother before he'd slit her soft white throat, or how his father had repeatedly begged for her life before Dannock himself had separated his head from his body. A cruel smile formed on his lips. Perhaps he would have his men hold the prince while he sampled the princess's virgin body.

He had only seen her once, but the sight had been enough to fire his blood—violet eyes flashing like pinpoints of fire, masses of flowing white-blonde hair and breasts to fill a man's hands. She would not be one to surrender easily, and there was naught he enjoyed more than the taming of a wild cat. He kicked his heels to his mount and rode on.

****

Kaden built up the fire and knelt beside Tannith, who was still sleeping. She was breathing evenly. He touched her face gently with one finger, stroking the soft skin of her cheek, then left to climb to the top of the nearby rise to stare out over the rolling plains to the south. The sun crested the Poniard Ranges; deep sandstone gorges, tall cone-shaped rock formations and long stretches of limestone swept into distant blue haze, as if the sky had joined and merged with the land. To the northwest, the defiant Carrum-Bahl Mountains pierced the clouds like sword points, blood red and glowing proud.

He watched as the sun's rays hit and aligned with the left eye socket of Skull Rock and speared a brilliant streak of light directly into a distant red cliff face. It was the sign that would lead them to the pass. He memorized the coordinates. If they made good time, they could make the hidden valley by late noon.

Already the day was growing hot. Kaden drew his cloak from his shoulders and dropped it to the sand. He glanced down at the garments he wore—a white loose-flowing tunic and white wide-legged pants. The tribesman who once owned the clothes had long ago stopped caring about worldly belongings. His eyes had been put out. His throat cut.

He settled onto a nearby boulder and unhooked the leather flask he had taken from the valley from his belt. If the hill tribes were famous for anything besides warring, it was distilling good rum. He sampled the brew with a hearty swallow. It warmed his insides like a brick from the Fiery Abyss and momentarily took his breath away.

Devoid of all human life, the landscape was stark and beautiful. His thoughts drifted haphazardly, but always Tannith's face returned to float before his eyes. Did he love her? Could love be born in such travail? Or was it only a passion felt between two people continually thrown together in circumstances of war? Would they feel the same when the quest was over? When all the pieces of the Cross were found, when Sernon had been dealt with, and their kingdoms restored?

He ran a hand over his jaw. He needed a shave and a good barber. Last evening Tannith complained about the stubble scraping her cheek. He smiled inwardly.

He looked to the east toward Dragonbane. Would he fit with her way of life…with her people? What would be expected of him? Would she want him as her consort? He laughed derisively and stared down at his callused palms. He had chosen the life of a soldier long ago. He despised the pampered dandies of the court and the way they lived, simpering nobles of all stations, vying for favor. He would suffocate in the opulence.

Tannith deserved better, someone who would revel in court life. Someone, like Etan…What was a princess doing out here anyway? What were any of them doing here? What was this madness threatening to engulf them all? He could kill Dannock-Shae—of that he had no qualms. Even Sernon he could kill, given the right circumstances. But what would it achieve? Would anything be different? Would it bring back his family? Would it take away the pain of the guilt he carried on his shoulders every morning he awoke?

He ran his hand over his eyes.

Probably not, but his fate was sealed from the moment he rescued the Elisian Princess in the forest. He knew that now.

He sensed the moment she approached.

"What are you doing?" she asked softly from behind him.

"Admiring the view."

She settled on the boulder beside him. "It is lovely out here." She sighed. "But should we not be leaving?"

He dropped a kiss on her nose and came to his feet holding out his hand to her. "I was waiting for you to wake." He stared at the ruby cliffs in the distance. "If we head due south by Ohma's reckoning we should encounter the pass before noon."

She took his hand and stood. Shading her eyes, she followed his gaze. "There is nothing there but a steep escarpment."

He nodded. "Then let us hope it is all Dannock-Shae sees."

****

Fifteen leagues away, three travelers sat around a campfire, focused on the fourth member of their party. He opened his eyes, slumped back against his bedroll, and stretched as if waking from a deep slumber.

Their leader, a man with hair and eyes of gold, stood and chose another log for the fire. He placed it on the flames and moved back to the old man to stare him in the eye. "How does my brother fare?"

"He is well," Ohma replied.

"And the princess?"

"She too fares well."

A collective sigh sounded from the other members of the party.

"Your brother is a man of extreme bravery, my lord, and is a worthy adversary to any who challenge him."

"Have *you* knowledge of the Living Dead?"

"No. But the weapons I ensorcelled will be enough protection should they catch them up, and both Kaden and Tannith are skilled warriors."

"How can you be sure of their survival?"

"You forget I am a seer. I have walked the pathways of the future, and in all, your brother and the princess survive long and prosperous lives. They are people of great destiny. The Gods of Creation protect them. Also, the Great Prophecy names them. They cannot perish while the prophecy stands unfulfilled."

"Pig's swill!" Etan leapt to his feet and began to pace. "You and your tales of the future. You are forever spouting on about visions and roads to the…gods know where. If you know so much, wave your magick wand and put an end to this farce." He stopped before Ohma. "Tell us now how this will end. Will we find the last pieces of the Cross? Will we defeat Dannock and Sernon? Or will we all perish? Answer those three simple questions."

And let me leave, he added silently. Let me escape the woman who torments my mind with thoughts of should have beens, and what ifs. His gaze slid briefly to Skylah sitting beside Erik, then flittered back to the old Mage Druid.

Ohma peered around the fire at the accusing faces.

Erik's eyes darkened. "Can you answer his questions?"

"Do you think I would not have told you if I could foresee the end?" Ohma spread his hands imploringly. "That one vision forever eludes me. The one thing the gods have denied me. Perhaps we were not meant to know. Perhaps it is something they do not know themselves. Maybe it is a saga that must be played out in its entirety and we in turn must make our own end."

Etan turned away and ran a hand through his hair. "Once again, old man, you speak in riddles that I am too exhausted to decipher." He grabbed his bedroll and the flask of leftover wine from supper and stomped into the forest where he hoped with a good drink and a good night's sleep, he could rid his mind of thoughts of the woman.

But the flask was soon empty—the night long—and sleep elusive.

****

Sometime after Etan retired to his blankets and Erik had excused himself from their company, Skylah and Ohma sat cross-legged, staring into the slow dying embers of the fire.

Ohma peered across the coals with a heavy heart. The former Faerie had seen much tragedy in her life, and still there was more to come.

"Do you truly love him, lass?"

Skylah frowned. "Who? Erik?" She glanced over to where the young king lay in the shadows.

He nodded his ancient head.

She smiled softly. "Erik wears his power so lightly. He has such gentleness. How can I not love him?"

Ohma sighed and lowered his gaze. "He is not the one for you. I have seen your future. He does not walk your path."

Skylah rose to her feet and glared down at him with eyes flashing like green fire. "Then you have seen wrong. Erik *is* my future, there can be no other."

" 'Tis no good towering over me in anger, lass. I meant no offense. You have no family to speak of and for some reason I feel a certain responsibility toward you."

"Then be released from it. I have Erik to look after me and wish for no other. You said there are many pathways to the future. Erik loves me and nothing and no one will keep us apart. So, you can take your vision, throw it into the deepest dungeon of your mind and slam its rusty door. Etan was right." She bent low her words soft yet powerful. "You are playing with people's lives, and I will listen no more."

Ohma remained silent, and Skylah looked away into the sputtering flames, wiping impatiently at the tears forming in her eyes. "We were meant to be together," she insisted, softly. "Why else would the gods have put us through so many trials to find each other?"

Ohma sighed, reached into his sleeve, and passed her a blue handkerchief. "Indeed why?" he muttered to himself. "Perhaps you are right, little one." He was sorry now he thought to meddle. "I meant no harm. I am old and images sometimes get muddled in this ancient head of mine. Forget my words. Go to your young man and seize what happiness you can. For in these times of desperation, who can say how each day will end?"

Skylah dried her eyes, bent to kiss his cheek, and tugged gently on the thin plait of his snowy beard.

"I am sorry I spoke so harshly. You frightened me. A long time, I have waited for someone to love. Surely the gods cannot be so cruel as to snatch away my happiness when I have just found it."

Ohma nodded and kept his own counsel. He had one vision of the future he wished he had never seen. Perhaps the gods would be generous and change the outcome, but he doubted it. The gods did what they did for a reason, but by all that was holy, he could see no reason in what was to come. "I am certain you are right." How could he tell her he had seen Erik's future in a vision of blood? He gave her a gentle smile. "Now, go."

Skylah glanced thoughtfully into the darkness of the trees to where Erik lay wrapped in his blankets. "I have a notion to heed your advice, my friend, and reach out for that happiness of which you speak." She bid him a comfortable sleep and slipped into the night.

Erik rolled onto his elbow and peered up at the dim outline of the woman standing above him. "What is it?" He pushed his sleep-tousled hair from his eyes. "Is there a problem?"

"Problem? Is it a problem when a lass seeks company?" Skylah peeled away her leather battle skirt, wrist guards and vest, and dropped them at his feet. "I am taking the advice of a Druid."

His eyes filled with knowing, and he moved aside. "Remind me to thank that old man sometime." He smiled softly and pulled her into his arms to welcome her naked form beneath his blanket. Rolling her over, he nuzzled her ear. "What else did you and Ohma discuss? You have spoken long into the night."

She shivered at the riotous sensations his lips evoked. She was barely able to breathe, yet still, Ohma's words haunted her. *Seize your happiness while you can...Erik is not for you...his path does not lie with yours. No.* She groaned, willing her mind to block out the Druid's words. It was not true. Erik was hers, and nothing, no one, would take him from her. In defiance to the words, she reached for the laces on Erik's breeches and deftly began to unravel them, but he placed his hand over hers.

"Are you sure?"

"I have long waited for this time. You do not mean to stop me now?"

He kissed her tenderly on the brow. "I had to ask."

"And for that you are even dearer to me."

He smiled in the moonlight and helped her with the laces, then all thought dissolved from her consciousness in a meeting of hands, lips, and the hard body of the man who loved her.

****

Well back in the shadows, Ohma sat cross-legged by the fire and turned his eyes to the starlit sky.

"Why?" he beseeched to the gods in soft anguish. "Why him? Has he not been through enough? Why not me? I am old."

But, no answer came, just the whisper of a gentle breeze as it picked up his words and scattered them to the lonely night.

Chapter Eight

Tannith stepped from the pass, her breath lodging in her throat at the sight displayed before her. At the center of the valley descending from a sheer cliff was a spectacular waterfall. She brought her hand to her face and wiped her eyes in disbelief. This was a heartfelt reward indeed for such a trying journey.

After traveling for a near full day, Kaden finally found the opening to the pass behind a fallen tree. The gap between the towering cliffs was barely wider than the width of Phoenix's flanks. The large stallion had panicked and reared onto his hind legs. After settling him, she was forced to lead him through blindfolded. Kaden trailed behind, eliminating their tracks. He arrived to stand beside her. Neither of them spoke. A brilliant rainbow arch of light was reflected in the spray.

"Surely the Gods of Creation themselves fashioned these falls." Her words were muted by the thundering water.

The tiny valley was fertile and wet, still glistening from recent rain. They mounted the stallion and followed a narrow track winding down into the valley to the foot of the falls. Palms, giant umbrella trees, and ferns of every description dotted the landscape; blue and mauve mountains towered around them, a swirling mist shrouding their peaks, giving them an aura of mystery. The falls pounded straight into a natural kidney-shaped basin. The spray of crashing waters smoked and hissed as it tumbled over black volcanic rocks.

Kaden dismounted and picked his way between boulders and fernery toward the edge of the pool. Undercutting the base of the falls, he spied a ledge leading into a dark cavern. He returned to Tannith, mounted the stallion, and leaned forward to take the reins. "I think that is what we are searching for." He pointed. "If we follow this path, it should lead straight to the entrance of the cave."

****

They continued along a narrow track that followed level ground around the inner rim of a gully, then began a slow steep ascent. The trail led to a small, crystal-clear waterfall and a cave where hundreds of multicolored Dillon birds nested in the crevices of an enormous rock chamber, then they passed over a rope footbridge strung across a shallow fern-filled stream.

By the time they reached the cave, the sun began to make its slow decent behind the blue-mauve crest of the hills. While Kaden searched for a place to tether Phoenix away from the drenching spray of the falls, Tannith moved ahead into the cave.

On entering, it took her night vision a moment to adjust.

The cave was shallow, no more than twenty feet long and thirty wide. The floor of charcoal-black rock gave the impression of having been seared by a thousand summers of ancient campfires. Rough antiquated drawings covered the walls, rendered in bright aluminous ochers, lending the cavern an aura of frightening intent. Images clamored to fill her mind. Screams of a million lost souls cried their despair.

Faces of creatures, bright and demon-like, swooped, howled, ascended, and descended, engulfing her body and soul in their fiendish game of madness. Whether an illusion or real, she cared not. Bending, she covered her ears, tried to shut out their screams, and fled. Kaden made to catch her arm, but her fear overpowered her. She wrenched free and ran refusing to answer his call.

Outside, drenching spray soaked her clothing, returning her to the present. The sting of the icy water felt real and invigorating after the strange imaginings that had invaded her mind.

Although unsure of what had happened, she knew she could not return to that unholy place that eve. She drew a ragged breath, then almost jumped as Kaden's arm came around her. It was warm and strong, lending her confidence. When he smiled down at her, she leaned against him, drawing from his strength.

He turned her gently to face him. "What happened? Why did you leave so abruptly?"

Tannith peered up at him, her hair and lashes dripping with moisture. She shivered. "Did you not feel it?"

His hands held her arms to steady her. "Feel what? I felt nothing. Tannith, there was nothing in that cave. I searched."

"There were…voices, screaming, the most hideous faces…spiders…You know I hate…" She shook her head and trailed off. "Just images, really. But know this, whatever is in that cave was trying to warn me or scare me witless."

"Perhaps the Dwarves had Ohma cast a warding spell over the cave to stop strangers from stumbling upon the entrance to the city."

"I am not spending one night in this place, even for you."

His arms came around her and he pulled her close to his chest, and she rested her cheek against his heart. "If you are worried, perhaps it is with good cause." He took her arm and led her out from the ledge behind the thundering water. "We will backtrack and set our camp at the base of the falls and try again come dawn. From my calculations, Dannock is about two moons ride behind us. We will be long gone before he and his creatures track us here—if they find this valley at all."

He led her out from behind the waterfall to where he had tethered the horse. He boosted her onto Phoenix's back and wrapped her cloak around her shoulders, then climbed up behind her. Grasping the reins, he headed the horse back down the mountainside.

****

Kaden awoke with a start. The two moons were high. A paradise of Hibiscus and Frangipani surrounded him. Night creatures played their orchestra on the periphery of the campsite, but none of this registered as terror struck at his heart.

She was gone.

Tannith's discarded blanket lay in a tangle beside him. Her weapons were still where she had stacked them, and thankfully, there was no indication of a struggle.

"Darn woman!" He grabbed up his sword and dagger and scanned the ground for a sign. It was not hard to find her tracks by the light of the twin moons. Her footsteps were deep in the fertile soil and led east along the bank of the small stream by which they camped.

She stood naked in a shallow pool, into which a narrow waterfall plunged. Droplets of water glistened over the swell of her well-rounded breasts, trickling down her flat stomach to meet with the flow of water swirling around her hips.

A bewitching goddess by moonlight.

His gaze slid over her slim curves in silent appraisal—breasts as white as the purest marble, a waist no larger than the span of his hands, and with a vision in his mind of what lay beneath the moonlit water, his loins grew hard and hot. The urge to reach out and feel the warmth of her perfect beauty burned deep in his gut.

****

Tannith watched him step closer and her eyes widened.

She thought she did well to leave the camp without waking him, but she should have known. The warrior never slept with more than one eye closed at a time. She wanted him to see her and made no move to cover herself. She wanted his hands on her body, touching her, bringing her to life. His dark gaze was a firebrand, searing her soul, marking her his. Some nights she dreamt of him with such intensity she had awoke hot and trembling.

Would he join her in the stream and make her his? She watched him warily, unmoving. Or would he scold and order her to return to camp? The feelings he evoked, the fire, the ice, the shivers of pure pleasure that racked her body and tortured her soul were worth a risk.

Taking her courage in both hands, she waded a step closer. "Are you going to stand with your mouth gaping all night, warrior? Or will you join me in the pool?"

"You should not be out here alone. It could be dangerous."

"Anywhere could be dangerous with you," she

assured, pushing a handful of silvery tresses back over her shoulder, giving him better access to her body. "I thought the risk would be worth the reward."

The emerald of his eyes blazed in the moonlight. "We discussed this."

"You discussed it. I listened. Now it is my turn to talk."

His brow rose. "I see." His emerald gaze never left her face. "If that is what you wish." He drew his remaining knife from his boot, lowered his sword to the ground, and pulled his knee-high boots from his feet, tossing them across to join his weapons.

Next, came his brown leather jerkin. The fastenings to his loose-fitting hill tribe breeches held no hindrance to his nimble fingers as he unlaced them and let them slide down over his well-muscled thighs to be kicked aside.

Tannith's breath caught, choking off her words. For what words could describe the sheer magnificence of his body—its masculine planes etched silver and gold in the moonlight? Like a bronze God of ancient times—sublime in his nakedness, hard, strong, unyielding.

She knew what she was about to do would change the course of her life. It was something that would go against every code of her upbringing, every law. She would be joining with a man from another race—an inferior being, according to her people.

It was a love such as this that caused the dilution of the Elven blood and the beginning of the Elisian Race. Did she truly love this man enough to put behind her all of her teachings and the elite bloodline her people now strived for?

He looked so vulnerable standing, awaiting her

decision. Even now he had stopped, was watching her, giving her a choice. In that moment, all doubts melted to insignificance. She knew she would give up her last breath to lay with this man.

Their eyes met. "Are you sure this is what you want?" he asked.

"I want you, that is all that is clear to me."

"Then by the gods, woman, you shall have me." Kaden stepped to the edge of the pond and dove into the water to disappear into its crystal darkness. Then as suddenly as he disappeared, he reappeared. His large hands spanned her waist to draw her toward him with slow assurance.

She ran her lips over his chest, the base of his throat, and across his shoulders, tasting, teasing. A groan issued from deep in his throat. Emboldened by her newfound power, she encircled his neck, drew his lips down to hers and took his mouth. His tongue filled her, seeking, finding, drawing forth a response from her, so complete, so thoroughly dazzling, she thought her knees would melt and blend with the water.

Then she was falling. Kaden must have felt it too, for he clasped her waist and lifted her, to slide her up the hard planes of his body. With one swift movement he pulled her thighs around his waist. Tannith felt his hard length pressed against her. It felt so good, right, as if it belonged. Pulling away, she trailed her hand down between their bodies, encircling him, feeling his heat.

In a sudden burst of strength, he thrust her to arm's length and flicked his long black hair from his eyes. "What are you doing?" He reached out to steady her. "Do you want this to be over before it starts?"

She slanted her head to the side and peered up at

him. "Did I hurt you?"

"No…of course not." He took a deep breath as her hands crept up his chest again. "As much as I love your touch, too much of that sort of thing can hasten a man along. It has been long since I had a woman."

She pulled away. "I thought—Druh Forest—" She left the sentence hanging and his arms came around her to draw her back into his embrace.

He smiled. "What gave you that idea?"

"Etan…"

"I should have known," he countered dryly. "I had consumed a little too much wine, but I swear I did not touch her, though the Elven wench tried."

Tannith laid her cheek against his chest, but Kaden shifted his stance and lifted her chin so he could see into her eyes. "I must have your trust."

"If you say it is so, then it is so," she answered simply. "I know now, you would not lie to me."

"Then all is well?"

"I am sorry I put you through so much. I mean…well…you know—"

He grinned, and she could see the white of his teeth in the moonlight. "I have not perished yet." His voice deepened. "But let me see if I remember what to do with a woman." He drew her closer against his body.

"First I put my hands here," he whispered against her ear, placing his hands on her shoulders. Then, he slid his hands to the soft curve of her spine and came to rest on her small derriere. "Then here."

Chills spiraled down her back, spread to the tips of her toes, then skyrocketed back up to settle low in her stomach.

"Then I place this hand around here," he continued

as one hand stole around to rest over the junction of her thighs.

She gasped.

"Relax." His lips ran from her collar bone to the base of her throat, his breath hot against her skin. "Trust me."

Relax! She groaned. How could she relax? His heat was all over her, his scent all around her. It filled her mouth, engulfed her, intoxicated, and made her faint. She could not breathe!

For a moment she struggled, then as suddenly as panic seized her, it drained away as she remembered where she was—who she was with. This was Kaden, the man she loved, the man she had fallen in love with the moment he had burst through the trees to aid her. She released her breath and wrapped her arms about his neck, pressing herself unashamedly into his hand.

****

"Whoa. Slow down." He laughed softly and shifted her position. Gently slipping a callused finger into her warmth, then another, and began a slow steady rhythm. She was tight, hot, and wet—a different kind of moistness than the water—smooth like velvet. Kaden prayed he could control himself long enough to bring her to fulfillment. There was nothing he wanted more than Tannith naked beneath him. Right now!

She moaned, bringing him back to reality, and he withdrew his fingers grazing his palm across her cleft. She threw back her head and a small sob escaped her lips. His left arm came around her to support her, the ends of her hair trailing the cool water of the pond.

"Kaden…" Tannith arched upward, offering more. Her body dissolving in liquid fire, a raging need like nothing she had ever imagined pooling between her thighs. Instinctively, she opened them wider, knowing only he had the power to ease the pulsing ache growing inside of her.

He tried again, rubbing, and flicking her tiny bud back and forth between his fingers. He leaned low and drew her breast into his mouth, grazing her nipple with his teeth, then soothed it with his tongue.

Tannith's whole body erupted into a thousand shattering pieces of intense delectation. So utterly terrifyingly pleasurable, it left her trembling in its wake. She collapsed against him and buried her head on his shoulder, waiting for her trembling to subside.

Kaden's arms came about her, and he scooped her up and waded quickly toward the shore. Lowering her to the grass, he came down over her and settled in the cradle of her thighs.

****

Adjusting his weight, he looked down into her eyes. They were dark pools of purple, and she appeared a delicate illusion of Fey, almost ethereal. He knew he had to ask one more time, even if the answer broke his heart. "There will be no turning back after this. Are you sure…?"

She put a finger to his lips. "I know what I am doing."

He searched her face for a heartbeat more, nodded, then bent to trail soft wet kisses down her breasts, stomach, and over her hips.

Tannith gasped as a strange tingling began in her navel and transcended to the secret place between her thighs. He hooked his arms under her legs, and drew them apart, then very slowly, lowered his mouth to press against her soft flesh and thrust his tongue into the tight warm opening of her body. She bucked and writhed, trying to pull away, but he held her firm and settled her with gentle words of love.

He returned his mouth to the place that burned between her thighs.

Rocking back and forth, her breath came in short sharp bursts, and the tension grew. She moaned for release, her muscles tensing and tightening. Higher, harder, like a spring ready to uncoil…she clutched at the grass with both hands and arched her body as his tongue touched her where no man had ever dared and worked magick with lips and hands.

She cried his name and grasped his shoulders, seeking, searching for a summit…Would this ever end? She wanted him to stop. She wanted him to go on forever. Her breath, hot and fast, she could barely breathe. Searching…for something only he could give.

He rose over her, and she arched up and pulled his body down hard into hers.

****

Kaden had wanted to take things slowly, not to frighten or hurt her, but just like his woman, she rushed in headlong, even into this. He watched her eyes widen, first with surprise, then pain, then with wonder.

His hands slid down to rest over the curve of her bottom. "Trust me," he whispered gently. "Allow your body to adjust to mine. We have all night and the rest of our lives. Can you feel me? I am inside of you—part of you—and you of me."

****

Tannith heard Kaden's words and gloried in them. She had entered a whole new plane she never knew existed, the initial pain of his entry already forgotten. She was so ready she hardly felt the tearing of her maidenhood. He was inside her, and she was hungry for the rhythm that would bring fulfillment to them both. His name came in a sigh, and she urged him on.

He began to move, teaching her, whispering encouragement, building the tempo layer upon layer. Yet still, he thought of her innocence and did not want to hurt her. He held back. Sweat ran freely, and his body grew taut, near to explosion—but he wanted more. He wanted Tannith with him. He rose enough to give him access to that place that needed to be touched. His fingers moved and he stroked her there. At the same time, he thrust, his strokes deep and powerful. Her nails bit into his back, but his pain turned to pleasure as he felt her respond, tightening and convulsing around him—straining into him.

Tannith became aware of strange sensations licking through her insides like quicksilver. Her breasts grew heavy, the urge to hold on, pull Kaden closer, climb into his soul, became overwhelming. Then it happened—her body spun away, racked with one continuous spasm after another. Great waves flowed over her, through her, picking her up, carrying her to their topmost peak then dropping her back down. Only to pick her up and start their wild ride over again. Her breath unraveled in a piercing scream.

"Tannith!" Her name splintered from Kaden's lips. A hoarse cry from somewhere deep in his gut. He felt the collapsing contractions of her body. With one final thrust, he poured himself into her with a heady rush of exploding senses.

With bodies joined, they rode out a maelstrom of pleasure so fierce, so tense it left them drained and breathless. They came down from their peak slowly, and for long heartbeats, neither spoke.

Kaden rolled onto his back and stared up at the heavens. "Now you are truly my woman," he murmured, taking a fistful of her fair hair, bringing it to his face. "Did I ever tell you I love your hair?"

She moved over him and stared down into his midnight green eyes. "Did I ever tell you, I love you?"

He grasped her and rolled her onto her back, then rose above her, his gaze mischievous as it swept her breasts.

She giggled and tried to push him aside.

He held her down and brushed his stubbled jaw across her nipples. "Prove it."

"Anytime." She squirmed, then her expression changed, and her violet eyes darkened even more. She lowered her hand between their bodies and felt his semi-erect shaft. "Still, I do not think you are up to it, yet."

He raised an ebony brow. "I take that as a challenge, woman. We shall see who is up to what.

As he spoke, her hands worked their magick and he gasped. His eyes transformed to an intense blue-green, and he grinned wickedly. "I told you not to touch me there."

Tannith smiled. "So you did, but I think you have noticed I am not much good at taking orders."

"Then I shall have to teach you." He began to ease down the center of her body. "Will I not?"

She smiled again and ran her hands through his thick black hair, letting it trail and coil about her hand. "Do you never tire?"

His reply was muffled as he turned his attention elsewhere. "Never of you, my lady, not ever of you."

Chapter Nine

Skylah's eyes widened in anticipation as the sun splayed from the mountains heralding a new dawn. She stepped through the open gates of Antibba. It was the first time she had been here as a full-grown woman.

Four cloaked figures blended furtively with the crowd milling their way toward the market square.

Erik explained that the market square consisted of tiers of shops built into a steep hillside, linked by walkways and a pleasant green park.

Novak's tavern, "The Tiger's Eye," was located at the bottom of a hill in the better part of the village, flanked by a silversmith and a blacksmith. Some of the more disreputable establishments were at the top of the hill, fringed by seedy brothels, or worse, trafficked in human flesh.

Erik strode ahead, keeping his face and hair well covered. He led the way down a narrow, ill-smelling lane, several more dimly lit streets, and across a small park into another lane.

Halfway down he stopped, peered over his shoulder, and made certain he was not observed. He knocked three times at a small side door displaying a snarling black tiger on a background of gold. He waited several heartbeats, then knocked twice more.

The door rattled and a metal slide pulled across to reveal a round, podgy face with a shock of red hair and salt and pepper whiskers. The man stared at them intently then rammed home the shutter.

"Be gone. Beggars are not welcome!"

Erik pounded again. "Open the door, Norvak, 'tis I, Erik."

"I know no Erik."

"Erik, your king! And if this door is not opened on the count of three, by the gods I shall behead you myself." Erik drew a deep breath. "One…two…"

The door crashed back on its hinges, the small party ushered inside, and the portal slammed behind them.

Norvak viewed his monarch in disbelief. "A welcome sight you are, Your Majesty. We thought you dead."

"Not yet, my friend." Erik pounded him affectionately on the back. "Though not for the want of trying on our enemy's part. How do my people fare?"

"I am well, milord, but there are many who are not. The Urakians are everywhere. The town is under martial law, and one called Sernon of Asomos sits on your father's throne. He has declared himself ruler of all Tarlis. The people live in fear. Any caught speaking against him are thrown into his dungeon or mysteriously vanish never to be seen again. They say he is a sorcerer of much ability."

Erik straightened as if struck, but it was no use being angry at Norvak, the man had always spoken frankly.

"Is it true, milord, your father the king, and Queen Morveena are…no longer with us? There has been talk…"

Erik's jaw clenched as Norvak's words trailed off. "My mother and father have journeyed the path to Elysium." Erik spoke in a tight voice. "However," he glanced away, "I would prefer not to speak of the circumstances just now. We are tired from our journey. And," he met Norvak's eyes. "I would favor not to spoil my homecoming with tales of sorrow."

"Of course, milord." The innkeeper nodded. "Forgive my foolish tongue. It does not know when to stop."

Erik stepped aside and motioned to the Elisian and the Druid standing behind him. "Meet my friends, Captain Etan Jarrisendel of Ellenroh, and Ohma of Merrum Island."

Norvak acknowledged them with a hearty handshake.

"And this," Erik brought the girl forward, "is my greatest treasure, Lady Skylah." He smiled down at the young woman beside him, his feelings written in his eyes.

Norvak slid her an appreciative glance. "A rare jewel indeed, my lord. Shall I have your usual rooms prepared?"

Erik glanced up. "Two will suffice. One for the Druid and the captain, the other for myself and my lady." He knew he could count on Norvak's discretion. He knew Kaden had brought several women here in the past.

****

"As you wish." Norvak did not think it strange the young king would be sharing with the woman. Many times, in days gone by, his brother had brought a wench to share a night in his establishment, as his father before him had shared with the witch Zoreena. Always Norvak had kept his counsel. He was a loyal subject to the crown and was not one to question. He grinned, showing his discolored teeth. There was usually a hefty purse to be had for his trouble at the end of their stay.

"Let me show you to my sitting room. I dare say you must be famished." He led the way out of the kitchen, through a brown beaded curtain into a small room, branching from a long narrow corridor. A faded green velvet curtain on the other side of the room separated the sitting room from the tavern bar. The room was warm and inviting with an open fire crackling in the grate and a wide elm wood table at its center. Oak paneling lined the walls, and over the hearth in pride of place hung a large moose head.

Norvak bent and tossed another log onto the fire, then stretched his back and turned to face Erik. "I will see your rooms prepared, and my Sara will bring you something warm for your stomach."

Erik nodded and took a seat at the table next to Ohma who gave a weary sigh, and Norvak gave a clumsy bow and scuttled from the room.

****

"Can you trust him?" Etan frowned leaning back in his chair across from Erik.

"With my life. He is a loyal subject."

"Even loyal subjects can be bought." Etan rose again and headed toward the green curtain separating them from the bar.

"Not this one. He was my father's man."

Etan peered around the side of the curtain. Two men looked around in surprise from their table, then quickly returned to their drinking. He grunted and moved back to his seat as a tavern maid entered by way of the hall. The girl served their ale quietly and efficiently, while casting several saucy glances at Erik and Etan.

Next came Norvak's wife with a venison pie, and

the maid exited quickly from the room

"It smells delicious" said Skylah, as Sara set a large portion of pastry topped pie before her.

Ohma dragged his plate forward. "Actually, I do not care what it tastes like. I am so hungry I could eat a wasteland toad on heat."

Sara shot him a daggered look.

"But of course, it would be nowhere as delicious as your wonderous pie." He stabbed a large piece of gravy covered meat and pushed it into his mouth making a show of chewing with gusto. The others chuckled.

Sara finished serving the food then departed and they ate in a companiable silence.

However, the uneasy peace between the two men was soon broken when Erik withdrew a heavy purse from his belt, weighed it in his hand, and threw it down in front of Etan

"When you have supped, take this and purchase clothing and weapons for yourself. The blacksmith next door is renowned for his crossbows; see him first."

Etan looked down his nose at the pouch and his jaw hardened. "What of you and the others?"

Erik took a hearty bite of his pie and washed it down with a draught of ale. After a moment he spoke again. "Norvak will see to our needs. And be careful, if what the innkeeper says is true and martial law prevails, you will not wish to be caught on the streets after dark. We will meet you here again just before sundown."

Etan shoved his plate aside and stood. It irked him to be beholden to the man. Grudgingly, he snatched up the hefty bag of coins and shoved it deep into his cloak pocket. Erik may be generous and a good leader, but to Etan he was no more than the man who stood between him and the woman he loved.

He was about to pull back the curtain to step through into the sectioned off part of the tavern when Erik spoke again. "One more thing." He waited for Etan to turn. "Something pretty for my lady." The sensual look he bestowed on Skylah was not lost on him, and his fist bunched involuntarily in his cloak. He was beginning to loath this man more every day. He had disliked him as a tiger, as a man he disliked him more.

"Something made of silk, I think." Erik's yellow eyes held Etan's for several long heartbeats, then he turned away to speak to Ohma as if in dismissal. However, his next words were again for *him*. "You should find a suitable gown in the market square."

Etan gave the curtain a violent thrust and stepped through into the bar.

Ohma watched the curtain fall back into place and frowned. He had not missed the look of animosity that had passed between the two men. Trouble was brewing as sure as dragons hatched from eggs. He did not need second sight for that knowledge.

****

Tannith awoke to the sun streaming into her eyes through overhead ferns, and the sound of Kaden's voice.

"Get dressed." He tossed her clothes into a pile at her side.

She stretched and blinked, shading her eyes. "What is it?"

"I must speak with you."

She frowned. "And I must dress for this occasion?"

He pushed a dark lock of hair from his eyes and met her gaze. "I would prefer it that way."

"You did not prefer it that way last night."

119

He looked away. "That was different. What I have to tell you may change how you feel about me."

Tannith grabbed her buff-colored tunic, dragged it down over her head and fastened the laces. "Turn."

"What?"

"I said turn around."

"Do not be ridiculous." He folded his arms across his bare chest. "I saw everything you had to show last night."

"That was different."

"How so?"

"If this thing you are going to tell me is so dramatic it may change the way I think of you, I do not want you gawking at me naked."

Kaden raised a brow. "Gawking? What kind of word is that?"

She laughed shortly. "A good enough word for you, warrior. Now turn."

Kaden expelled a long breath and swung to stare into the trees, and Tannith gave a small half smile. At times, he reminded her of a child. What could be so important he would be in such a hurry? And how could he imagine it would change her feelings for him after the passion of last night?

She finished pulling on her soft leather breeches, laced her shirt, then moved to hug his waist and lean her cheek against his warm back. "Now, what is this thing that cannot wait?"

He turned to face her, then dropped down onto the blanket, pulling her down with him. For a moment, he remained silent, then he began to speak, his voice deep and unhurried.

"I wish to tell you a story."

"But—"

"Hush and listen." He took her hand and squeezed it gently. "Once upon a time, there was a king who was married to a very beautiful queen."

Tannith chuckled. "Oh yes, and what was her name?"

"That is not important." Then changing his mind, he said, "Morveena. Now be quiet, or I shall have to gag you."

Tannith gave a half laugh, but otherwise remained silent.

"The king and queen were married for five summers and in all that time had only one son. It was thought the queen had become barren. As much as the king loved his queen he was worried for his kingdom, should something befall the young prince. His gaze wandered, and he soon became smitten by a comely peasant woman, by the name of Zoreena-Rah. It was said she was a witch and she had bewitched him, for she wanted a child, and no one would do but the king himself to sire it. Nine months later a child was born.

"The king wished to take the boy to live at the castle, but the woman would have none of it. She wanted the child close to her, and she coveted the king for her own, for he was handsome and strong, and she had fallen in love with him. But he spurned her, telling her he only wanted the babe, that he loved her not, and could never leave his queen. So, she cursed him, and ensorcelled his eyes so that he could never again be unfaithful, and no other woman could be deceived in the way he had deceived her. From that day forward you could always read the king's feelings from the color of his eyes. But that is not all. She bewitched the boy in the same manner,

121

so all would know he was the son of the cursed king."

Tannith cupped his face. "You were that boy?"

He nodded. "So, do you see now the wrong I have caused you? Not only am I not of your race. I am the bastard son of a cursed king."

She knelt and encircled his neck and stared into his sea-green eyes. "Hear me now, Dorrachian, and listen well. Do you think my feelings so shallow I would permit a matter of so little worth to rob us of our happiness?"

"But the laws of your people are so strict. You are certain you do not want to end this now before it is too late?"

She smiled. "I fear it is already too late. Do you not know that?" She pulled back and ran her hands up over his bare chest.

"Two can play at this." He pushed her back onto the blanket and came up over her, but she scrambled from under him.

"Not yet."

He shook his head and there was laughter in his eyes. "What is this new game you play?"

"No game, just a few small details I would have clarified."

He grimaced and pushed his hair from his face. "You are not going to make this easy, are you?"

She shook her head and he fell back, and she moved to straddle him.

His hands went to her hips, and he looked up at her. "What is it you wish to know?"

"If your mother wanted to keep you, how was it you were raised by your father?"

Kaden's eyes darkened and he looked away. "I was

six when my mother found she was dying. Not even her magick could save her from the wasting disease attacking her body. When she could no longer care for me, she took me to Wolveryne Castle to my father, who was then faced with the dilemma of explaining me to his wife."

"The queen never knew?"

He shook his head. "When Zoreena refused to give me up, the king wanted nothing more to do with her or her child. There were rumors of course, but Morveena had chosen not to believe. She told me that once when I asked her."

"What happened?"

"The queen accepted me without question, trying everything to win me over. I was quite a villain." He grinned.

"I can imagine." Her lips curved in a smile. "Go on."

"I hated her then…my father…and anyone who tried to get close. I blamed them all for my mother's death. It was Erik who eventually won me over. An eleven-year-old boy pointed out how grateful I should be to have someone who cared for me. He called me a selfish street brat. I gave him a bloody lip that day, and we became friends and brothers for life.

"Finally, I settled in and began to forget about the young boy who once ran the streets of Glen-Dorrach. After my father formally adopted me, I became the prince he wanted me to be, trained in all the princely arts. Then, when I was old enough and skilled enough, he put me in charge of his army."

"But if the queen was barren, what of Asleena?"

"She never *was* barren. The physicians were wrong. Asleena was born when I was twelve. To Asleena, I was her true brother." He smiled as memories floated to the surface. "She would tag along behind me everywhere, wanting to do everything her big brother did. I used to pretend to be cross and scold her, but she would just chuckle, give me her big green-eyed smile and my heart would melt."

"You must have loved her very much."

She moved aside, and he leaned forward, resting his forehead against his upraised knees, his hair falling forward like a black curtain shielding his face.

"I loved them all. Morveena, my father, Asleena—and now they are no more. They did so much for me, and I could do nothing to save them." He raised his head, his eyes deep green pools of pain. "Why was that Tannith? Why do you think I was spared and not them?"

She put her hands to his face and stared into his eyes. "I cannot answer that. Perhaps it was not your time. Perhaps this has made you a stronger and better man. Or the gods had something more important planned for you and watched over you that day. I wish I could take away your hurt, but I cannot. Only time can heal deep wounds to the soul." She stroked his hair from his face. "There is nothing wrong with remembering them or loving them. It is part of the healing process. But do not allow it to make you bitter." She looked into his desolate green eyes. "And remember, you have my love."

Someone clapped their hands. "How delightful."

In unison they both spun to seek the owner of the voice, but Tannith already knew who it would be. The dark personification of evil itself.

The Dorrachian grabbed up his sword and leapt to his feet, and she followed suit. Dannock-Shae stepped from the shadows and into the dappled sunlight filtering down through the throngs of large Tropical Fern Trees. "I never thought you two were so close. "The mocking voice continued as the priest took another step toward them.

Kaden raised his sword. "Come no closer Priest. Or taste the steel of my blade."

Dannock stilled his steps and laughed without mirth. "All in good time, boy. The last time I viewed you in the crystal of illusions, you were bickering like children." He looked pointedly at the prince. "Have you taken her yet?"

Kaden pushed Tannith behind him. "Shut your foul mouth, demon swill, or I will cut out your rancid tongue."

Dannock's eyes glittered. "Ah, I see you have. What a pity, I would have preferred that pleasure myself. However, I am sure the princess has other charms."

Tannith pulled from Kaden's grip and moved up beside him throwing the priest a look of scorn. "I would rather die first."

"That can be arranged." Dannock smiled coldly.

Kaden stepped forward, but Tannith's hand lashed out to stop him. "It is what he wants—to make you overreact and cloud your judgment."

"Clever, Princess. Brains, beauty, and spirit, a rare combination in a woman." Dannock switched to Kaden. "Your sister was much like her in that respect," he crooned. "I would have liked the opportunity to tame her. Unfortunately, that was not to be. She had a predetermined date with destiny." He chuckled, but his pale blue eyes were akin to chips of ice. "Such a tragedy."

A killing light entered Kaden's eyes. "You are a dead man."

Dannock gave an exaggerated yawn. "Such threats only tend to bore me, whelp. Your sister threatened me. How did it go? Ah, yes. 'Kaden will cut your black heart from your chest and feed it to the Reamer Jackals,' " Dannock mimicked. "A trifle dull, do you not think?"

Kaden took another pace toward Dannock. "Today you pay for the suffering you have caused. The innocent lives you have ruined."

The priest stepped to the side and snapped his fingers. "I think not." *The Five* appeared from the trees to flank him. They wore full black and silver battle dress and their silver visors flashed in the newly risen sun.

"First you must pass my men." Dannock gave a mock salute.

Kaden ignored him. "How did you find us? I was certain I covered our tracks."

"*The Five* track by scent," countered Dannock, "not sight. They can smell the blood flowing in your veins, and they will feast upon it when you are dead."

Tannith slid the sword Ohma had ensorcelled from its sheath and stepped up alongside Kaden.

"Kill him!" The priest pointed and *The Five* drew their heavy cutlasses and charged as one.

"And keep the woman! You can have her when I am done."

Kaden took the first warrior, leaping and kicking out with both feet. He landed at an awkward angle but managed to roll and draw his dagger. Flipping to his feet, he punched it through the warrior's eye, killing him instantly. His enchanted sword snaked into his hand, and the fight began in earnest.

Tannith, with a double-handed thrust, stabbed the second demon through the gut. Black blood sprayed from the wound, reeking of death and corruption. The injured warrior grabbed her legs as he fell, knocking her to the ground. She landed hard, her sword flying from her outstretched hand. Scrambling, she snatched it up and looked up to see a creature looming over her with a raised sword. She screamed and watched the blade descend, but Kaden blocked it and pushed the warrior back hard with his foot. Then he spun and brought his sword down in a powerful sweep, taking the head from the corrupted soldier's shoulders. It rolled several feet then stopped, its visor flying open revealing a rotted, maggot infested face.

A shiver travelled through Tannith and she almost gagged, but Kaden kicked the head away and pulled her to her feet.

The next two demons charged in rapid succession. The prince dropped to his knees and slashed deeply across the thigh of the third creature, almost cleaving his leg in half. The man fell to the side and lay still, then Kaden twisted, and made to drive his dagger through a gap in the fourth warrior's armor just beneath his helm, but the demon pulled back, and their blades locked.

For a moment they faced each other. Through the slit in his visor, the eyes of the demon glowed bright red. Then the twin blades sang again. Kaden drove forward, his silver blade stabbing through his opponent's guard, into his heart finding the blood it craved.

The last of the walking dead rushed at Tannith. She parried his blade and spun away to regain her breath. Then charged with a forward thrust to the heart. The warrior blocked and slammed his fist into Tannith's jaw. She staggered and the creature came again.

****

Kaden rounded to help, but found his ankle gripped by the creature with the gaping leg wound.

"My lord…I beg you."

Kaden bent to pry the man's skeletal fingers from his leg, raised his boot and landed a blow to the warrior's head. Then turned to find Tannith.

She was holding her own with her attacker.

The thing he had just kicked away clawed his way toward him again, stretching out his hand. "My lord…be merciful."

Kaden frowned down at the man, caught by his pleading tone. "What is it?" he growled.

The soldier pulled the visor from his ruined face and met the prince's eyes. "I beseech you, take my life. I cannot live like this."

Kaden released a hiss and swallowed the threatening bile in his throat. The flesh was peeling from the man's devastated face, bearing skeletal bones beneath. The eyes, sunken into their sockets, were a milky white. His nose had been eaten away completely. Even for a battle-hardened warrior such as he, the sight was too much. His flesh crawled as he turned away from the man's pale eyes.

The wound the soldier received must have served to release the Demon Spirit from his body. He could feel nothing but pity now. It was not the soldier's fault he had become such a wretched creature. He was just another pawn in Sernon's fiendish game. Only someone completely evil could wreak this savagery upon another living being.

He twisted and with one mighty blow of his sword released the man from his pain.

The remaining demon battling Tannith twisted in

time to see his comrade fall. If it was a sudden urge for self-preservation, one would never know, but the sword dropped from his gloved hand, and he fled into the dense jungle behind him.

Dannock swore loudly and straightened up from the tree he was sitting under. "Always I am served by fools. I suspected they had no fire in their bellies." His black basket-handled sword glinted as he dragged it from its scabbard. "So, it is down to you and me, my prince." The last word was spat like an obscenity.

Tannith's eyes narrowed. She readied her sword, but Kaden lay a hand on her arm.

"No. This is between him and me. It started long before I met you."

She nodded and lowered her weapon. "If you should need me, I will not hesitate to kill him."

Dannock gave a bark of laughter. "Beautifully spoken, Princess, but your words only serve to spur me on. I can almost feel your soft white body writhing beneath mine. Just wait there until I deal with your lover." He paused and a cold light entered his eyes, and he switched his gaze to Kaden. "Shall I wound him and make him watch, as I did his father?" Another pause for effect. "He may even beg for your life as the king begged for the wife's when I threw her naked to my men."

Kaden's sword flashed above the priest's head. "Bastard scum!"

Dannock's teeth flashed, and he lunged, his blade nicking Kaden's right forearm.

The prince steadied, regarded the priest with hard eyes, and wiped the blood from his arm. "You have struck first blood, priest. But it will be your last."

He drove forward and opened a gash down

Dannock's long cheek bone.

The priest hissed and jumped back, bringing a hand to his face. His ice-blue eyes held a wealth of pain. "You will die for that, you princely bastard."

"Now who is threatening?" Kaden slashed and his blade cut into Dannock's side.

The priest fought back with a savage riposte that sliced across Kaden's thigh. It stung like a burning coal, but luckily the wound was shallow.

His hands tightened on the hilt of his sword, and he pushed forward.

Dannock checked his next rush as Kaden stooped smoothly and slid his dagger from his boot, offering that point as well. They circled each other in the clearing, their blades weaving, kissing, and tapping lightly, each seeking an opening.

The priest stared into his eyes. "Do you recognize this sword? I took it from your father before I took his head. Now I shall take yours!"

"I will never fear my father's sword whilst the man who wields it is a coward."

Dannock's jaw clenched, and he charged, his sword raised.

Kaden stepped to the side and elbowed Dannock to the side of the head as his momentum drove him passed. But the priest spun and lunged again barely faltering with speed belying that of an older man.

He barred the blow and steel sang and trilled on steel as time ceased to exist.

The prince slashed at the priest's robe, exposing and slicing into the man's bony chest. Then spinning on his heel, Kaden whirled and brought his sword around to cut across Dannock's upper thigh.

The priest grunted. His face flushed and beaded with sweat. He retreated a step, then another and stumbled on a tree root. He righted himself and hacked wildly at the air above Kaden's head, all the while, his wounds leaked blood.

With a reckless lunge and a mask of hate marring his face, Dannock turned the fight by raining down blow after desperate blow at Kaden's head. He drove him back to the edge of the clearing.

His injuries were beginning to tell. His sword arm ached. Blood flowed from the gash in his arm and the cut above his knee with each blow to his sword. Every time Dannock's blade crossed his, fire ate into his wounds.

Then the unthinkable happened. His arms flayed out, and his legs went from beneath him, and he sprawled backward across a fallen log. He grappled to regain his sword, but too late. Dannock's sword came down to rest lightly at the base of his throat.

"Kaden!" Tannith's voice filled his ears and from the corner of his eye he saw her stagger toward him, her sword in her hand.

"Hold, Princess, or I will skewer him like a boar." The priest laughed softly, chilling. "But what am I saying? I am going to skewer him. Then, you and the Cross will be mine!" He shifted his gaze from Kaden for a breath to glance at Tannith.

It was a breath too long.

Kaden rolled to the side and powered a kick into the priest's knee.

The priest shrieked and sprawled backward, his sword slipping from his grip as he clutched at his knee.

Kaden scooped up his dagger and leaned over Dannock, the knife to his throat.

The priest's eyes widened as he felt the steel against his flesh. "You do not want to do this Kaden." The priest's words were rushed. "I have known you since…since you were a boy."

"You should have thought of that before you murdered my family." His tone was deadly. "Nothing you can say will save you."

He held up his hands. "Please. It was Sernon…Sernon made me do it."

"I do not think so. This is for my sister and my mother," he said, driving the dagger deep into Dannock's stomach. "And this is for my father and brother," he ground with a final savage twist of the blade. "May your dark gods have no mercy on your wretched soul."

****

Pain like a million tiny needles spiraled through Dannock's innards. His breathing grew ragged as he strained to free the knife causing liquid fire to flow throughout his body. With numb fingers, he clutched the hilt, dragged the blade free and dropped it to the grass. He pointed a shaking hand at the Wolfhead Prince. "You think this is over?" He laughed, a chilling sound in the eerie silence that had befallen the glade. "It will never be over as long as *he* lives."

The Wolfhead Prince looked down at him in silence, his jaw hard and implacable.

Dannock's hand lowered to his side and his breath rattled in his throat, his words coming on a whisper. "It will not end here." His mouth held the metallic taste of blood and another breath rattled in his throat. He closed his eyes.

How had things gone so wrong? All the scheming and planning over the long years. He gave a mental laugh. He was supposed to be the ruler with Sernon standing at his side advising him. "Sernon will send others," he said, not opening his eyes. "He will not rest till he sees you and all those with you dead." A shiver ran the length of his body, and he cracked his eyes open, but his vision grew dim, and a soft sigh escaped from his lips as he slipped into darkness...

****

Tannith hurried to Kaden's side. "Is he dead?"

"No such fortune." With a motion born of hate, Kaden swept up Dannock's sword. "But I will see him on his way." He raised the great broadsword that had belonged to his father above the head of the man who had brought him so much grief.

"No!" Tannith's hands shot out to stay his arm.

"What!" He shook her loose. "Leave me be, woman." He cast her a look of exasperation. "You would deny me this? After what this man has done to me and mine?"

"If you slay him now, you will be no better than him. He is a dead man anyway." She pulled at his arm. "Leave him. Let this act of savagery not weigh heavy on your soul."

"I tell you now woman, this will leave no stain on *my* soul."

"Then, for me."

Kaden stared down at her hands on his arm, then down at the priest. Even as his life's blood ran from his mouth, he could swear the man was laughing at him. He pulled away from her and strode back to their belongings, snatched up his tunic and dragged it down over his head. He would not look at Tannith. He could not trust himself not to do her physical harm.

133

His blood ran hot in his veins threatening to explode. How could she ask him to do such a thing? Did she not know what this man had done? The grief he had caused. At last, he spoke. His words measured. "Do not think that I will thank you for this. Perhaps you may have saved my soul, but you have consigned me to a life of knowing I could have done more to avenge my family."

Tannith made to speak, but he held up his hand. "Say no more. You have said enough. Leave me and take the horses. I will find you on the trail."

She glanced back at Dannock. "You promised."

"I give my word as a Prince of the Wolfhead." His tone was hard almost violent. "Is that not enough?"

She stood for a heartbeat longer, then gathered up the bedrolls and tied them to the horses.

He refused to look at her as she started up the trail with Phoenix and Dannock's black stallion in tow. When she rounded the bend, Kaden picked up his cloak and tossed it over the prone body of the priest.

"If the Gods of Creation have any mercy in their hearts, they will know what to do," he said out loud. He cast a look at the heavens and turned to follow in Tannith's footsteps.

It was not long before his long strides found him at her side.

****

She could tell by his carriage he was furious, was alerted to the fact with every glance of his bottle green eyes. She knew he thought himself denied his revenge, but…

A cry rent the air, and she stopped. A man's scream—a terrible awful sound that penetrated her ears even through the thunderous pounding of the falls ahead of them. Again, it rose from the valley, then ceased, leaving only the dense crashing of water.

She looked at Kaden. He had stopped beside her, his jaw hard, his scar standing out white in the tan of his face.

"The last of the living dead has returned." Kaden gave her a stony look, daring her to speak. "May Dannock rot in the Void for all eternity."

Tannith walked on. She could find no answer. To her, the priest had been the driving force behind his own destruction.

"I am going back."

"What?" She looked over her shoulder at him. "He will be dead. I thought that is what you wanted."

"There is something I promised to do. Keep going. I will find you."

She nodded and watched him sprint back down the way they came. "Be careful!"

****

Kaden returned to the scene of the melee, drew his sword, and checked for danger. There was no sign of the demon warrior. He moved to the body of the high priest, sheathed his broadsword, and drew his dagger.

He searched the face of his nemesis for a last time. The man's features were twisted in a hideous mask of death. He had been torn from throat to groin. However, his heart was still intact.

He bent and sliced the still warm organ from the priest's ruined chest and pegged it to a nearby tree, using a stick he carved into a spike.

"Now you are trapped in the Void for all time," he whispered to the wind. "And never shall you walk in the place of your gods."

He had fulfilled the promise made to his sister at the monastery.

Chapter Ten

Skylah pushed her pewter plate across the table and rose to warm her hands by the fire in Norvak's sitting room. She wondered at the absence of her companions.

Etan had not yet returned, and she worried for his safety as evening approached. Strange he was never far from her thoughts, yet it was Erik she loved. Perhaps what they say is true—old habits die hard.

Ohma and Erik had met her earlier as planned, but Norvak had arrived with an urgent message. With a caution from Erik to stay and finish her meal, he and Ohma had left with the innkeeper.

She glanced at the curtain separating the sitting room from the tavern. The noise of laughter, music and the occasional squeal of the tavern maids filtered through the faded partition.

Curious about what went on inside such an establishment, Skylah edged closer to the curtain and peered through the slit at the side. What she saw filled her with revulsion and curiosity.

Two men arm-wrestled at one table while others watched, quaffing ale, and placing bets on the outcome. At another table, three warriors played a game consisting of one man sliding three shells around on the surface. Under one shell was a bean. She realized the object of the exercise was to choose the shell hiding the bean.

But what horrified her most was the third table. Two

blue-skinned Urakians held a bar-maid sprawled across the tabletop, fondling her breasts while their comrade unfastened his breeches.

Skylah's hand closed around her short sword, and she pushed through the curtain only to be confronted by two scruffy men who shoved her back roughly into the room.

"Well, what have we got here, Will?" asked the first man, a gangly warrior with a shot of red hair which sprang out in various directions from a balding pate, and set of black and broken teeth.

"Looks like ol' Norvak's been 'olding out on us, Vermos." The second man, chubbier than his friend with a matted, black beard, grinned at his companion while scratching at his crotch through his dirty brown, too large leggings. "She's right pretty, she is."

"Aye." Vermos nodded. "And I bet she's got plenty for us." He closed in as his friend circled behind Skylah.

"Stay where you are." She spun, attempting to watch them both at the same time. "Or I will hack off your shriveled balls and toast them on a spit."

Will lunged, knocking her sword from her hand. Vermos stepped in, grasped her waist, and forced her arms to her side. "Now you aren't so cocky, are you, bitch?" He slammed her down hard over the table, knocking the breath from her lungs.

" 'elp me strip off her breeches, Will, and I'll show her what it's like to 'ave a real man."

Skylah kicked out, connected with Will's face, and heard him grunt. He rubbed a hand across his bloody nose and tried to drag off her boots. She kicked again with both feet but knew she did not have the strength to defeat them. She had not been trained to fight against a mortal enemy. Also, she was beginning to realize a man with lust on his mind could be a terrible enemy indeed.

"Step away from the woman." The voice was cold, implacable.

She heard his voice, and her heart missed a beat. She knew he would come.

Will spun and grappled for his knife but it never left its sheath. He slumped face down over Skylah's legs, a crossbow bolt in his throat.

His friend spun, his face a mask of rage. "Bastard! You've killed him." He lunged at the warrior, but Etan's hand was a blur as a crystal dagger flew and lodged in the man's chest. Will was dead before he hit the floor.

Etan stepped over him and made his way to Skylah. She had pushed the body aside and sat trembling on the floor. He dropped his bow on the table and reached for her hand. She took it, and he helped her to stand, his arms closing around her, crushing her to his chest. His warm breath touched her ear. "Did those vermin hurt you?"

She could barely breathe. She pulled back to see his face. It was almost as pale as she knew hers must be. His lips were but a whisper from the sensitive tip of her slightly pointed ear. She raised her head and his eyes captured hers. His eyes—how could a man have such beautiful eyes? As deep and fathomless as a blue summer sky. She pressed her cheek to his chest, listening to the racing beat of his heart. It matched hers. She luxuriated in the strength of his arms and his hard body against hers. It felt so right…but her thoughts were broken as a cold voice spoke from behind. "Is there a problem?"

They both stilled, then slowly, Etan took his arms from around her waist. "Here, take her." He pushed her toward Erik. "You might do a better job protecting her next time."

She whirled, giving them both daggered looks. For some uncanny reason, she felt guilty, and she did not like the feeling. "I am not a sack of goods to be bartered from one man to another, and I will not be spoken about as if I am not here."

"I was worried for your safety," soothed Erik, closing the gap between them, pushing her tousled hair from her face.

She stepped away. "These men attacked me." She indicated the men dead on the floor. "Etan came to my aid. I was shaken by the incident, and he offered me comfort. That is all there is to it. I am grateful he arrived when he did." She threw Etan a hesitant smile.

He ignored her and spoke to Erik. "She is your woman, Dorrachian. In the future, watch after her. She is too precious to be left on her own." He smiled but it did not reach his eyes. "A man does not deserve such a treasure if he cannot protect it." He paused then spoke again. "Someday, someone might take her from you."

Erik's hand moved to rest lightly on the hilt of his sword. A touch of iron laced his next words. "That man could try, but he would surely die in doing so."

Ohma, who had entered the room unknowingly, moved to Erik's side and laid a firm hand on his arm. "You do not want to draw attention, my lord."

Erik's expression darkened but his golden eyes never left Etan's. "The Elisian should have thought of that before he killed two men."

They stood silent, faces like granite, bodies alert, hands resting lightly on their weapons, neither wanting to be the first to back down, neither wanting to show the other a weakness to be used against him.

Finally, Etan swore softly and bent to wrench his dagger clear from the ruffian near his feet. Blood gushed from the man's wound and spilled out onto the floorboards. He wiped his blade clean on the stranger's shirt, then moved to the other body. Kneeling beside the corpse, he recovered his crossbow bolt, and strode without speaking through the faded curtain into the bar.

Skylah stared after him, a hard lump in her throat. "Why is he like that? So ready to anger, so—"

Erik began to speak, but Ohma shook his head. "Etan carries many demons in his soul, lass, unfortunately only he can rid himself of them." He took Skylah's arm and tucked it in his own and patted her hand, then he guided her back to the table. "Sit." He looked to Erik. "Do not think too harshly of him, my lord. I am certain the boy meant no harm." He filled a mug with mead from a pitcher on a sideboard and slid it across the table to Skylah. "This is Mistress Norvak's finest. It will settle your nerves."

She glanced down at her trembling hands. "I do not much feel like mead, Ohma. I do not feel anything." She pushed her thick hair from her eyes. "I am weary. I will go to my room." She stood and walked past Erik, casting him a look daring him to stop her.

****

Erik watched her go, then settled at the table, picked up the mug of mead and stared down into the dark warm liquid. *Was Skylah really his? Yes, she gave her body freely, but can anyone really own a creature as elusive as a Faerie? Had she really rid herself of her love for the Elisian, or would he always be there, standing in the shadows between them? Waiting.*

He downed the mead and reached for another, as

Norvak bustled into the room, followed by two young red-haired men. They could have been twins.

"Sorry, my lord. The captain sought me out in the bar. Me and my boys 'ave come to clear away the bodies. Apologize to Lady Skylah for me, please. I had no idea…"

Erik held up his hand. "You are in no way to blame old friend. I am certain she knows that."

Norvak pressed a hand to his chest trying to regulate his breath. It was not good for a man of his bulk to be running. "I am only glad the captain was in time to save her."

His hand tightened on the handle of his tankard. He was only grateful it was made of pewter and not clay, or it would have broken in his grip. Erik gave what he thought might pass for a smile, but he really was not feeling it. "Indeed," he murmured, standing to move to the fireside and sink into an overstuffed chair facing away from the Inn keeper. He was in no mood for idle chatter.

****

Skylah sat cross-legged on the four-poster bed she would share with Erik and tugged at the tangles in her hair. It had been almost two notches of a time-candle since the attack and her hands just now stopped shaking. She felt bad about what happened between Erik and Etan, and still a little surprised over Erik's display of jealousy. She had never seen a man jealous over her before and it left her slightly unsettled.

Out of patience with her hair, she tossed the tortoiseshell brush onto the coverlet and stood to admire the long white shift Etan had purchased at Erik's request. It had been laid out on the bed when she entered the room.

The gown was woven from the sheerest of silk transported from Aquador, a small island off the northwest coast of Glen-Dorrach. The fine cloth ran through her fingers like water and its transparency brought a blush to her cheeks. The enormous amount of skin exposed above her breasts seemed indecent, but if it were what mortal women wore in their bedchambers, she guessed she would get used to it.

She shrugged and lay back on the pillows. She would have to become accustomed to such matters as grooming, washing, and dressing well now that she was a real woman. Still, it seemed strange.

To a Faerie, trivial matters like a smudge on her cheek, a hair out of place, or a rip in her skirt seemed inconsequential. The people who viewed her and took notice were her own kind, and she had always been known as a bit of a tomboy, much to the despair of her mother. Now that she was a mortal, there were certain standards to which she had to adhere.

The young king had grown up surrounded by beautiful women—Erik. Good, kind Erik. How he loved her. It was only right she try to be what he wished her to be. She should be grateful someone as handsome and regal as Erik wanted her. She tried to bring his face to mind, but it refused to appear.

In its place came another face...a face she had seen in her dreams many times. The face of a man, straight and tall with the uniform of an Elisian Captain. Pale blonde hair she itched to brush back from his eyes, deep blue eyes, which filled her with longing as they had stared down into hers.

Her musings ceased with the intrusive banging on

143

the heavy oak door.

Believing it to be Erik returning from his business with Ohma, she moved across the room to drag it open, only to come face to face with the man whose image had filled her mind only heartbeats before.

He raked her body in cool appraisal. "Do you always open your door to men when you are half naked?" He stepped past her into the room. "I suggest you close the door before you issue an invitation to every man on the first floor."

Skylah's lips tightened as she closed the door and moved toward the bed. Her hands shook as she busied herself picking up her skirt and folding it over the rail. She saw how his gaze slid over her body as he stood in the doorway. What did he want? Why did he not say what he needed to say and leave? Moments before she was thinking of him; now he was here, and she wished it not. She was frightened of what he made her feel, afraid what she might notice in his all-seeing eyes.

****

She jumped when he spoke from behind her.

"I thought I might speak to Erik, see if he wishes me to scout the perimeter of the town while we wait for the others." Etan's lips curved in a cynical smile. Did she think because she was not facing him, he could not see right through that flimsy rag she wore? The sight of her small, rounded bottom was making him so hard he could barely think.

Her voice was even. "As you see, Erik is not here. He is still in the bar with Ohma."

He stepped closer, encircled her waist, and drew her back against him.

****

She stiffened but did not move away. The thick rug had muffled his footsteps. She felt the warmth of his skin through the fine linen of his shirt and the silk of her gown. She wanted him; by the gods, she wanted him.

And she knew she should not.

"If I had a woman like you," he whispered in her ear, "I would not make her wait while I enjoyed an ale with an old man."

Skylah's breath labored. His scent was all around her, his warmth enveloping her. She was trapped by her own weakness. This was Etan, the man she loved, the man she would always love.

She breathed deeply trying to hold onto her composure, but when she spoke her voice sounded husky and fragile. "What is it you really want, Etan?" She held her breath again. Longing for the answer she wanted but knowing it would come too late. She was committed to Erik.

He pushed her long hair to the side and ran his lips along her nape, sending tingles down her spine. He slid his mouth to the curve of her ear and rested his lips there, breathing hot words that left her pliant with need.

"What do I want? Let me see...I want these." His hands slid up her sides to cup her heavy breasts.

Her breath filled her lungs and caught in her throat.

"And this." His hands slid down and lingered over her flat stomach. "To fill and swell with my child."

A rush of warmth radiated out to heat her skin from beneath his fingers.

"Ah yes, and this." One large hand trailed lower still to cover the mound between her thighs. "To melt into my fingers and cradle my aching body."

He spun her abruptly and caught her in his arms. His

lips claimed her mouth, bruising, mind-bending, emotion-filled. He conquered her completely, searching, seeking, and finding the desperate response he sought.

A frenzy of mixed emotions raced through her mind. This was Etan…Etan whom she had loved for so long with such intense longing—holding her, kissing her, wanting her. He touched her where she longed to be touched, where she needed him to touch her. Her breath came in short sharp bursts as his lips sought her eyes, throat, and cheeks, then savaged her mouth again.

His arm hooked under her thigh, drawing her leg up around his hip, giving him better access to her body. She groaned into the heat of his mouth as his fingers found her sweet, hot core.

Then they were falling.

She hit the bed at a sickening rate, sinking into the soft depths of the mattress. Etan sprawled across her, crushing the air from her lungs. He rolled onto his elbow and came up laughing.

The sound was enough to sober her, and she smiled hesitantly. Never could she remember a time when she heard Etan laugh. The sound made him appear softer, younger, carefree, and it filled her heart with sorrow for she knew he could never be hers.

****

He noted her frown and his laughter died. He reached to touch her, but she pulled away. He gave her a long, pain-filled look. Swinging his legs over the side of the bed, he bowed his head to rest his face in his hands. "Have you any idea what you are doing to me?"

Skylah remained silent.

"I cannot sleep because all I see is your face. I cannot eat because I imagine the taste of your skin on my tongue. Every breath of air I breathe fills my head with your scent." He pushed his long fair fringe impatiently from his eyes and spun to touch her, but she scampered to the far side of the bed.

He circled the bed and dropped to his knees, taking her hands in his. "Leave Erik; come with me. Now. Tonight! There are tall ships to carry us to the Far Islands. We can leave this land—its wars, its turmoil. We can start over." There was a desperate plea in his voice. "Say you will come…I love you. I have always loved you. I know that now."

Skylah pushed him away and scrambled to her feet, glaring at him with brilliant green eyes. Her red-gold hair crackling and writhing around her face.

Noting her expression, he knew before she spoke, he had lost her. He came to his feet. "Go on, say it, I am a fool."

He was surprised when her words came on a whisper.

"How could you? You told me you did not love me. You told me with every action, with every word you ever spoke to me. How many times had I longed for some small kindness?"

"I—"

"No!" She slashed with her hand. "Let me finish. I was not the dullard you believed me to be. I knew for us there could be no future. Yet deep down, I believed something would happen to make it possible. But you would not believe, would you, Etan? You would not give us a chance." She glanced away. "It was Erik who helped me accept if you wished hard enough, all things were possible. He loved me even when I was tiny, and him a tiger." She swung back. "Now I have betrayed him—his love—his trust. May the Gods be merciful and forgive me." She swiped at her eyes. "Yes, I love you. I have always loved you, and perhaps always will."

"Then why—"

She cut him off. "Because never again will I betray Erik or his faith in me. I have made my choice, Etanandril Jarrisendel, and I will stand by it."

****

He took a step toward her, his hands outstretched. "Let me explain—I—"

"No!" She stepped back. "There is nothing you can say to change my mind. I want you to leave." She pointed to the door. "Now, or I shall scream loud enough to bring everyone in this establishment hastening to my aid."

Etan opened his mouth to try again, but the brittle light in her eyes stopped him. He turned and moved for the door.

"And Etan?"

He stilled but did not turn. He was afraid should he do so, he would never be able to leave her. He straightened his back. "Yes?"

"Do not come here again while I am alone."

He reached for the door, stood for a moment, then opened it, stepped through, and closed it softly behind him.

The sound of finality rang loud in her ears.

****

Erik stared into his ale long after Ohma departed for his room. He had watched Etan storm down the stairs and rush out of the tavern. It was still curfew, yet he did not care. He knew the Elisian loved Skylah, he had known since their meeting with the Dragon, yet he had been selfish and taken her for his own.

But she was beautiful, in that Etan was correct. He noticed it the first time he watched her across the clearing on that day long ago. In miniature, she was a vision of loveliness he could not dismiss from his mind, even in sleep. He wondered if she realized how much he loved her and longed to make her his queen. He knew he should tell her, unburden himself, but he could not. He was afraid of her reaction. What if she rejected him?

If he lost her now, after loving her—after feeling her body wrapped around his, he would surely die a myriad of deaths. Never would he find another with the rare gift to give everything she had and still more. Those she loved would always come first with Skylah.

He thumped his fist onto the table. He could not let her go. He would not. She was his. He would kill anyone who tried to take her from him whether the man was friend or foe. He had to find a way to bind her to him, a way she could never leave him. With his mind set, he drained the dregs from his tankard and placed it deliberately on the oak table.

****

Skylah heard the key rattle in the lock, the sound ominous in the dark room. Lying quiet, barely breathing, she watched through narrowed eyes as Erik entered, made his way to the dresser, and lit the candle lamp. The smell of tallow was strong in the air, and she forced herself not to cough as he lowered the lamp to peer into her face. The flame was warm on her cheek.

Satisfied she was sleeping, he extinguished the lamp and placed it on the blackwood dresser. She heard the rustle of fine silk, the sound of his breeches dropping to the floor, and regulated her breathing. Lying still, she prayed he would not reach for her. The mattress sagged as he slowly eased in beside her.

He pulled her back gently into his arms, holding her spoon-fashion against his hard body.

Guilt paralyzed her and she lay unmoving, willing him not to speak, not to touch her. How could she give herself to him now after what had happened with Etan?

His hands cupped her breasts through her sheer gown and her nipples hardened. One hand slid down over her thigh to bunch her gown in a fist and draw it up over her hip. She tried not to move. If she feigned sleep long enough, perhaps he would cease.

His fingers began their familiar magick, and she was unable to contain the moan of pure pleasure issuing from her lips or the traitorous shivers raking her body. His hot mouth, the touch of his hands, the smell of pine on his skin all blended to weave their spell about her body, driving her senseless of any thought but finding release to the intolerable need building between her legs.

Erik moved over her. "Say it," he demanded.

She could feel the ends of his golden hair trailing across her breasts, his sweet breath laced with lager, hot on her face, his amber gaze boring down at her in the dim light. She knew the traitorous feeling of a body in need and heard herself utter the words that would bring her torment to an end. "Anything. Take me—fill me—do what you will." The words slipped from her tongue on a sigh.

Were they really her words, so passionately uttered? Disgust warred with lust. Was she so weak she could go from one man's arms to another, and not only enjoy it— beg for it?

All thought ceased as he fit his body against hers and her breath fled as he sank into her. He moved and swelled and filled her completely. He took her with hard, fast thrusts as if trying to stamp his brand upon her soul. She held him tight and met each stroke with compelling hunger, longing for the pleasure never to end.

When she thought she would surely die from the rapture he aroused, a great swelling of pure forbidden lust washed over her. Nails raked his sweat slicked back, and she rocked side-to-side, riding out the tide of ecstasy. His name splintered from her lips. He surged and drove deeper, lifted her thighs, dragging them higher up and around his waist, then shuddering, spilled into her, wave upon wave, flooding her womb with his seed.

Slowly their bodies grew still.

Sated, Erik rolled to his side and gently lifted a strand of her hair to his face. He tasted, sniffed, and tested its fragrance as she lay staring at the darkened ceiling. He leaned over to light the candle on the nightstand, then looked down into her face, frowning when he saw the tears in her eyes.

He wiped them away gently with his thumb. "Why do you weep, little one? Did I hurt you?"

She shook her head and turned away.

"Is it because we are not wed?" He took her face between his hands and forced her to face him. "Tomorrow I will send for a brother from the Temple of Glen-Dorrach. It cannot be a large service with the eight days of feasting as is custom, but you will be no less my wife. Now smile and tell me you love me. For tonight you should be happy. Have I not asked you to be my queen?" He lowered his head and touched his lips softly to hers, but she pulled away.

Tenderly, she stroked his damp hair back from his face. "Do not be foolish, my lord. Now is no time for a wedding, there is much we must do. You have a quest to resolve with your brother, and I have a need to find my people. There will be no more talk of marriage until this war is over and we are free to spend the rest of our days together in peace." She took his hand and kissed it. "At the moment it suffices that you care enough to ask."

The look he gave her was long and penetrating. Finally, he nodded. "You speak wisely, my love. We shall wait until I can seat you upon the throne of Glen-Dorrach. Then all my people shall see the beauty I have chosen to rule beside me."

Skylah sighed and lay back in his arms only half listening as Erik spoke of Wolveryne Castle and the childhood antics of him, Kaden, and their sister Asleena. Finally, his words gave way to the even rhythm of sleep.

It was long hours before she was so blessed. Thoughts of two men kept running through her mind, mingling and merging, and giving no quarter. How could the gods have been so cruel as to grant her wish for true love and deny her happiness all in one? How could she be truly happy when she was in love with two men? And today she had been forced to choose between them.

Chapter Eleven

Late afternoon found Tannith and Kaden inching their way along the narrow ledge behind the waterfall. All the time, they were conscious that one false step could put them over the edge to certain death on the dark volcanic rocks hundreds of feet below.

Phoenix remained passive as Tannith led him carefully along the slick rock.

Dannock-Shae's gelding, whom Kaden was leading, became more skittish with every step of its massive hooves. Without warning, the horse reared. Its hooves skidded and its eyes bulged in terror as its back legs began to slide over the edge of the ledge.

Kaden double wrapped the reins around his fist and grasped the tightening leather with his free hand. Bunching his powerful muscles, he struggled to hold the entire weight of the destrier, but his strength soon ebbed and every muscle and sinew was strained to its ultimate point. He realized with a sinking heart he would have to let the stallion go to his doom. Inch by inch, he painfully unraveled the reins from his bound hand, and the great war horse slid over the edge.

Its screams hung in the moist air as it crashed into the pounding water below. Kaden, exhausted and spent, collapsed against the rock face, and sat trembling, knowing how close he had come to death.

Tannith left Phoenix inside the cave and hurried

back along the ledge to gather Kaden in her arms, kissing his cheeks and forehead. "I thought I had lost you. Never frighten me like that again."

He pulled away and searched her face. She was shaking as much as him, and tears glistened in her eyes.

They had barely talked since Dannock's death, but the gravity of the situation brought home to him how frail life really was and how foolish he had been. He pushed his hair back from his face.

If matters had gone differently with the horse, he might never have seen Tannith again. He hugged her to his chest. "Neither man nor beast has the power to separate me from you," he whispered against her ear, waiting for her trembling to subside and his own heart rate to steady. Then he drew back and slipped his dagger from his boot, making a small nick in his palm.

"What are you doing?"

"Something I should have done long ago."

Waiting until the blood dripped freely onto the wet rocks at his side, Kaden lifted Tannith's palm. He made a small cut, matched their hands together, and mingled their blood as one. "Do you swear to love me for all time?"

"You know I do."

"You must swear it."

"May my blood run the breadth of Tarlis should I ever be untrue to you. And may my shade follow you into Elysium."

He brought her hand to his lips and gazed into her beautiful violet eyes glistening with tears. "I pledge my love, my soul, to you. I will walk the hills with you. I would lay my soul at the door of the Abyss to protect you." He touched his lips to hers. "Now you are truly mine from here into eternity." He rested his forehead against hers. "We are handfasted in the Dorrachian tradition. You are my wife."

****

Hammer Deathwielder, Son of Lêr, stood cross-armed before a transparent wall of blue rock. A frown marred his craggy features, and he ran his thumb over the runes on the haft of the black and silver hammer hanging from the harness at his waist.

The hammer's haft, one and a half feet long, sported a nine-pound head of solid iron, cast in the shape of a fist. Most men would have found the weapon heavy, awkward, and imprecise. But in the hands of the young, dark-haired dwarf, it swung through the air seemingly as light as a rapier.

Hammer had been named for his ancestor Deathwielder, who fought alongside Magus in The Mage War. *Shae,* his war hammer, was handed down four generations before it had finally come to rest in Hammer's hands.

It was told that when Deathwielder swung *Shae,* the enemy had trembled, and the earth had shaken. Hammer had yet to know if that were true, for he had never fought in a real battle, but he had trained aplenty and was ready for the day when he would prove himself. Then he would see what *Shae* could do, and blood would flow.

Hammer stared into the blue crystal wall, watching with a frown as a tall, black-haired warrior studied the trigger to the entrance of the city. Who was this man? What did he want?

He knew exactly where to find the rocks that triggered the entrance. Hammer's hand closed tightly over *Shae's* haft.

Only one man knew where the gateway of the city lay. The man who had designed it, and this man was not he.

Deathwielder had watched the previous day as the strangers had entered the cave. The man had seemed obsessed with searching for something, but the woman, upon entering, had gone uncommonly still. It was almost as if she were entranced. Then suddenly she cried out and fled. Could it have been she had seen the spirits of the Slave Age? Hammer knew a few had borne witness to the souls of the ancients, but it was a limited few.

He had never been privy to them in all the time he had guarded the gateway.

In ancient times, slaves were bound with golden chains and thrown into the falls in sacrifice to the great Water God, Ahgoss. It had been the belief that the ritual would appease the God and stop the flooding of the caves. The practice died out centuries ago. The Dwarves no longer took slaves. However, it was said that on a certain day of the year, the spirits of the dead would gather in the place of their doom and inhabit the body of any unfortunate found there.

The woman's aura must be strong indeed if she had resisted the entering.

Which brought Hammer back to the present. Who were these people? Only Ohma and the Dwarves knew how to activate the device that would give access to his city, yet the stranger was doing just that. Hammer watched the man through the one-way transparent wall with a scowl on his face.

****

Kaden stood centered between two blocks of granite. The stones of the gateway, well over seven feet tall and three feet in width, were identical. Each inscribed with a bygone language he found illegible. A palm print was carved into the inside face of each rock. He placed his hands into the impression and pressed, at the same time speaking the ancient words Ohma had entrusted to him. *"Balloc, Harkem, Naradoor."*

Immediately, his hands tingled, and an eerie scraping sound echoed through the cave. His palms grew warm, and a strong blue light encompassed him, radiating from the cave wall in front of him. Then, as if it had never been, the wall vanished and, in its place through a mist of blue light, stood a small man.

Kaden faced the first *Hill Dwarf* to be seen by one of another race for one hundred and fifty summers.

With short-cropped, black hair and beard, he sported a brown fringed shirt, leather leggings, and knee-high moccasins. In his fist, he clasped a large black and silver war hammer, and Kaden realized he was none too pleased to see him.

The dwarf planted his feet squarely in front of Kaden and hefted his hammer. "Come no closer, *Tall-One*. What is it you seek in the Poniard City?"

"I am Kaden of Glen-Dorrach, and this is Princess Tannith of Ellenroh." Kaden indicated Tannith standing behind him in the shadows.

She stepped into the light. "We have come to reclaim the third section of the Cross of Tarlis. We were told it resides in your city."

"I know of the Cross, but how do I know you speak the truth? Where is the Mage?"

"Ohma has sent us in his stead. There is much he has yet to do. Tarlis is in peril. Sernon of Asomos has risen from the dead and means to take all of Tarlis for his own and enslave its people." Kaden searched the dwarf's face. The eyes were shrewd but sparkled with an inner warmth. He liked what he saw. "Should nothing be done to stop him, Sernon's reign of terror will soon encompass us all, even your people. The princess can use the power of the Cross to bring Magus down from Elysium. It is our hope he will defeat Sernon and set all kingdoms to rights. Will you help us?"

The dwarf relaxed his stance, but his expression remained guarded. "Enter," he growled, stepping aside, "but be warned. The gate spell will not hold for more than a few heartbeats once you take your hands from the stones. You must pass beyond the wall before the light fades."

Kaden nodded to Tannith. "You go first."

The princess pulled at Phoenix's reins to lead him forward, but the stallion reared and refused to cross through the blue light and dragged her further back into the cave.

"Leave the horse!" yelled the dwarf. "I will send someone to collect him."

Tannith hesitated for a heartbeat, then grabbed the packs from the horse and ran through the light to join the dwarf.

"Now, take your hands away slowly and run!"

Kaden took his hands from the stones and dove through the false wall, hitting the ground in a blink of an eye as the stone began to solidify. He rolled over and landed at the dwarf's feet, and the smaller man leaned down and offered his hand.

"Well met, Dorrachian. You may call me Hammer."

Hammer pulled him up with more strength than he would have given credence to.

"Well met, indeed." Kaden nodded. "Now, take me to the one in charge. We can lose no time."

Hammer drew himself up to his full height, which was a little over four feet, and puffed out his barreled chest. His deep, brown eyes held a glimmer of pride. "I am second in line to the Kastan."

"Then it is your father I must speak with."

Hammer regarded him for several long moments, scrutinizing his face, then turned, relieved Tannith of her pack, and strode in silence from the cavern.

The cavern door led them down a network of glowing tunnels which branched off into a myriad of different directions. Each passage was lit by softly glowing phosphorus rocks suspended from the roof of the tunnels. Rounding a corner to the right, they were met with a tunnel lined with miniature doorways of polished timber. Hammer explained they were the dwellings of his people—each home having been carved into solid rock. Several Dwarves hurried passed, staring at them with open curiosity.

"You must forgive my people. Like me, they have never seen a man so tall. Except Ohma of course, and he would barely be taller than the princess."

Tannith smiled briefly, and Kaden nodded peering into the gloom ahead as strange noises came floating toward them. The passageway gave way to a huge cavern with a high ceiling carved in the shape of magnificent cathedral arches supported by large intricately carved columns of stone. The craftsmanship exhibited rare beauty unlike anything he had ever seen on the surface.

The cavern hub was alive with bustling activity. Crowds ebbed and flowed through a small marketplace, which sold everything from squealing piglets and flapping chickens to fine cloth and succulent fruit.

Several Dwarves stopped to stare at them, some casting looks of hostility.

Kaden ignored them and paused to see Tannith admiring a bright red scarf spun from silk so soft it ran through her fingers like quicksilver. She glanced across at him and smiled.

"The silk comes from a giant arachnid," informed Hammer, at her side. "The spinners risk their lives every day gathering it, but they tell it is worth it, for no silk could make finer garments."

She dropped the silken square back to the table and hurried on to the next stall.

Hammer quirked a bushy brow. "The princess dislikes spiders?"

He grinned, remembering their conversation at the cave where they found Verbena's body. "She has an aversion to them, yes."

"That may pose a problem."

"Oh yes. Do tell?"

Hammer looked up from examining a wide leather belt at the stall before him. "I am not at liberty to say. First, I must speak with my father."

He noticed the way the dwarf avoided his eyes.

"I wish to keep nothing from you. 'Tis just that my father is the Kastan—you understand?"

He nodded and changed the subject. "How did you achieve this?" He gestured with his arm, encompassing the whole market square, interspersed with the enormous carved pillars reaching to at least an eighty-foot ceiling.

Hammer twirled his drooping moustache between two stubby fingers. "This is a natural cavern which was cleared and is lit by many torches, as you see." He pointed around the walls. "The *Ancients*, who were ingenious tunnel builders, built the dwellings you passed earlier, and the stone carvers worked on this cavern for almost two centuries. Excavation is still undertaken on the outer reaches of our kingdom, but not as much as it was once. Unfortunately, stone carving is a dying art, and I fear within the next hundred years, the art will be lost entirely. The young dwarf men of today prefer other occupations.

"All the produce you see is grown or created underground." Hammer smiled with pride. "When my ancestors left the world above, they knew they would have to become self-sufficient."

Hammer indicated another tunnel hewn out of living rock, and they slipped into the entrance. The pungent odor of ground spices, fresh fish, cooked chicken, and a thousand other smells drifted in their wake. More phosphorous rocks, suspended at intervals above their heads, lighted their way.

Rounding a corner, Hammer stopped in front of a small door and drew it open. Kaden stood aside for Tannith to enter, then ducked and followed.

The room was oval and filled with women of all ages—some engrossed in weaving, others spinning, while the rest sewed or worked on tapestries. Sunlight streamed through several rough-hewn, circular holes cut into the roof. Natural light flooded the man-made cave, enabling the women to work without the aid of candles. Several of the dwarven women lifted their heads and smiled, and Hammer introduced Kaden and Tannith as friends.

Moving to stand beneath one of the holes in the ceiling, Kaden peered upward. "Amazing. What stops the rain from pouring in?"

"Simple. Large crystals are polished then placed at the top of the holes, blocking them off completely, while allowing the light to filter through into the caves below."

"Ingenious."

"It was Ohma's creation. He is a man of extraordinary talents."

Kaden raised a brow. "More than we would know, it seems."

Hammer gave a soft chuckle and, after bidding the women good day, led Kaden and Tannith back out into the tunnel. Finally, after another long walk and another corner, he stopped in front of a large door stained red with silver runes and stars painted upon its wood.

"This is Ohma's room when he spends time with us." The dark-haired Dwarf took an iron key from a large ring of keys hanging at his waist and fitted it into the lock. "We have only one bed of this size," he explained, opening the door, and stepping into a room of good proportions. "The princess can sleep here. I have ordered a large pallet to be placed on the floor of the men's dormitory. You must forgive our lack of hospitality Prince Kaden, but only married couples are granted a room of their own. It is our custom."

Kaden stood just inside the room. "That will be fine. Now I do not wish to be rude, but the princess and I have much to discuss."

"Of course." Hammer backed toward the door. "I will have supper arranged to be sent and organize an audience with my father."

Tannith watched him close the door behind him, then tumbled back onto the wide feather bed. "I hope you will enjoy your pallet on the floor, Warrior. This bed feels wondrously soft." Her violet eyes glittered mischievously. "Why not tell him we were handfasted?

"You looked tired, and I did not want to delay the meeting with his father any longer. I will rectify the situation later." He gave a low growl and came down over her, pinning her arms loosely above her head. "And no wife of mine sleeps alone."

"And do you have more than one wife?" she countered, rolling him over to straddle his chest.

He grinned. "Why would I want another, when the one I have is the greatest beauty in all of Tarlis?"

"Right answer."

He groaned, meeting her lips as she leaned low, and his hands found their way up under her tunic.

****

The arachnid's body consisted of two large portions. Pincers at least two feet long sprouted from its forehead. Its eyes protruded, blood-like and luminous. A tough, leathery hide and coarse, black hair covered its grotesque body, supported by eight long, powerful legs.

Tannith stood on a ledge in front of a board spanning a gaping chasm. The beam measured no more than three hand-spans wide, two finger-lengths thick, and twenty feet long. The chasm of black nothingness yawned cold and daunting on both sides. On the far side of the cavern, the giant arachnid crouched. The piece of Cross was guarded by *Sharsnak*, the Dwarves' name for spider— the mother of all spiders.

Kaden blocked her path. "No, Tannith. Let me go in your stead."

"Get out of my way, Dorrachian. I must prove I am not a coward."

"I know you are no coward after the trials we have

faced."

"I must face my fear."

Kaden's fist tightened. "Then you are a fool, woman."

"Call me what you will, but all my life I have feared spiders. Now I have a chance to break free of that fear." She glanced over his shoulder at the giant spider. "My people have a saying. 'Once you have faced your fears, you will rid yourself of them forever. Fear is only as strong as the beast in your mind.' The time has come for me to face the terrors of my imagination. Step out of my way and let me pass."

Kaden gave her an assessing look. Her face was set in determined lines. She appeared without fear, but was she? One false step could see her gone. That is what frightened him most. Could she defeat the spider? Was she strong enough—fast enough? Could she tread the beam without slipping into the nothingness below? He shook his head and stepped from the plank. "I will watch your back, but do not take your eyes from the spider."

****

Tannith did not intend to allow the hideous beast to leave her sight. She nodded and placed one foot carefully onto the board. At the far side of the beam, there was a narrow ledge and an enormous spider web. In front of that web, on the same ledge, lay the third part of the Cross, glowing dimly in the shadows.

The board groaned and gave fractionally under her weight as it adjusted to her next step. She took another. A cool breeze seeped through the crevices in the ceiling, and the torches flickered on the perimeter of the chasm. Tannith's hair lay lank and damp on her neck, and perspiration trickled down her spine. A foul stench wafted across the pit from the arachnid's nest. Small rodents and bats and the remains of a dwarf lay suspended, his face half eaten and rotted, his body encased in treacherous woven silk. With one wrong step, she could share the fate of the dwarf above her.

She paused to still her churning stomach. All her life, spiders had been her one weakness, and here she was, about to face the grandmother of all spiders…a spider seven times her size. Drawing on the courage of the God, Magus, she mumbled a quick prayer and inched along the beam another two paces.

Natural light streaked bright through large cracks in the cavern roof, turning the silken web into a rainbow net of beauty and duplicity.

Was it only an hour ago that Hammer had knocked on the door of her room with permission for her and Kaden to speak with his father? The meeting had been short and to the point. Kastan Lêr was happy to see them, yet he was a man of caution and perceived the seriousness of the situation. Permission was granted for them to procure the missing section of the Cross—if they could.

Hammer and a company of men had led Tannith and Kaden deep into the mountainside through the ancient tunnels of the Elders. There, they found the third part of the Cross guarded by the spider.

She drew a deep breath and glanced down at the beam. The treasured icon was a mere sword's length away. Two more steps and she would seize her prize, and the spider had yet to move. She eased to one knee on the plank, her gaze never leaving the giant arachnid nestled high in the corner of the cave. Clutching the piece of Cross with one hand, holding her dagger in the other, she prepared for an attack. However, she was not equipped for the swiftness or the accuracy of the creature when it struck. The spider dropped behind her, blocking her path to safety. With expert cunning, it nudged her slowly, directing her into the path of the web.

Tannith straightened and held her ground, but the spider moved in, and she had no choice. Blocked, she could not move forward. She had to go back. She stared helplessly across at Kaden as he shouted her name.

A backward step found her stuck to the web, soft as silk and strong as iron, holding her entrapped in its silver threads of death. Her mind numbed. She struggled to reach her knife, but the more she tried, the tighter the silken strands adhered to her. Screams rose in her throat. Her lungs ached as she fought for breath. Fear akin to a raging beast swamped her, and a roaring filled her ears. Her own screams! She was sinking…sinking into a quagmire of her own making.

The last thing she remembered was being completely covered in sticky silk, and the dreadful black maw of Shasnak looming toward her. She closed her eyes and sank into oblivion…

****

From the moment the spider dropped from the ceiling, Deathwielder and his men kept up a heavy rain of brass-tipped arrows. The shafts pummeled into the back of the arachnid, but the arrows were mere pinpricks to a creature of such magnitude and only proved to antagonize the creature more.

Shasnak turned her head. A dreadful hiss emanated from its maw, and yellow bile streamed across the chasm, striking a young dwarf. He clutched at his face and dropped to his knees screaming, and his comrades ran in and dragged him from the edge.

Kaden bent to examine the young man's wound. The skin was rapidly peeling away, revealing bone and raw sinew. He ordered two dwarves to take their friend to safety. Another dwarf ran onto the beam, but a slash of one hairy leg swept him screaming into the chasm.

Kaden was worried. He knew he had to stay calm, yet he was terrified for Tannith's life. The spider had not harmed her yet, but it was only a matter of time. Spiders preferred their prey fresh, usually breaking it down with secreted fluids, then sucking it in.

Hurriedly, he sifted through plans in his mind, skimming them then discarding them for some fault or other. Finally, he came to a decision. Hopefully, luck would be with him. He turned to Hammer. "Can you distract the spider?"

"You have a plan?"

"You draw the spider's attention. I will leap onto its back and cut its dragline. It will drop into the pit and be killed."

"How do you know it will work?"

"I do not."

Hammer grinned. "I like the plan."

Shasnak sat suspended an arm's length above Tannith, seeming uncertain of what to do.

Hammer signaled to his warriors. Each notched a burning arrow to his bow, and a volley of flaming shafts flew across the pit. The spider scrunched up its eight legs and spun on its dragline, her gaze following the flaring shafts into the far wall.

It was the signal for which Kaden awaited.

He raced across the beam and leapt onto the spider's back. The momentum of his jump set the arachnid swinging. He wrenched himself up and with all the force of his mighty shoulders, drove his sword down into one of the monster's red eyes. The creature hissed, thrashing its legs wildly trying to dislodge him. Yellow fluid burst from the orb, staining Kaden's clothes, burning holes into the cloth.

The pain from the gaping wound must have made her clumsy, for she missed his face and hands.

Kaden tore his blade free, and with a broad sweep, severed the dragline suspending the grotesque creature above the void, hurtling it into eternal darkness. At the same time, he leapt for the edge of the narrow beam. One hand caught around the plank, but his legs dangled free above the pit. He started to slip and knew he had to act. Dropping his sword, he threw his other arm up over the beam.

However, his strength spent from battling the spider, his right arm aching profusely from the wound he received from Dannock, and the wrenching from Dannock's horse on the mountain, all culminated to weaken his grip. Cold sweat broke out on his forehead, and his breath seemed solidified in his throat. A cold knot of realization formed in his stomach. He knew he did not have the strength to heave himself onto the board.

Then a hand clutched his wrist.

"Let go," called Hammer. "I will bear your weight."

Kaden groaned. A burning pain turned his arm to fire, but still, he hesitated. Did the dwarf have the strength? Could Hammer hold him?

"Trust me."

Kaden's bad arm lost purchase, and for several heartbeats, he seemed suspended in mid-air.

Hammer caught his second hand and started to drag

him up.

The dwarf's muscles bulged. His face reddened, and sweat beaded his wide forehead, as his strong shoulders strained to take on Kaden's full weight. Then, with a mighty heave, he swung him up onto the beam.

Kaden lay catching his breath, thanking the gods for his delivery. For someone who did not believe in the gods, he was doing an awful lot of thanking them of late. He glanced up to see Hammer sitting in front of him, grinning.

He breathed deeply and pushed to his knees. "We did it."

"Yes, my friend, we did it, but now you must leave the beam while I fetch your lady. You are still weak, and the board will not hold the weight of three."

Kaden looked to where Tannith hung encased in the cocoon of silk, then back to Hammer. "Can you carry her?"

Hammer raised a brow. "I carried you, did I not?"

He nodded and gave Hammer a last studied look before pushing to his feet. He took a few unsteady paces to solid ground, then rounded to watch Hammer closing the gap between him and Tannith.

With deft precision, the dwarf used his hunting knife to slice through the silken shell and release the princess. Catching her as she collapsed into his arms, her face pale, and her body unmoving, he tossed her over his shoulder sack-style and carried her across the board to sanctuary. It was not until he lowered her to the ground and Kaden held her in his arms, that they discovered she held the piece of the Cross clasped firmly in her fist.

Chapter Twelve

Out the window of the tower room, Sernon stared at the indigo clouds thickening in the night sky. He cursed loudly into the silence. Where was Dannock-Shae? He had been missing now for two full moon cycles.

He lifted the crystal decanter of ruby wine, poured a goblet, and swallowed it in one gulp. It tasted bad, as bad as he felt. He should have been pleased. The two main kingdoms were within his grasp. His men had taken most of the smaller forts and outlying villages. Thousands of slaves now worked the richest mines in the land—all belonging to him. He was living in the largest and most luxurious castle in all Tarlis, next to Ellenroh. However, even that prize would soon be his.

A special sacrifice had been planned for the fourteenth day of the fourteenth month of the Year of the Gods. In eight weeks, the moons and stars would be in alignment on the astrological charts, and once more, the gates of the Abyss would be thrown open. All who tried to stop him would be dealt with in accordance.

Soon, all the power, glory, and strength of the Dark Gods would be his! His power would be limitless. He would be as a God—invincible. Only one thing stood in his way—the Cross of Tarlis!

His fingers tightened on the stem of his goblet as a knock sounded at his door. Ruby wine splattered onto the deep Argeasian carpet at his feet. For several heartbeats, he stared down at the stain, then raised his voice and bellowed for the intruder to enter.

A barrel-chested man of indiscriminate age and full red beard stepped into the room and raised three fingers in the salute of the Urakian. The soldier knelt to await leave to speak.

"By the wrath of Arahmin! Do you know what hour it is? What do you want?"

"I am Kraal, Sire—Captain of the Urakian Imperial Army. For these past four seasons, my lieutenant and I have been on a special mission for the High Priest, Dannock—"

"You have news of Dannock-Shae?" Sernon cut him off.

"Yes, my lord." Kraal hesitated. He had heard stories since entering the castle that this new Lord of the Urakians was quick to anger and easily took offense. "I—"

"Spit it out, man, or I will rip it from your worthless tongue."

Kraal lowered his eyes. "The news is not pleasant, Sire."

"I shall be the judge of that."

Still, Kraal hesitated.

Sernon looked down at the filthy man at his feet. He was sure the warrior was riddled with fleas and lice. He took a step backward, and, as if on cue, the man scratched at his groin.

"Speak!"

****

Kraal, not usually a man to quail before another, reached with a shaky hand into his cloak pocket. He found that for which he sought, made to draw it out, but it slipped from his fingers and rolled across the flagstone floor. Casting a quick glance at the sorcerer's impatient countenance, he dove after it and managed to grasp it before it slid beneath a gilded chair. He came to his knees and handed it to the sorcerer.

Gingerly, Sernon examined the gold ring. Chunky, with a pale moonstone in its center, the sorcerer recognized it as Dannock-Shae's. He grasped Kraal by his tunic, all thought of his filth forgotten. With uncommon strength, he dragged him to his feet. "Where did you get this?"

"The priest lives no more, my lord. I have been tracking the Princess of Ellenroh for weeks. Her last tracks led to a hidden valley in the Poniard Ranges. There, we found the mutilated body of the high priest. He was only recognizable by his ring and the cross he bore around his neck."

Kraal took the cross from his other pocket and handed it to the sorcerer. "The priest's face was missing, and his innards spilled from his body. Around him lay four more corpses. They were so decomposed and stank so vile, we reasoned they had been there for several weeks. Strange—as Dannock-Shae's blood was still fresh, as if he'd only died that morning."

Sernon cursed beneath his breath. "Pity," was the only word he spoke aloud. "You have done well, Captain." He dismissed Kraal with a wave of his hand. "Leave me."

"What are your orders, Sire?"

****

Sernon hesitated and ran his gaze over the man before him. He had the build of a warrior and the look of a hawk about him, keen and strong with just a touch of

172

cruelty about the lips and eyes. Now Dannock was dead, he would need someone he could trust, and this man had proved his worth by reporting the priest's death. "Clean yourself up," he ordered. "You stink worse than a black toad on heat. Then take over the training of the conscripts. A battle is brewing, as sure as I sit on the throne of Tarlis. I want my men ready when the time comes."

Kraal came to attention. "It will be done, Sire." He saluted and strode from the room, shutting the door behind him.

Sernon held his slender fingers to his throbbing temples. Why did the darn priest have to get himself killed right now when he needed him most? He had received word only that day, the rebels had amassed an army in the hills and were preparing an attack against Wolveryne Castle.

He snatched up his goblet, and it crashed heavily into the gilt-edged portrait of the Wolfhead King hanging on the opposite wall. Wine ran down the painted face, staining it blood red.

Sernon stared at the portrait, transfixed for several heartbeats, then wrenched it from the wall and swung it down over the corner of the oak table dominating the room. The corner of the table protruded through one green eye while the other glared accusingly back at him.

Cold fingers of fear played down his spine. Was it an omen? Was it a sign that his dark gods were deserting him? He lifted a shaky hand and pointed toward the painting. Blue fire sprang from his fingertips, setting the portrait alight. Still, the king's face stared through the flames. Sernon caught up the burning portrait and hurled it through the nearest window, watching as the fiery spectacle splashed into the moat below. Then he slammed the shutter and collapsed onto the nearest chair.

It would be a long time before he could rid his mind of the accusing green eyes of the Wolfhead King.

****

Kaden and Tannith stood on a wooded hill overlooking the sprawling city of Antibba. The gates were closed. Seven days ago, they had left the Poniard City with a promise from Hammer to rally to their aid should they muster enough men to launch an attack on Sernon. In fact, the young dwarf had almost begged Kaden for the honor to do so. Hammer Deathwielder and his dwarven warriors were itching to prove themselves in real battle.

A great restlessness grew among the young men. Tired of mock battles and the sparring they were forced to undertake to keep fit, they wondered what the use of learning strategies and skills was if they never used them. They yearned to fight in real battles like their ancestors had fought before them.

In honor of slaying the giant arachnid, the great market square lay cleared, and a feast was prepared. Shasnak had long been the bane of the dwarven people. Kaden and Tannith joined in the celebrations for two days, and the cavern had overflowed with feasting and revelry of all kinds.

Tannith watched while the natives of the city danced around a huge fire with wild abandon. She wished she could have given herself over to the music, but her strict upbringing had conditioned her mind against such pursuits.

The women presented her with a long flowing skirt and silk blouse, akin to theirs, in thanks for her part in ridding the Dwarves of Shasnak. She smiled and accepted the gift graciously, grateful for the opportunity to relieve herself of the breeches she had worn since leaving Druh Forest.

She came from her reverie as Kaden touched her arm. "Are you all, right?"

She nodded and peered up as soft rain sifted down from the cobalt clouds overhead. She pulled her cloak more snugly around her shoulders. "What do we do now that the gates are closed?"

"I thought this might happen." He rolled up one of the field blankets. "Allow me." He grinned and stuffed the blanket up under her russet tunic to make her look as if she carried a child, then he pulled her cowl close around her face. "Just follow my lead. They probably have our descriptions from here to Lemma. So, keep your face down."

He took Phoenix's bridle and led Tannith down the hill to stop before the ironbound gates. Two sentries, high atop the wall, peered down on the travelers.

"Papers," called one of the soldiers.

Kaden shifted restlessly, feigning cowardliness, imitating the voice of a peasant. "I beg your forgiveness sirs, but my good lady is havin' trouble birthin.' She 'as need of a midwife quick, or she's as good as gone. And she is soaked to the bone from the rain and most likely will catch a fever."

Tannith cried out and clutched at her swollen abdomen. "The babe is coming!"

"The city is under martial law. No one leaves or enters after dusk unless they have papers." The dark-haired sentry shaded his eyes from the fading light and struggled to get a clearer view of Tannith.

Kaden removed a brass coin from his pocket and flipped it up to the guard.

The sentry pocketed the coin. "They're only peasants," he said to his comrade.

"And we don't want 'er dropping no squalling whelp at our feet," his friend agreed.

The wheel turned above Kaden's head, and the iron portcullis groaned and lifted. He led the stallion through the gates of Antibba, its great metal-shod hooves ringing out on the black, slick cobblestones as it stepped into the city.

"Halt!" ordered the guard again.

Kaden tensed, his hand slipping to the hilt of his father's sword concealed beneath his cloak. His eyes remained focused on the ground, not daring to raise his face to the reddish glow of the torch in case recognized. "Aye, what is it?"

"Where did you get that horse? Too grand for one the likes of you."

"The beast was won in a fair wager," Kaden called back. "Jockan Deevah, be no thief. The nag be mine by law." His rough words were met by silence.

The sentry waited for several heartbeats, then slowly lowered the torch, and wound down the portcullis, waving them on.

Along a narrow cobblestone street and around a corner, Kaden led Tannith and the horse. Wending their way into the hushed city, they made sure to stay clear of patrolling sentries. They followed the road until finally, Kaden drew to a halt before a stable. He thumped on the double green doors twice, and the door was eased open to display the face of a small boy. A lad of around ten summers ushered them inside and Tannith slid from the stallion to pull the field blanket from beneath her skirt, tossing it over Phoenix's rump.

"Thank the gods that is over. I felt like an overstuffed pheasant."

"I thought it suited you." Kaden's intense green eyes met hers across the back of the horse.

****

What would it be like to bear the prince's son? She wondered. Would he be dark like his father or fair like her? The boy tugged insistently on her arm, interrupting her thoughts.

"My lady, you must go, it is not safe for you to linger—the soldiers. Sometimes they stop here."

She touched a hand to his head. "You are right, but first, would you care to earn a silver deemah?"

He grinned, showing several white, crooked teeth. "What must I do?"

"Guard this horse with your life and tomorrow you shall have your coin. Agreed?"

The boy nodded, took Phoenix's reins, and led him into a back stall.

Tannith watched him go uneasily. "Do you think he can be trusted?"

"I would trust the boy with my brother's kingdom. He is Norvak's youngest son." He dropped a small kiss to her forehead, tucked her arm into his, and led her from the stables through a rough, wooden side door. They crossed a narrow alleyway where the prince stopped at an arched door, the sign overhead reading "The Tiger's Arm." He knocked, and for several long heartbeats, came naught but brittle silence, then a clatter as the metal shutter slid aside.

"State your business," came a muffled voice.

****

Kaden hesitated. He had heard the voice of the jovial innkeeper many times and knew it well. This was not he. Yet, in all the time he had known him, none bar Norvak had answered the side door. It was for select customers only.

Kaden palmed his knife. "Stand behind me," he said in a low voice. "This could be a trap." He reached back and gave her hand a quick squeeze. "If I say run, run like a demon is on your tail."

Tannith squeezed his shoulder in reply, and he gave the door another bang.

The voice came again, this time louder. "State your business, or I shall call the watch."

"Where is Norvak?" Kaden demanded.

The bolt rattled, and the door dragged open. A hand grabbed his shirt and pulled him inside and Tannith followed behind. The door slammed shut.

Kaden could barely believe what he was seeing. Before him stood not the tiger he had left several moons ago, but his brother in human form. "Erik—what the—" Kaden hugged his brother, and they both laughed. Then he released Erik and brought Tannith forward. "Tannith, meet Erik." He grinned. "The real Erik."

Tannith was at a loss for words. He was the exact replica of Kaden, or almost. He was minus the scar and a little older, and his hair was yellow gold. "How?" she asked at last, searching Erik's face.

Erik gave Tannith a gentle hug. "I will explain later. First, come see the others. They feared for your safety." He led them from the kitchen down a hall into Norvak's sitting room. There, another surprise awaited them.

A tall, red-haired girl rushed forward, enveloping

Tannith in her arms. "We knew you would come," she said, laughing and crying at the same time. She pushed Tannith to arm's length, wiping hastily at her tears, but still did not release her.

"Skylah! May the gods be blessed? This is incredible. First, Erik. Now, you. Who wrought this miracle?"

Skylah and Erik looked at each other and laughed. " 'Tis a long story," they said in unison, then laughed again.

"I would know it anyway."

Erik shook his head. "Later." His tone brooked no argument, but he softened his refusal with a smile as his arm closed possessively around Skylah's waist.

Tannith had to force herself not to frown.

"We would prefer to hear of your travels," he said.

"And that you shall, but first I must speak with my friends."

She glanced across the room to the young man leaning against the hearth. Etan met her inquiring look with a brief shake of his head. Hurt clouded his eyes. She excused herself from the others and made her way toward him. He stepped in to meet her and take her hands, but she ignored them and went straight into his arms, hugging him warmly. "What is going on here?" she whispered in his ear.

"Nothing time will not heal." He kissed her cheek, then released her to thread her arm through his. "Come, I am sure Ohma is impatient to speak with you. He has done naught but fret over your safety since he last saw you."

The old Mage stood as they approached, his weathered face breaking into a smile. "My lady."

Tannith stretched up and kissed his brow. "Well met, old friend."

He flushed and drew out a chair from the table and waited for her to seat herself, then took the chair opposite. "You look well, my lady, a little paler than I remember, and wet, but…" He smiled. "And your trip…was it profitable?"

"Did you not look for yourself?"

"I could see nothing once you entered the valley. Did things go as planned?"

Tannith blushed and glanced at Kaden.

"Very," replied the prince, overhearing Ohma's remark as he walked to join them. He covered Tannith's hand with his and gave it a gentle squeeze. "We recovered both pieces of the Cross, and Dannock-Shae is dead."

"Then our family is avenged." Erik's voice sounded behind them.

"Aye." Kaden released Tannith, stood, and turned to his brother. "Now our parents and sister can rest in peace. I am only sorry you were not there to share in the bastard's death."

Erik clutched Kaden by the shoulders and looked into his eyes. "So am I brother. Did you take his heart?"

"Pegged to a tree in the hidden valley. Dannock-Shae will never see Paradise. Or his version of it."

"Good. Then our revenge is complete, and you can live again." Erik seemed to relax. He took Kaden's hand and pushed both their arms into the air, making an inverted V. "Norvak! Food and ale for all. Tonight, we celebrate!"

****

Tannith and Kaden had been given a room to bathe

and don clean clothes. And not long afterward, they joined their friends in Norvak's private dining room. There, another of Norvak's sons served them a large haunch of beef, potted pig's tongue served with a rich gravy, and suet dumplings. Several vegetable side dishes accompanied the main meal, followed by a sweet of various stewed fruits and clotted cream.

After the hearty meal and several rounds of Norvak's finest ale, the companions sat around the table and exchanged stories. Ohma told of the Dragon and the transformation of Skylah and Erik. Then, Kaden went on to relate the story of the Poniard Dwarves and Tannith's adventure with the giant arachnid.

"Where was our innkeeper earlier?" Kaden inquired, lowering his tankard to the table when the stories came to an end. "I have never known anyone but Norvak to answer the side door."

"Our friend has formed an underground resistance," replied Erik, his gaze trained on the curtain adjoining the other room. "His men are smuggling food to our allies in the hills and have recruited warriors from the breadth of Tarlis and even beyond to join the Dorrachian cause. There is a force of over five thousand training in the Carrum-Bahl Valley, awaiting you to lead them."

Kaden's eyebrows rose. "They were so sure I would come?"

Erik met his look. "I told them they were not to march without their general, that you would be here."

"General?" Kaden grinned. "I have been promoted?"

"General Lars died at the battle of Wolveryne Castle. You are the only other I trust to lead them."

"What of you?"

"I am no warrior, you know that. I can take care of myself in a fair fight, yes, but I am neither the strategist nor the soldier you are."

Kaden's eyes darkened, and he placed his hand on Erik's shoulder. "Then for my king, I shall lead his army."

"Good, that is settled."

"And Sernon? Have you knowledge of him?"

"He has taken Wolveryne Castle and crowned himself ruler of all Tarlis."

"By the gods, he has not!" His fist came down on the table, and the tankards rattled. "That serpent shall rue the day he sat on my father's throne. I will cut out his entrails!"

"Not if I get there first," countered Erik.

Ohma cleared his throat and placed a hand on his shoulder. "I know this is unsettling news lad, but there is more yet to discuss. We still have the last piece of the Cross to find." He leaned toward Tannith. "You have the other three pieces. I can feel their power. May I see them?"

"Yes. Let us see," urged Skylah. "Is the Cross as beautiful as pictured on the wall in Magus's shrine?"

"Even more so." Tannith pulled the leather pouch from around her neck and emptied the contents onto the table. A faint green glow emanated from the three jewel encrusted pieces.

Ohma's eyes sparkled, and he reached to take a piece into his hand, but small lightning bolts struck from the part closest to him, searing his fingers. Hurling himself backward, he avoided further bolts, but his chair crashed down, and he fell sprawled out with his blue robes hiked up around his knees.

Etan leaned over and helped the old man to his feet. "So, who is on the floor now?" He asked with a raised brow, and laughter erupted from his comrades.

Red faced, Ohma accepted his help to regain his seat and dipped his scorched fingers into his cool ale. Straightening his robes, he leaned forward. "As I thought, the power becomes stronger as the pieces are brought together. Assemble it Tannith. You are the chosen one."

Tannith took up the first part of the Cross. It tingled in her palm. She had not thought to join the Cross as she collected the pieces. She had not even taken them out to view, afraid of the power they bore. The only time she had touched them was when Kaden lay dying.

She remembered how the pieces of the Cross burned its image into Kaden's chest. He still carried the mark, yet, it had seared her not at all.

The second piece of the Cross felt cool to her touch as she fit it to the Key. Then she locked the third into position.

When finished, she held up the incomplete Cross, suspended from its chain. Roughly three inches long, inscribed with intricate gold runes and small precious gems, it glowed with the brightness of green fire lighting up the room.

"So now, except for the Eye of Magus, we need only the fourth piece," stated Ohma. "Skylah, you said you might have knowledge of it."

The former Faerie grimaced. "It could be in the treasure cave, but I cannot be certain. As a child, I played there, though I cannot remember seeing the Cross. The cave is vast and deep, and there is much treasure."

"Tell me," Ohma went on. "If it were there, do you

think the Bearah would give it up?"

"He is unpredictable and easily upset. If I am with you and he recognizes me in this image, then perhaps."

"And if not," Kaden said. "We will just have to take it."

"There will be no need for that, I am certain," Skylah said, giving the Wolfhead Prince a dark look.

Chapter Thirteen

In the dead of night, guided through the vast maze of sewer tunnels by one of Norvak's people, Kaden and his comrades slipped silently from the city.

The tunnel emerged in a dense thicket of bushes adjacent to the city walls. The party of six traveled through the forest for the next twelve days, skirting the base of the Carrum-Bahl Mountains and dodging marauding Urakian patrols. They followed the Argon River to where it joined with the blue waters of the Tarlis River. After fording the river, they cut north into the tall silver pines and pink cherry blossom trees of the Sabiah Woods.

Seven days later, and seven leagues from Antibba, Tannith found herself camped under a star-filled sky a day's walk from the legendary Valley of the Faerie. Up until now, she had been unable to speak with Etan alone; however, tonight she was adamant he would avoid her no longer. She was curious to know what had caused the animosity between her friend and the young king. Though she guessed Skylah was at the center of the matter, judging by the long-suffering looks Etan threw her way when he thought no one watched.

Each evening after supper, he would head into the trees and not return until dawn. When she questioned him, he stated he was keeping guard on the perimeter of the camp. She was certain he was not telling the whole truth.

She watched as he rose, threw his pack over his shoulder, picked up his crossbow, clipped it to his belt, and strode into the woods. She scrambled to her feet to follow, but Kaden's hand shot out and clamped down on her wrist. "Let him go."

"No." She stared down at his hand. "We are like family. What hurts him hurts me."

"First, I would know, what it is between you?"

"His father saved my father's life and was killed for his trouble. The king adopted him out of friendship for the man who gave up his life. We were raised as brother and sister. That is all there is." She held his gaze.

Kaden watched her face, a brittle silence settling between them, then he set her free. "Go if you must, but I will tell you now, there is no cure for what ails him."

Ohma shook his head as she ran into the forest. "Women are certainly most wondrous creatures, my lord."

Kaden fed a stick to the fire and smiled softly. "Most wondrous indeed. They think they hold the answer to the world's problems."

Ohma chuckled. "Perhaps they do."

****

Tannith came to an out of breath halt. She had been searching for quite some time and finally found Etan sitting with his back to a tall blackwood. He had not answered her calls. She knelt and snatched a leather flask from his hand. He tried to grab it, but it was too late, its contents forming a black stain on the forest floor.

"What are you doing?" His eyes darkened in his pale, handsome face. "Are you insane?"

"No, are you?" She glared down at him.

He looked past her into the darkening shadows. "Can a man not get drunk when he wishes?"

"No. Not when it affects his mission and the lives of his friends." She sank down beside him and touched a hand tenderly to his cheek to turn him to face her. "Talk to me Etan? What is it that hurts you so?"

"You would not understand." He glanced away and ran his hands through his hair, pushing it from his face.

Tannith noticed for the first time how long it had grown since leaving Ellenroh. "You need a haircut," she told him. "And a shave. Soon you will be as uncouth as Kaden." She sighed. "What is happening to you? It is as if you do not care anymore about anything or anyone. In fact, why are you still here?"

He looked back at her. Pain reflected in his eyes. "I promised to see you through this, and I will."

She picked up his empty flask. "Is this what you do every night, sneak off and get drunk? Drown your problems in cheap spirits?"

A shadow of a smile crossed his face, and for a moment she thought she saw a flicker of the old Etan. "I will have you know that was good Reamer Whiskey."

Tannith shook her head. "What can be so bad that you must blot all thought from your mind?"

He came to his feet in a rush and smashed his foot into a nearby sapling. "Curse you Tannith. Curse you to the Pit! Must I bare my soul to you? Can a man have no secrets?"

"And since when have there been secrets we needed to keep from each other?" She rose and covered his hand with her own. "What happened, Etan? We used to be so close."

He rounded on her, grasped her by the shoulders,

and brought her face within a hair's breadth of his own. "Yes, Tannith, since when have there been secrets? How long have you and the Dorrachian been sleeping together?"

The blood rushed to her face, and he did not wait for a response. He rounded to lean his shoulder against an oak and hung his head. "Forgive me. I had no right. But what is it with these Dorrachians? Do they not have women in this god forsaken kingdom that they must steal mine? First you, then Skylah."

Tannith circled his waist with her arms and laid her cheek against his back. She could feel the heat of his skin through the fine linen of his shirt. She spoke quietly. "You know I was never really yours. It was what our parents wanted and what our people expected. Deep in your heart, you knew you never really loved me other than what a brother would feel for a sister. Or you never would have fallen in love with Skylah so quickly."

He spun and enfolded her in his arms, holding her close as if she were a lifeline in his pit of despair. "I know, Tannith, but it was not until I knew I was in love with Skylah that I realized. I love that woman. I love her so much I can hardly bear the sight of her. Every time I see him touch her, my innards twist, and it is everything I can do to stop myself from slicing those yellow eyes from that pretty face of his." His hands tightened on her arms. "Now you know why I make excuses to get away. Why I need to drown my soul in liquid fire—to deaden my brain and my heart."

"Etan, you are hurting me."

Tannith pushed from his arms.

"I am sorry." He threw himself to the ground and dropped his forehead to rest on his bent knees. "See what she does to me?"

"Have you told her how you feel?" Tannith crouched beside him and stroked his white-blond hair. "I know she used to care for you. I think she fell in love with you the first time she saw you." Her mind drifted back to the wistful looks the tiny Faerie had cast the Elisian Captain. What could have changed Skylah so much while she was away? "I cannot understand any of this."

He looked up. "She loves me, which is what makes this harder. She admitted it when I asked her to come away with me."

"You were going to leave without saying goodbye?" she asked in a small voice.

"Sorry, but all I could think of at the time was Skylah and how much I care for her. If the only way I could have her was to creep away in the dead of night, then yes, I would have done it without hesitation. But she refused me. It appears she has some misguided notion that she owes Erik her loyalty and her trust because he loves her. He saw in her right from the beginning what I did not. So here you find me," he patted the grass, "getting quietly drunk. If the only thing that will make her happy is to leave her alone, then so be it. But I do not have to stay and watch."

Tannith rose and looked down at him. "If I could take away your pain, you know I would. You are dear to me."

He gave her a shaky smile. "For that, I will always love you."

She met his smile with a gentle one of her own. "But not like you love Skylah?"

"No," he murmured. "Not like Skylah."

Tannith watched him slip another flask of whiskey from his pack and pull the stopper. She moved toward camp, leaving him alone in the moonlight under the stars.

This was one war Etan would have to battle alone.

Chapter Fourteen

The travelers separated late the next afternoon.
Ohma took the women further upstream to bathe in a
brook that ran through the forest while the men went on
to locate the cave of the Bearah.

Etan studied the imposing statue blocking the
entrance to the treasure cave. "So, what do we do now?"

The Bearah stood head and shoulders above Kaden,
who at six foot four was the tallest of the men, and its
breadth was at least three times his width.

"We could try to move it, or we could wait." Erik
shrugged. " 'Tis nearly dusk."

Etan spat in disgust and shook his head. "Wait! Wait
for what, for that thing to awaken and kill us? I say we
crush it with our swords while it sleeps and be done."

Erik's lip curled in barely disguised contempt.
"Typical." He dropped onto a flat-topped boulder and
eased his pack from his shoulder. "Skylah said to wait
for the creature to wake, and she will speak with it. We
were merely to locate the cave."

Etan glared at him. "I say you are soft to take orders
from a woman."

"And I say you are all too ready to kill anything or
anyone that stands in your way."

Etan's hand flashed to his dagger. "Do you want to
try me? Do you?"

Erik drew his hunting knife and took up a fighting

stance. "Any time, *boy*."

Kaden stepped between them. "That is enough! We all know this is not about the Bearah. If we get out of this mess, I will be only too happy to let you slice each other to pieces, if only for the calm that will follow. Until then, I suggest you keep your jealousy under control." He looked from one to the other. "Both of you." He walked toward a large oak, settled under it, and stretched out with his hands beneath his head. "We will wait for the others, then decide. Now sit."

Grudgingly, the two men sheathed their knives and followed suit.

****

The tips of his pointed ears twitched, his eyes flickered, and the stench of man flesh filled his nostrils. He growled and shook, brought one clawed fist to his gray, scaly chin, and scratched. He could feel their eyes boring into him and imagined the sweet warm taste of their blood.

For a thousand summers, he had guarded the treasure. Did these man-beasts never tire of trying to take it from him? Even though the wee folk had vanished, he was still the guardian, and he would protect the treasure until they returned. For what else could he do? He was the last of his kind.

His heart filled with a sadness that threatened to overwhelm him. Soon there would be none of the Ancient Creatures left. First, the Horned Horses were hunted to extinction because man believed that their horns, when ground down and blended with wine, could restore their flagging virility, or promote everlasting life. What nonsense. Then the Roc Trolls had perished after being hunted purely for sport. The Bearrahs tried to help, but then Man had turned on them as well.

He believed there were a few Roc Trolls left hiding in the remote peaks of the Carrum-Bahls, but Xhargos was beyond caring. Now the Faeries had been attacked and the rest disappeared. Would Man never be satisfied? With a sigh, he stretched his bat-like wings and stepped from the mouth of the cave to face his enemy.

A tall man with black hair rose from beneath the oak tree nearby and strode forward. "Guardian of the cave, we mean you no harm." He held up his hands. "We are in search of the lost Cross of the God, Magus. We believe the last piece lies in your cave."

"And if it does, the corrupt hands of Man shall never fall upon it." He bared his sharp, white teeth and growled to emphasize his point.

****

Kaden drew his sword. "If you do not surrender it, we will have to take it from you."

"You can try, and you will die." The Bearah snarled, a harsh grating sound that cracked the silence of the valley.

Erik dragged forth his broadsword and stood beside his brother, as Etan released a bronze-tipped bolt from his crossbow.

The shaft hit the Bearah's shoulder, snapped, and dropped to the ground as if it had struck solid rock. The creature roared low in his throat, crouched, and sprang.

Kaden and Erik charged as one. Their swords struck the Bearah's neck, but their blows deflected, leaving their shoulders jarred and their fingers numb.

Etan sprang onto the Bearah's back, riding him hard for several long, dizzying heartbeats. The creature bucked, spun, and snorted, trying to dislodge the man from his back. Then, the Bearah bucked higher still, twisted, and tossed the Elisian through the air headlong into his comrades, sending the trio sprawling.

At that moment Skylah appeared. "Stop this! I told you to find the Bearah, not attack him. Cannot a woman bathe in peace?" She stood, hands on hips, glaring down at the three warriors.

On hearing the cry of the Bearah, she had donned her dress and used her light-travel to arrive at the scene. She was unsure whether she still possessed the power to perform such a feat, but apparently, she did. Her hair dripped water down her leather and plate battle dress, and a shiver ran the length of her body, but she refused to acknowledge it. "Cannot men do anything without resorting to violence?"

The warriors had the audacity to grin.

Ohma rushed from the trees, his chest heaving, his wrinkled brow beaded with sweat, Tannith at his side. The Druid of Merrum glanced pointedly at the warriors, then at Skylah.

"What happened here?" He breathed raggedly. "I thought Skylah was to do the talking. The Bearah is a creature of her people after all."

The men rose to their feet, all speaking at once.

"We tried to explain—"

"They were trying to kill the Bearah," Skylah broke in.

"There was no reasoning with the creature." Erik shook his head and strode over to retrieve his sword. "The creature said we would have to take the piece by force if we wanted it." He grinned. "We were only doing as he bid."

Skylah noted the Bearah watching them with

interest.

"No one enters the treasure cave except the Faeries of Sabiah." His voice boomed across the clearing. "You know that, Princess."

He spoke directly to Skylah, and she cringed. In all the time she had been with them, she had never disclosed to her friends her true identity. She wished now she were still a handspan in height as they stopped speaking and stared at her.

She rounded on the beast, snapping out several words in Faerie dialect in rapid succession—words unintelligible to the others. The Bearah dropped to his haunches, and she turned back to her comrades. The first face she saw was Etan's—his eyes azure-blue and accusing. She should have told him. She should have told them all that she is the Lady of Sabiah, daughter of King Oberon, instead of one of the common populace of Sabiah as they believed her to be.

Erik threw her a bewildered look. "Why the secrecy?"

She raised her hand to halt his words then glanced from one member of her party to the other. "I wanted you to care for *me*, not for what I was. If you had known I was the daughter of Oberon would that have been possible, or would you have reacted on the power of my title?"

Tannith stepped forward and took her friend in her arms. "Of course, and I do not blame you. I know how it can be, never knowing if you will be accepted for your true self, or that for which you can be used. At times, I have felt the same."

Erik moved to Skylah's side, and Tannith released her into his care and stepped away to speak to Kaden.

Erik gave her a quick hug and took her hand.

She smiled hesitantly. "I am sorry, but the longer I kept the secret, the harder it became to share." She stood on her toes and kissed his cheek "You are not too furious with me?"

"How could I be?" He smiled. "You are a piece of my soul."

She looked away. "You are too good to me."

"I know." He raised both hands and turned her to smile into her eyes. "But that is part of caring for someone."

An awkward silence fell between them. "I must talk to Xhargos."

"Of course." He released her, and she stepped out of his embrace. "I will join you at the river when we finish speaking."

Erik looked toward the Bearah, and the beast scowled back at him. "He is an ugly brute. Are you sure he is safe?"

She patted his arm. "Do not fret so. Xhargos and I are friends. I grew up playing in this cave."

Erik left her, and she watched him stride away. He really did deserve someone better, someone who could offer him all her heart. She sighed, turned, and joined the Bearah.

They walked until they found a flat-topped boulder within the cave, then she settled and faced the enormous creature. "Now Xhargos, why have you been harassing my friends?"

The Bearah, the faerie name for gargoyle, crossed his well-muscled arms over his massive chest and regarded her with steely intent, yet Skylah could tell from the way his ears twitched he was nervous.

"They intended to steal the treasure." He growled, low in his throat.

She raised a brow. "Is that entirely true?"

Xhargos shifted his feet and brought his heavy tail down with a thump. Thick dust rose into the air. She moved aside and smiled at the Bearah's agitation.

"They wanted the *sparkly* your brother, Prince Cahan, brought here before the attack."

"Why do you call it that?"

"King Oberon ordered me to guard it with my life. He said it was precious, and that one day, evil would come for it. The *sparkly* is so pretty, my lady. It fills the back cavern with light. I am sick of the darkness."

Skylah sighed and moved to the boulder beside him. "You were right to do what you promised my father, but your *sparkly* is needed. It could mean the saving of our world. There is one who is evil, a sorcerer, who wishes to rule and enslave all Tarlis, man and beast. He does not care how he does it. If the Cross of Tarlis should fall into his hands, he will have the power by which to achieve his awful plan."

"Why should it affect you, my lady? You are not of their race. You are a Faerie…" His words trailed off and his demeanor changed. With extended talons, he reared up and loomed over her in a threatening manner. Suspicion was thick in his tone. "What happened to you? Why are you so tall? Where are your wings? You appear out of nowhere claiming to be the lady, but how do I know you are really she?"

Skylah spoke to him gently, as if a child. "If I were not, *she*, then how would I know your name, which only one of the *Royal House* would know? How could I understand the language of the Faerie if I were not such a creature?" She shifted to touch his arm. "Also, it was you who recognized me. I never claimed to be anyone important."

The Bearah scratched his head. Relaxing his stance, he sat back on his haunches, a frown wrinkling his forehead.

"Do not fret, my old friend, 'tis I." She threw her arms around his hard, gigantic shoulders the best she could, and his face twisted into the semblance of a smile, as if glad to have the matter closed.

"Now, Xhargos?" She stepped back.

"My lady?"

"Have you seen Prince Cahan…or any Faeries?"

A deep sadness filled the beast's eyes, and he shook his head. "Nay, I very rarely venture from the cave. Yet, as time passed and nobody came, I began to worry. I made my way to the village. What I found brought tears to my heart—the mutilated bodies of hundreds of Faeries. Of your brother, and the rest of your people— no trace could I find.

"I searched for three nights after I buried the bodies, having to return each morning before daybreak. But to no avail. It was as if they had never been. And to this day, I thought you were lost as well." He released a heavy breath. "I hoped someday, someone would return. Where have you been all these long days? And where are your people, if not with you?"

Tears welled in Skylah's eyes, and she stared at her toes. "Of that I have no knowledge. When the Urakians attacked, my father told me to flee—to hide. I saw him taken, and, in my terror, I flew. I should have stayed and fought with the others, but the enemy were so many. For one moment only, I hesitated. In that instant, I saw

Tobias, my brother's squire, picked up, his wings plucked from his back and his body dropped to be crushed beneath the massive heel of a hobnailed boot—the picture, even now, haunts my dreams."

Xhargos patted her shoulder gently with two large fingers. "Where did you go?"

"I flew until I could fly no longer. Exhausted, I hid within a hollow log like a loathsome bug, the screams still echoing in my ears. The next morning, I returned to the village to find our homes crushed and mutilated bodies littering the grass of Sabiah. My parents had been tortured in the most horrendous way. I buried them, and although I searched for days, I found no trace of my brother or the others.

"Those days passed in a blur. I must have wandered for leagues without even knowing it. Eventually I gave up hope, not caring if I lived or died. In my grief, I imagined it was a sign from the goddess that I had been left alone. It was my punishment for deserting my people. I wanted to die. It was then Tannith of Ellenroh found me and took me to Dragonbane Castle."

Her voice grew stronger. "In her, I found a true friend. She gave me the courage to go on. She convinced me to keep searching."

"But now you have taken on the image of a man-beast?"

"Yes." She touched his hand. "An Elisian. They are not as long-lived as a Faerie or an Elf, but almost." She smiled hesitantly. "I decided if I could not find my people, my only chance at happiness would be to become one with the people I knew."

"Why did the ugly men attack Sabiah?"

"I have no idea, Xhargos. Perhaps they thought we

had Magus's Cross. Which brings us back to, why I am here." Skylah put both her hands into his great scaled paws. "Where did you say the fourth piece lies? Even now, as we speak, the moments are costly. Sernon and his minions are destroying Tarlis. Cities are burning, people are being tortured and enslaved, fields and villages drenched in blood. Why? So that Sernon can sit upon a throne and call himself king. It will not be long before his followers find you, my friend. The sorcerer has a way of knowing where we are. I only hope, unwittingly, we have not put you in danger."

Xhargos reared up on his back legs. "Do not fear for me, my lady. Should they come, I shall be ready. For a thousand summers, I have guarded the Faerie treasure-hold, and for another thousand, I will stand fast. Not until my body is crushed and turned into dust, will I let an enemy pass me by. You and your friends may enter and take that which you seek. But mind, warn them, touch nothing more or I shall know, and the penalty for stealing from this cave is death."

She was about to turn away when he called her back. "Wait."

For several long heartbeats, he disappeared into the darkness of the cave. When he reappeared, he had a golden pendant in his hand which he dropped down over her head. "Your father said to give you this should the day come that he is no longer here to guide you, or something should befall your brother."

She picked up the pendant and studied it. Round, it was inscribed with runes of a different language than Faerie, and at its heart was a large clear jewel. Having no time to decipher the writing, she tucked it down her shirt. "Thank you, dear one, and thank you for your loyalty to my family. I shall treasure the pendant all of my days."

The necklace was soon forgotten as she hurried back to join her friends.

****

After gaining the last piece of the Cross, Kaden held the torch high. It lit the darkness as he led the way back through the cave to where Ohma and Xhargos waited outside. Skylah and Erik came next, and Tannith and Etan trailed, unhampered by the dimness of the cave because of their ability to see in the dark.

Tannith noted as they traveled, the mountains of gold coin, plate, precious objects of art, and glittering mounds of cut and uncut gems littering the walls and floor of the cavern. Torchlight reflected and bounced, illuminating the surface of the treasure, giving it the brilliance of the sun and stars. It was a wonderment even the most stoic of people would have been hard pressed to resist.

Etan's eyes filled with hunger. "Have you ever seen anything so magnificent? There is more treasure here than in all of Ellenroh."

Tannith grasped his arm. "You must touch nothing. You heard what the beast said."

Etan pried her hand from his arm. "Why? What else have I, Tannith? You have Kaden. Erik—Skylah. What have I when this quest is done? Answer me."

"The knowledge that you played a part in saving your people, delivered them from Sernon's evil. Even now, Ellenroh could be under his control, our people working the mines. We have had no word from anyone in months."

He glanced away and ran a hand over his eyes. "I have gone beyond caring for others. With a handful of this," he indicated the gold and precious gems around him, "I could start over, travel far from here—build a new life. Perhaps go to Nildor and help. I hear there is a war there. I could *be* something. Not just the Captain of the Elite." He grasped her shoulders. "Can you not see that?"

Tannith refused to look at him, afraid of what she might see in his face, and twisted out of his embrace. "All I know, Etan, is that riches are not the answer. You could be the wealthiest man in the whole of the land, but what then? Would you be happy?"

His face reddened, and his lips set in a tight line. He refused to answer.

"Be stubborn and do as you will. But I would think long and hard about what is important. You have your life and friends that care about you. You touch this treasure, and you will end with nothing." She swung away and left him standing alone in the dark as she hurried after the waning torchlight. She hoped above hope, her childhood friend would take the right path.

Once outside the cave, she joined the others and stood, waiting anxiously for Etan to emerge. Their conversation kept running through her mind. Would he accept her advice and leave the treasure behind, or would he follow the misguided dictates of his heart?

Etan was a long time emerging.

The sun completed its descent, and the stars blanketed the night sky. Tannith's palms had grown clammy, and she wiped them down the front of her tunic, then glanced up as she heard a movement at the entrance of the cave.

He stepped over the threshold, filthy, his hair disheveled, and his clothes torn and mattered with dirt and cobwebs, but on his face, he wore a charming smile. "Sorry, I got lost. I stopped to remove a stone from my boot and found myself literally left in the dark. It took my night vision a while to adjust. I guess I must have taken the wrong fork." He made to join Tannith, when Xhargos stepped to block his path.

He looked up at the Gargoyle. "Is there a problem, beast?"

Xhargos stood his ground, his body rigid, his agate-colored eyes implacable as iron.

Etan's hand crept toward his baldric and his brace of knives.

Xhargos snarled low in his throat, his pointed teeth flashing in the dim light. "Empty your pockets, man-beast."

Etan laughed and shook his head. "This is ridiculous—Skylah, call off your friend. Tell him this is unnecessary." He spread his arms and looked at Tannith. "I have nothing. I promise."

"Do it."

His smile dropped, and he stiffened as if struck. Unhurriedly, he turned out one pocket, then the other. Both proved to be empty.

Xhargos relaxed and stepped aside. "Go."

Etan stepped toward Tannith, the few paces separating them seeming like leagues. She could see the pain in his eyes, but also something more, triumph, and her expression hardened. *You lied*, she mouthed.

The blood rushed to Etan's face, and he looked to Ohma, who stood at her side. For several heartbeats, he and the old man stared at one another, then he cried out and sank to the ground. "Wait. I think I have something in my shoe." He pulled off his black military boot and upended the contents onto the ground. An uncut diamond, roughly the size of a bantam's egg, rolled onto the grass. He scooped it into his hand, held it up to the moonlight, then tossed the stone to the Bearah.

Xhargos caught it in his gigantic fist, eyed him with a growl, and looked at Skylah. With a nod of his lady's head, he pitched the stone over his massive shoulder into the cave, then he rounded on Etan.

****

Ohma stepped in front of the creature and helped Etan to his feet. "That was quite a performance," he whispered. "But I knew you would make the right decision."

Etan pulled away and looked at Skylah and Tannith. They refused to meet his gaze. He turned to Erik and Kaden, and their faces were masks of undisguised anger, however, nobody spoke.

The Bearah growled and Skylah raised her hand.

****

Etan rounded and fled—hurt pride and disgust raging within. How stupid could one man be? Tannith was right. He had almost lost his life and now he had alienated his friends. He stopped at the river's edge and leaned his heated forehead against the trunk of a willow. Where had he lost his way? When had he become the self-centered, selfish creature who inhabited his body?

He closed his eyes and sent a prayer to his God. He prayed for the strength to become a better man.

Ohma reached out with his mind, listening to the young man's thoughts, and smiled. To think something was one thing, to follow through was another. However, he had always liked Etan, always knew there was a heart beneath that layer of arrogance and thick pride. He saw the boy's path clearly in his mind and great deeds lay ahead of him.

One deed would see a country freed. One deed would break his heart.

Chapter Fifteen

Five nights later, Kaden camped alone beneath the stars in the treed foothills of the Carrum-Bahl Mountains. He lay quietly gazing up at the heavens— heavens so vast and unconquerable. If only Tarlis were so.

His thoughts flowed to his brother and friends. They had come a long way together, in distance as well as deed. Tannith had found her true self, overcame her fears, and became his soul mate. His brother was a king his father would be proud of, breaking from the mold of the court dandy to become a leader.

Skylah put her faith to the test and found love—even though it might not have been where she expected. And finally, Etan accepted himself for what he was and had risen above it, to put his comrades first. Then there was Ohma, whose powers had returned to their former glory, and without whom, they most likely would have perished.

Kaden's last meeting with the group was a solemn occasion on the bank of Edan River, near the Bearah's cave. They had shared a meal of smoked fish and washed it down with Norvak's best wine. They agreed that their wisest course was to separate. Kaden would search for Radoch and the rebel army, then send word to Hammer.

To Etan, Kaden had entrusted his second black-hilted dagger, the one to which Phalae held the twin. The

Captain of the Elisians would seek out the Chief of the Blue Panther to repay his debt of honor and Ohma would summon *Gahna-Tah*, the Dragon.

It was hoped the Dragon would carry a message to Etan's grandfather, Loden, at Dragonbane Castle. He in turn would convince the Council to send the Elisian army on the backs of the dragons, to Wolveryne Castle for the destined battle against Sernon and his forces.

Erik had devised a plan to enter the castle from a secret entrance in the sally port. It was an entrance unknown to Kaden. As part of his inheritance when Erik came of age, their father had given his brother a chart mapping all the underground passages. The king exacted a promise its existence was to be kept secret, and that he was to use it wisely.

Erik had not understood the importance of the maps at the time. Now he did. He told Kaden in private that the only tunnel he had ever used was the one leading into his bedchamber from the sally port. Kaden had not questioned his brother further but knew a pretty woman would have been involved.

The plan would be for Erik to lead Skylah, Ohma, and Tannith into the passage. Erik and Skylah would branch off and open the castle gates. While Ohma and Tannith searched for the Eye of Magus—the gem that fit the heart of the Cross and activated its power. Kaden was aware it would not be an easy task and had been reluctant to leave the princess in danger. He planned to arrive back at the castle with his army in time to be of assistance.

He rolled his cloak into a ball, tucked it beneath his head, and pulled his blanket to his chin. Then, taking the dagger he had borrowed from Etan from his pack, he laid it across his chest underneath the blanket and closed his eyes.

Unable to sleep, his mind filled with half-formed thoughts and the sounds of the night. A lonesome Wolveryne howled in the distance, and somewhere in the darkness, a shriek owl hooted. A shiver ran down his spine. It was said among his people that if you heard a shriek owl cry on a night with two quarter-moons, somewhere someone close by would die.

It was then he heard another sound. Light footsteps. Two men. One tall and heavily built, the other slight. A twig snapped. He smiled. These thugs had all the stealth of a lame Dragon. Instinctively, he braced himself. Any moment now, they would make their move.

His hand tightened on his dagger as a shadowy figure loomed over him. Kaden twisted, then rolled back and grasped the man around the legs. He flipped him over onto his chest, with his head pulled back and a knife pressed to the base of his skinny throat.

"Drop your weapon or your friend is dead," he called to the other assailant, hiding in the bushes.

A Black man, a mountain tall, took a step into the open, his face wreathed in shadow.

"Who are you?"

The man he straddled tried to answer, but Kaden pressed the blade a little deeper into his throat. It drew a trickle of blood.

"Ouch, you're killing me!" the boy cried.

Kaden was enjoying himself. "Good. Now, quiet."

The lad mumbled something unintelligible and lay still under the knife.

He knew he could easily take out this younger one, but the large one could pose a problem. "Now, what was it you were saying?" he asked, conversationally.

The swarthy warrior stepped from the shadows into the light of the fire and raised his hands. He was taller than he had first imagined, but he hid his dismay. This might take longer than expected.

"There is no need for violence." The dark man's voice rumbled into the night. "We saw your fire and were curious. Few travel these parts alone. The mountains are dangerous in times of war."

"Then why are you here?"

The man ignored the question. "I am Demise of the Swaithilands. This is Yole from Isamp." He indicated his comrade. "We mean no harm." He spread his hands. "We are travelers like you."

Kaden loosened his hold on the young man's neck and rolled him over. A child. He frowned. "You are Elisian?" However, the question needed no answer, the boy's almond-shaped eyes, slightly pointed ears, and braided silver-white hair, told Kaden all he needed to know.

The Elisian's jaw drew hard, and he wiped at his throat. "Now will you let me up?"

Kaden relinquished his hold, climbed to his feet, and stepped aside. He offered the Elisian his hand, and the boy accepted it, then dabbed at his throat with the sleeve of his loosely woven gray cloak. "How did you know I was there, anyway?" he asked sullenly.

"You have all the subtlety of a Lemma Bear."

The boy straightened and puffed out his chest. "I would let you know I am a warrior of great valor. I fight for Prince Kaden and the resistance."

He raised a brow. "Do you now?" he searched the boy's face. "And is this prince as great a warrior as they say?"

"Greater. I once saw him take on twenty Urakians singlehandedly and slay them all."

"Slay them all, you say?" he laughed again. "He must be mighty indeed—almost a god to achieve such a feat." He looked into the boy's eyes, and the boy looked away. "You actually saw him with your own eyes?"

The young man reddened and dragged out his sword. "You call me a liar?"

His hand flashed forward, and the sword spun from the boy's hand and fell to the ground.

"Of course not, lad." He bent and retrieved the blade as if nothing had occurred and handed it back to the youth. "But I find the incident hard to recall."

Yole's eyes narrowed. "Why should you remember it at all?" He frowned. "Who are you?"

He crouched and unlaced his pack and removed an intricately engraved, golden headband. Slipping it over his brow, he stepped into the firelight. "Perhaps this might explain."

The Black man, overhearing their conversation while building up the fire, stopped and dropped to his knees. He pulled his axe from the holster at his hip and offered it to Kaden with both hands. "My axe and my life. Yours to do with as you will, Sire."

Yole's face paled to the color of parchment. "What are you—"

"Get down, fool," the Swaithia growled. "Do you not know a prince when you see one?"

Kaden grinned, then laughed outright as the boy stumbled and dropped his sword in his haste to scramble to his knees.

"Sorry, my lord," the boy said, his tone urgent. "Forgive me."

"There is nothing to forgive, Yole." He ruffled the boy's silver blond hair. "You were not to know."

He ran a hand over his stubbled jaw, removed the gold circlet, dropped it back into his pack, and grinned. "I realize it is probably hard to recognize me as your prince with this seven days growth and three days dirt on my tunic. Now stand. I will have no man on his knees before me—not even when I have restored my brother's kingdom and seen every man who fights for me back on his own soil." He sank onto the worn stub of an ancient tree trunk. "Did you really see me take on twenty men, Yole?"

"Well not...exactly," the boy hedged, still not able to meet the prince's strange, green eyes, "but a friend told me..." He left the sentence hanging as Kaden chuckled.

"Never believe everything you are told. Not even by a friend. Now..." Kaden said, gesturing to the two. "Come, sit by the fire and share a flask, and we will talk of things that have passed, things that are, and things that will be."

He passed the wine to Demise, and the tribesman squirted a goodly portion down his throat. "Ah." The big man sighed, wiping the dregs from his chin with his tattooed arm. "Time has long passed since I tasted such wine." He handed the bladder to Yole.

The boy glanced from one man to the other, then tipped the wineskin to his lips in anticipation. The wine hit his gut with the bite of fire, and his face reddened. Tears swam in his silvery eyes, and he choked on an apoplexy of coughs.

"How old did you say you were?" Kaden leaned forward and gave him a hearty thump between his shoulder blades.

Yole finally brought his spasm under control and found his voice. He passed the wineskin back to Kaden. "Fifteen summers, my lord."

"So young. I have children fighting for me?" he asked softly. He searched Yole's face and shook his head. "Why are you here, anyway, and not home with your family? Are your people daft?"

The boy's expression hardened, and his silver-mauve eyes grew cold, bringing a chill to Kaden's heart.

"I have come to spill the blood of those who murdered my parents and sacrificed my sister to their dark gods."

Kaden felt the boy's pain. He knew what it was to lose a family in such a manner. "And so, you *shall* have your vengeance," he soothed, "and soon." He looked to Demise. "And your story, my large friend. You are a long way from the Swaithialands. Sernon's power could not have reached so far, surely?"

The Black man glanced into the darkness. Kaden could see he carried a deep sorrow in his eyes.

"I would prefer to keep my thoughts my own, my lord, if you are not offended?"

"As you wish, tribesman, for I am not one to delve into another man's secrets, when there are many secrets in my heart that I would not divulge." He changed the subject. "I have traveled far in search of a man named Radoch. Have you heard of him?"

"There is a Colonel Radoch who leads the resistance," countered Demise, taking a round of bread from his pack, breaking it in three, and sharing it with Yole and Kaden. "Could be the man you are seeking."

"Can you take me to him?"

Demise hesitated and eyed the young Elisian who looked as if he were about to answer. He frowned and shook his head. "We will leave at first light. The pass is narrow and not for journeying at night."

Kaden rose and wrapped himself in his blanket. "Sunrise it shall be then." He settled beside the fire and stretched out with his cloak beneath his head. "Colonel Radoch and I have much to talk about." He closed his eyes, and his deep even breathing soon filled the night.

Demise took first watch, scanning the edge of the trees. After contenting himself all was well, he drew his weighty battle-axe from its leather harness and methodically began running a whetstone along its gleaming blade of death. His mind raced ahead to the coming battle. The Wolfhead had returned. It would not be long now before his dreams of revenge were no longer dreams.

Chapter Sixteen

Kaden strode into Radoch's tent a little after dawn.

"My lord!" The older man hobbled forward, his hands outstretched. "My eyes deceive me. Can it really, be you? I thought you were surely dead."

Kaden laughed and shook Radoch's hand. "You are not that lucky, my friend. And you, you big lummox…the last time I saw you, you professed to be dying."

Radoch collapsed into his chair, stretched out his leg, and rubbed the top of his thigh. "The leg still aches on the cold morns, but I fare well for an old dog." He looked expectantly at the tent flap behind Kaden. "And Erik, is he with you?"

"No, but he is well."

"Were you able to break the—"

"Spell?" Kaden finished with a smile. "Yes, he is his handsome self again. Our king is on his way to open the gates of Wolveryne Castle."

"So, the time has come?"

Kaden sank onto Radoch's field bunk, pulled off his boots, dropped them one by one to the black and gold carpet, and lay back on the bunk. "Aye, my friend, it is time to see to that cur sitting on my father's throne choking on his entrails. I have waited patiently for this day, Radoch, and nothing will stop us now."

"We are five thousand strong, scattered throughout

the valley. No, I am wrong." He grinned. "We are five thousand three hundred troops strong. Three hundred Elven archers rode in from Druh Forest yestermorn. I have never seen the likes before. Deep green tunics and beautifully scrolled silver breast plates, grieves, and pauldrons."

"I thought they were allergic to silver."

"I as well. But I asked their leader, and he told me the armor had been ensorcelled eight centuries ago by a Druid Mage named Brekan, but I cannot believe so. To me, it looked like it had been wrought yesterday. He said the armor had been stored ready for a time such as this."

Kaden nodded, remembering the young Lord of Druh Forest whom he helped with the fortification of his city. "Does their leader have white-blond hair and silver-gray eyes

Radoch grinned. "Looks to me like he has not been long out of swaddling rags, but he can hit a bird on the wing at three hundred paces with his Ash bow."

"That is Jerak Montielle. "I believe he is a couple of hundred years old.

Radoch ran a hand over his chin. "Well, that is something. Had it been anyone else telling me that, I would have thought them a liar."

"And Jerak's men, are they as accurate?"

"Every one of them. Their lord gave me a demonstration and not one missed their target. I have never seen the likes. It was incredible. Yet I have never met one Elf, let alone three hundred en mass."

Kaden laughed and swung his legs over the edge of the bunk. "Good, I have plans for them. How long will it take to gather your men?"

"*Your* men, you mean." Radoch folded his arms and

leaned back in his rattan chair. "I have nurtured this lot long enough. It is your turn to take the reins. If I send out scouts now, the army could be assembled within two days."

Kaden eyed his friend. "How many cavalry do we have?"

"Around two thousand horses are penned high in the mountains. I'm not too sure about good riders though."

"We will manage. And weapons, have we enough?"

"Aye, the blacksmith in Antibba loathes the Urakians as much as we. His son died in the Battle of Wolveryne Castle. Most men brought their own fighting implements, and the women have been instructed in how to make arrows. A forge has been built to produce bronze arrow heads."

"You have done well, Radoch." Kaden smiled. "It seems I left the right man in charge. This would not have been possible without you."

"I hate that monster sitting on your father's throne as much as you do. The king was not only my monarch but my friend. He did not deserve to die in such a contemptible manner." Radoch filled two earthen mugs with rum from the flask on his table and pushed one toward him.

Accepting the drink, he took a hearty swallow. It burned all the way down and set a fire in his belly. "What of enemy activity?" He wiped his arm across his lips.

Radoch grinned. "They stopped coming. I guess they are waiting to see what our next move will be. Apart from the mine at the base of the mountain, the Urakians have kept away from this place. At first, they sent in scouts, but finally realizing whoever they sent would not be returning, they ceased."

Kaden finished the last of his rum and breathed out heavily.

Radoch chuckled. "Packs a punch, does it not?"

"Where did you get it? I haven't tasted a brew like this for an exceedingly long time."

"Bought it off a Swaithia Tribesman. He told me it was imported straight from the Far Isles. Showed up here twelve days ago with a wagonload of the stuff—said he was unable to fight without fire in his belly."

"Sounds like a bit of a scoundrel."

"Good fighter, though, carries a double-sided battle-axe and swings it as if it is no heavier than a short sword. He led a raid on an Urakian supply train a few days after he arrived. Wiped out the lot and brought back eight wagons filled to bursting with grain, armor, and food."

"Headed for the castle?"

"That was my guess."

"With few serfs left to work the land or cottagers to steal food from, and no food for his men or grain for their horses, the morale of Sernon's troops must be getting mighty low. Good move, Radoch."

"The idea was the tribesman's, not mine. The Swaithia has the mind of a natural brigand."

"What name does he go by?"

"Demise."

Kaden put back his head and laughed. " 'Tis a good name. I have met this man. He nearly killed me last night at the foot of the mountain." He sobered. "Have someone fetch him."

"Why?"

"I need to send word to the Dwarves."

"Dwarves? I thought they were—"

His sentence trailed off as the air around him began

to pulsate with the sound of a thousand beating wings.

"What the—" Kaden strode to the entrance of the tent and threw back the flap.

All around, men were crying out, dropping to their knees, cowering to the ground as the beating noise rose to an intolerable pitch. A shout went up as a multitude of dark winged creatures crested the rugged mountain peaks, filling the sky, blocking the morning sun with their humongous shadows.

Feeling as if a mighty weight crushed his shoulders he stared up at the sky. Was this Sernon's last ingenious stroke? Had the master sorcerer conjured winged demons to destroy them? Defeat lay on his shoulders like a living beast. He had come so close—only a few more days.

He tried to rise but the high-pitched whirring of the wings was intolerable. Again, he fell to his knees, covering his ears beside Radoch. Thoughts of failure filled his mind. Sernon had won, and all was lost. No man could stand against this mighty force of evil. He closed his eyes and bowed his head.

"Kaden! Ho! Why does the Wolfhead cower so?"

The prince's eyes flew open. Dragons filled the sky, circling above the camp. Upon each of the Dragons' shining backs sat three dwarven warriors, each fully armed. Hammer Deathwielder rode their leader.

He leapt to his feet. "Hammer, you whoreson. Get down here!"

Hammer let out a laugh and called something unintelligible to the dragon he rode. The whole heard of mystical beasts began their descent.

The Wolfhead army pushed back to clear a space for the dragons to land, and the Dwarves dismounted.

Hammer slid down from the back of a large green and gold dragon. He said a few words of thanks to the great beast then strode toward Kaden, his hand extended in greeting.

Kaden thumped him on the back and hastened him into his tent. He introduced him to Radoch, and Hammer told Kaden how Ohma had already gone with *Gahna-Tah* to carry the two thousand Elisians from Dragonbane Castle. Ohma decided the Dwarves would be collected in the same manner if they were to be at Wolveryne Castle in time for the rendezvous with Erik. "He hoped you would not mind him taking the liberty."

"Indeed not." He thumped the dwarf on the shoulder. "It was a brilliant idea."

"He said to tell you that *Gahna-Tah* and her kind will not be fighting in the battle as there are so few dragons left. They cannot be put at risk."

Kaden nodded. "She has done enough already, and we would not care for any more of her noble kind to perish. Now come, we have much to ready in three days."

****

All day, men, women, horses, and wagons trickled into the valley. By nightfall, thousands of troops sat around blazing campfires on the valley floor. Over the hundreds of fires roasted game of every type from pheasant and fowl to wild elkow and White Mountain deer. Strong liquor flowed freely. It was a balmy night, but the fires were essential, serving as a light and a means to cook their food, this night before battle. The air fare crackled with anticipation of the following day. The whole of Glen-Dorrach and most of Tarlis hinged on tomorrow and their victory. There would not be another chance. Tomorrow, it would be for him and the Tarlisian people, all or nothing.

A young lass with fiery red hair approached Kaden as he crouched to hack a portion from a haunch of roasting venison.

The girl touched her small, warm hand to his bare shoulder. "If you are lonely, milord, I could warm your bed."

Kaden rose and stared down at the woman-child with dark eyes. She was no more than fourteen summers with mussed fire-colored hair and the slim body of a youth. He recognized the girl as the Baker Nilard's daughter. Her father had died in the attack on Wolveryne Castle.

"Galena, is it not?"

"Yes, milord." She gave him a tentative smile.

"I have a woman, Galena, but I am honored by your offer."

The smile vanished from the young girl's face and the sparkle left her green eyes. She hung her head and began to trudge away.

"Wait."

"Milord?" She swung back, her face brightening. "You have changed your mind?"

"No, Galena, I have not. But why do you do this?"

She seemed to slump. "A person must eat, milord."

His lips tightened. He sliced several large slabs of meat from the roasted haunch before him and thrust them into her hands. "Here, take this."

Galena's teeth tore into the warm meat, and she stuffed great chunks into her mouth, almost gagging. He moved quickly to thump her hard between the shoulder blades. "Slow down, lass, you will choke."

She wiped the meat juice from her lips with her bare arm. "I am sorry, milord. I am just so hungry. I have not eaten in three days."

Kaden shook his head and took in the girl's slight appearance with a frown. "I can see that. Are there others like you?"

She nodded as she crammed more meat into her mouth.

"When you have finished, gather the other youngsters who are in need and send them to this man." Kaden signaled to Demise standing nearby. "He will see them fed."

The girl glanced up at the big Black man shyly.

He smiled kindly into her eyes and touched a gentle hand to her hair. "Do not be afraid, little one. I fear my face is not as pretty as yours, but I will bring you and your friends to no bad end. I promise."

Hesitantly, the girl slipped her slender hand into his larger one and brought it to her cheek. A grin spread across his face as she turned, and he watched her run off into the night.

"Wait!"

"Milord?" She glanced over her shoulder.

"No more sleeping with the soldiers," scolded Kaden. "Your father would have expected more from his daughter. He was an honorable man."

Her smile faded, and a twinge of guilt niggled him. It was not her fault she had been forced into prostitution. "You need anything, anything at all, you come to me. Soon the fighting will be over, and all will be as it was before Wolveryne Castle fell." He stared into the distance at the moons. "The Dorrachians will prosper again, and there shall be plenty for all."

"Yes, milord." The girl nodded, dropped a small curtsy, and disappeared between the hub of warriors and the bright burning campfires.

Kaden settled beside the fire, staring blankly into the flames, his appetite long gone. In his heart, he knew he had lied to the girl. Things would never be the same. The country may thrive again, but those who lost their lives and those who would lose their lives in the days to come would never see the prosperity. "It is a sad day indeed, when a child has to prostitute herself to eat," he said to Demise.

"Aye, it is, my lord. Then again, all days are sad when a man must slay his own countrymen to gain freedom."

****

Two days later, Kaden called Radoch to his tent. It was just after dawn and heavy mist wreathed the campsite.

"Are they all here?" he asked, lowering his father's sword to the bed.

"The last just rode in. Are you ready?"

"I was born ready." Kaden grinned and picked up his shining metal breastplate and held it in place while Radoch tightened the straps. "You worry too much."

The older man snorted and reached for the golden pauldrons, buckling one at a time into place. Jerak had brought the armor from his village for Kaden. Golden in color, the Elf Lord had said that the same mage who had ensorcelled the Elves three hundred suits of armor had left this one with Jerak, saying that he would know who to give the armor to when the time came. The elf said he was certain it was meant for him.

"I am not the one who has to convince six thousand

222

men to ride against an enemy of ten thousand," returned Radoch.

Kaden broke from his meandering thoughts and stepped away as the older man finished his task and rested a hand on his shoulder. "Have you no faith, my friend?"

"Not when it comes to *felo-de-se.*"

His jaw hardened. "I force no man to fight at my side, Radoch. You know that."

Radoch remained silent. He helped him on with his leather gauntlets and lifted his sword from the end of the bunk to strap to his waist. When Kaden looked into Radoch's eyes, they were cold. "Try leaving me behind," returned the older man. "Then you *will* see war."

Kaden laughed and picked up his shield. He exited the tent, and Radoch followed, carrying the helmet that matched the golden armor.

Outside, Radoch signaled to two officers who pulled an empty wagon forward. The wagon stopped before them, and the prince of the Wolfhead climbed onto the tray to face the massed ranks of his rebel army.

****

Radoch took his stance at his prince's side on the ground. The older man felt tears form in his eyes and quickly wiped them away. This was a proud moment for him. He had worked long and hard to repay the prince for saving his life at Wolveryne Castle. Now perhaps, he would see his labor bear fruit. This was the testing time. Could Prince Kaden lead these men? Would they follow him?

Kaden threw back his black cloak. His specially wrought golden armor shone upon his chest as the sun chose that moment to break through the over-hanging mist. He raised his arm and sunlight ran along the blade of his father's sword. To Radoch, he looked like a Sun God of old.

"Friends…brothers of Tarlis." His voice rang out, strong and clear. "For those who do not know me, I am Kaden, Son of Farramon, Prince and General of the Dorrachians. In my veins runs the blood of Ambroch of the Wolfhead, the greatest king of all time, and Mareeka Alendronate, the Witch Queen, who it is told, led eighteen thousand men into battle against thirty thousand and wrote her name into the history scrolls of Tarlis. I am here now to lead *you* to victory against Sernon's hordes of evil. Together we will free this land from tyranny!" He punched the air. "Together! Victory!"

The warriors took up the cry. "Victory!"

Kaden stopped their cheering with a raised hand, and his next words boomed into the silence. "Like you, I have felt defeat—dawns of steel and blood. You have bloodied your swords, your shields, and your bodies! You have faced fear and dealt with it, seen death and risen above it!

"The time has come. The time is now to band together as brothers.

"Fight as one for freedom! Freedom from the oppressor who would see your children slaves!

"Freedom from the monster who plunders our land, takes the bread from your mouth, steals our women, and would see us dead!"

A roar sounded as thousands cried out in unison.

"Come with me now!

"Follow me!

"Fight for what was taken from you!

"And by the gods, I swear, we will take it back!"

"We are with you!" boomed Hammer Deathwielder from amidst the crowd. "Death to Sernon! Death to the usurper!"

The dwarf and his men punched out the words with their fists. "Death to the Urakians!"

The rebel army took up the cry. "Death to the Urakians! Death to Sernon!"

Kaden leapt from the wagon and joined Radoch where he waited with Phoenix. Climbing into the saddle, he took his golden helmet from Radoch and pulled it down over his head and brought the stallion around. He waved his sword in the air. "Come!"

And six thousand men followed.

****

It was mid-morning when Kaden halted the cavalcade and scanned the valley floor. They journeyed two leagues, and still had two to go.

Twenty cottages were scattered along the banks of a narrow, winding river, smoke rising from their small stone chimneys. "Why has Sernon left these people in peace and not others?"

"They supply him with grain and meat," Radoch informed, urging his mount in line with Kaden's. "They also supply us with information."

"They are informers?"

"How do you think we knew when to attack the supply wagons?"

Kaden regarded the cottages with renewed interest. "Would they join us?"

"I would stake my life on it."

He called to Hammer sitting upon his small hill pony, and the dwarf rode up beside him. "Take some of your people down to the valley. Tell the cottagers the

225

Wolfhead has returned. Tell them the time has come to fight."

The dwarf nodded and rode back along the line, and the rest of the cavalry rode on.

Around noon, Kaden sent word down the long cavalcade that he needed to see Jerak. Within the hour, the elf's white stallion pulled in alongside him.

"What can I do for you, General?"

Kaden met the Elf Lord's gaze. "I fear we will not make the castle by dawn. I must split the ranks and take the cavalry ahead and leave the foot soldiers to follow. I need you and your men to go on before us. Erik is to open the gates at sunrise tomorrow. He will need a diversion. You will fire a volley of lighted shafts into the first courtyard at the same time the gate is opened, thus the diversion. Find the princess. She and the others will be in a cave this side of the castle."

He gave Jerak the directions. "Take care. Sernon will know we are on the move." He thumped the elf on the back. "Good luck, Jerak, and may the power of your god be with you."

"I make my own luck," said the elf. "But thank you, and may your journey be a safe one." He kneed his charger around and rode back down the line.

A little later, three hundred Elven archers in the dark green and silver garb of Druh Forest cantered past in the direction of Wolveryne Castle.

Radoch watched the last of the green cloaks disappear over the rise. "Let us hope they get there in time."

He nodded. "Our world depends on it."

Chapter Seventeen

The plan worked perfectly. After dispatching the sentries guarding the perimeter, Jerak and his men slipped silently up to the east wall in the pre-dawn shadows.

Erik watched from his position along the overhanging wall.

On the signal, the Elves let loose a volley of blazing shafts over the battlements. He heard the screams of the enemy and smelt the smoke as arrows showered the thatched roofs of the stables.

Erik and his companions picked their way through the tunnel. Small rivulets of water trickled constantly down the side of the walls. Slime and mud squelched beneath their boots, and the stink of mold hung thick in the air from the tunnel's many summers of neglect.

Ohma flicked his fingers and a flame leapt from his palm, filling the man-made tunnel with light.

"Ohma, you had best come up front with me," called Erik, peering over his shoulder at the Druid.

Skylah dropped back beside Tannith, allowing Ohma to light the way. Together, they traveled on in silence until the tunnel branched right, eventually coming to a narrow staircase.

Erik motioned for Ohma to climb. "This is it."

The steep, narrow, winding stairs only allowed them to ascend in single file. At the top, it broadened onto a long rock platform where they could all stand comfortably. A stone panel measuring three feet wide and twice as high blocked their path.

Erik slipped his hand into the mouth of the wolf effigy at the bottom of the wall and found the lever. The panel rolled laboriously aside. He ducked his head around the edge, checking to make sure the room was clear, then stepped into his old bedchamber.

It felt like coming home, and he was forced to gather himself as childhood memories flooded him. The room was sparse. The only furniture remaining was his ornate four-poster bed. All else had been looted. The bed must have been too heavy to carry. Even the place high on the west wall lay bare, and with sadness, he noted his parents' portrait was missing. He breathed deeply and turned to signal his friends.

When the others entered, he locked the panel back into place then told Tannith to listen at the door while he crossed to the far window. "Let us hope the map is still here."

He watched Tannith tiptoe across the room and put her ear to the door. She nodded. "All is clear."

Erik took his dagger, ran the tip beneath the windowsill, and inched a large block of stone slowly toward him, drawing it from the wall. He slid his hand into the dark opening, and his fingers touched parchment. He drew out the map, unrolled it, and spread it on the wooden floor.

Tannith leaned down to look at the scroll.

"Here." Erik pointed. "This tunnel leads to the gatehouse."

"Good, now find the passage that takes us to the tower room," she said.

He glanced up. "There is no such passage."

Tannith dropped to her knees beside him. "There has to be. She scanned the map herself, then sighed. "Ohma and I will just have to be careful we are not seen." She looked at the old man, and he nodded. "Now, let us run through the plan one more time. Ohma and Skylah come join us." She waited for the others to settle across from her and Erik, then went on. "Erik, you and Skylah will find your way to the gatehouse and wait for Jerak's next signal. At the start of the disturbance, you deal with the sentries and open the castle gates. Understand?" She looked at Skylah, and she nodded.

"While you and Ohma search the tower room for the *Eye*," finished Erik, praying everything would go as planned.

****

Ohma and Tannith crept along the tunnel to the king's chambers, certain Sernon would have claimed it for his own.

Erik had given them directions to the rooms and Ohma pressed his ear to the panel leading into the bed chamber. Finding no sound, he slipped through the door and whispered for Tannith to follow.

On entering, he moved quietly to an oak closet running the length of the wall while Tannith strode over to the four-poster bed. She dropped to look beneath the bed, then tossed open the lid of a large carved wooden trunk.

Ohma rummaged through drawers and cupboards and continued to search systematically, finally concluding the Eye was not among Sernon's belongings. "He must have hidden it somewhere else, unless he has it with him."

Tannith agreed and disheartened, they abandoned the room and proceeded along the corridor toward the east wing and the tower room.

He hoped the rare jewel would be in the king's chambers, and there would be no reason to seek.Sernon. Many decades ago, he had witnessed the duel between Magus and the sorcerer, and the sorcerer's power had been formidable indeed. He had no wish to face him. His own magick had strengthened with use since leaving Merrum Island, but Sernon's power was near godlike—invincible. The only one Ohma knew who had a chance of standing against him was Magus. So, his thoughts were brought a full cycle. Where was the Eye?

He looked to Tannith. "Assemble the Cross."

She spun, with her mouth open. "Are you daft?"

"Trust me."

She went to object but seemed to have second thoughts. Shaking the pieces from the pouch onto her hand, she set them on the sideboard next to her and began fitting them together.

As she did, the joined pieces of the Cross began to hum.

****

Jerak's Elves, the Elisian army, and Phalae's six hundred tribesmen fringed the green hills surrounding Wolveryne Castle. As dawn broke red on the horizon, they swarmed the valley and charged headlong into the opening gates—three thousand battle-hardened warriors, raging for blood, crying their war chants.

But there was no sign of Kaden and his Dorrachians.

Etan, Phalae, and Jerak had been unable to wait. They had to attack on the signal or miss the element of surprise.

Jerak sprinted into the courtyard, squinting against the rising sun. His first arrow took a Urakian in the eye. His opponent fell, clutching at his face. The enemy was everywhere. He called to his archers, and they formed a tight-knit circle in the center of the inner courtyard, letting loose a volley of bronze-tipped shafts into the ranks on the battlements.

Then the Elven warriors raised their long narrow shields in a protective circle, awaited their moment, and sent up another volley.

Below the stairwell leading to the gatehouse, Phalae and his men fought as a unit to the right of Etan's Elisians. Not one Urakian broke through, but to the left, the Urakians were forging an opening.

Phalae charged into them, slashing, hacking, and slaying. Like a lion among jackals, he hammered his way through their ranks dividing them. The men of the Blue Panther gathered behind him roaring their defiance, pushing the Urakians back.

Etan joined them at their center, plunging his blade into a warrior's chest.

As the man fell, he lashed out, his sword slicing a shallow cut across the captain's cheek. Etan stumbled and another man lunged. Erik hurled his dagger to hit the assailant, hilt first, behind the ear. The man half slipped and dropped his sword.

Erik finished him with a two-handed cut to the neck and pulled Etan to his feet.

"Behind you!" The Elisian cried. A warrior leapt from the stairway, his axe raised. Erik spun on his heel and brought his sword around and opened up the man, shoulder to gut, but his sword snapped in his breastplate.

Two Urakians dropped down from the stairs. He

dove, scooped up the fallen axe, and rolled to his feet. He blocked an overhead cut, then backhanded a warrior across the face with the axe handle.

The first man lanced his blade at Erik's shoulder but missed by a breath.

Etan ran behind and hammered his new, found sword into the attacker's neck.

The Urakians fell back.

****

Tannith and Ohma moved with stealth down a dim, narrow corridor lit only by a lone torch in a sconce at the end of the hallway. In the harsh silence of the castle, the humming from the Cross at Tannith's throat rang out unbearably loud.

As they rounded a corner, all pandemonium broke loose. In the distance, a scream sounded, and then another.

Footsteps scudded on the staircase at the end of the corridor, and they hurried into an unlocked bedchamber.

Tannith ran to a narrow window and threw back the shutters.

Ohma moved up beside her and shaded his eyes. "Erik has succeeded. The gate is open, but there is no sign of your prince."

"He will be here; this is too important to him." Tannith creaked open the door. "Come, we need the Eye." She peeked into the corridor, then quickly pulled back shutting the tall oak door again as a soldier ran past.

Her back against the door, she sighed. "Why does the Cross make this noise?" She clutched at the icon around her neck. "It is getting louder and driving me insane. Is there no way to stop it?"

"Unfortunately, not. I had an idea this might happen

once we came within range. It is calling to the Eye."

"You could have told me."

He sighed. "It cannot be far now." He opened the door and peered out. "The guards must have joined the battle. Hurry, this is our chance."

They ran down the corridor and through an archway to a spiral staircase, and the scraping of their leather boots echoed back eerily through the empty hallway as they climbed.

****

Sernon stood on the balcony of the tower room, his eyes bright.

Blood surged hot in his veins as he peered into the killing fields below.

"How many of these fools do you think there are?"

"My informants counted almost twenty-four hundred Elisians and Elves, and six hundred tribesmen. How they persuaded those black devils to fight, I cannot begin to imagine. They hate the round-eyes, and they fight like demons unleashed."

"No matter, they will die the same as any other. The Wolfhead Prince is among them?"

"No. My spies tell me he is a league away with two thousand cavalry and three thousand foot soldiers following a half a league back. Prince Kaden should be here within the hour, the rest of his rabble around noon."

"Good. You have done well, Kraal, everything is going as planned. When the prince and his cavalry enter, bar the gates."

"My lord?"

"No enemy of mine will leave here alive this day."

The newly appointed general was about to speak again, but Sernon signaled him to silence. "We will split his force. When we have annihilated those inside, let the others through. We will be ready for them." He gave a cold smile. "Soon these swine who dare to defy me will be wiped from this land, enslaved, or imprisoned in the mines. With the Urakians by my side, I will rule unopposed. With the power of the Dark Gods, I will be invincible! Did you know there are other realms that are invisible to our eye?"

Kraal shook his head, but Sernon saw his mind racing.

"Today I will perform a rite which will have one of those worlds opened. When these cretins are defeated, my army will march through the gateway and crush that world also. We will be the greatest force in the Universe. Just think, Kraal. Slaves, power, riches beyond anyone's imagination."

Kraal's black eyes gleamed with greed.

Sernon's lips curved into a cruel smile, and he spoke again. "Order my priests to bring in the prisoner. " 'Tis time for the ritual."

****

Kaden topped the rise. He sat on his black destrier, staring down into Tinsliegh Valley. The sight of it brought a sense of deja vu.

He had been here and done this before. That day the Dorrachian army had been crushed. That day Wolveryne Castle had been lost. He vowed to himself today would end differently.

Distant screams like those in a recurring nightmare echoed through the valley. Glancing over his shoulder, his gaze swept the cavalry lined up behind him. He stood in his stirrups and signaled to a young, dark haired Dorrachian several horses back. The war horn sounded, and Kaden punched the air with his fist. "Attack!"

And two thousand horsemen followed him into battle.

Chapter Eighteen

Sernon stood on a raised dais beside the black altar and watched the prisoner being dragged into the tower room.

Three priests emerged from the shadows and roughly fastened him to the heavy stone.

"You will die for this, heathens!" The King of Ellenroh's voice echoed off the thick, blue-stone walls. Even after months of imprisonment, his will to fight was not broken.

Sernon leaned over him. "Do not threaten me, cur. Has the darkness you now dwell in not taught you that, if nothing more?" He ran a finger down the king's cheek, burning a scar where he touched. The king screamed and cowered back as Sernon laid a gentling hand on his brow. The fight went out of the king and his head sagged to the side.

"So much better." He smiled coldly at his high priest. "Now I can think. Gag him. We do not want him waking during the ceremony and shouting for help."

The bald priest rushed forward to do his master's bidding.

Sernon watched the proceedings, unseeing. His mind raced ahead. To him, the king was not just a prisoner, but a pawn in a greater plan.

Victory was close. He could taste it. He had worked hard and long, serving the Prince of Darkness over the past year, planning this moment. Now it was time to seek his reward and see his enemies crushed.

With the sacrificial ritual of the Seventh Moon, power equal to the God of Blood would be his. He had only to perform the rite, and the knowledge of the *time portals* would be within his grasp.

Everything was in place—the day, the time, the location, the sacrifice. The necromancer's lip curled in contempt—a king. If this was the best Tarlis could breed as a ruler, then the realm was as good as his.

All he needed was the final ingredient—the Cross of Tarlis. Yet even now, that ancient icon of power was wending its way toward him.

Raising his hands to the heavens. Thunder cracked overhead, a fissure opened in the ceiling, and the roof vanished.

He signaled another of the bald priests. The man stepped forward and struck a giant brass gong, which peeled throughout the castle, the sound traveling out the tower room window.

There was not a body in the courtyard that did not cease their fighting to look up.

The heavens opened, thunder boomed, forks of lightning streaked across the leaden sky, and spilled its pain in torrential rain down upon the helpless mortals below.

The fighting began again in earnest.

****

Kaden leapt from Phoenix's back at the front of the castle gates. With his sword drawn and the war cry of the Dorrachians on his lips, he led his troops through the outer bailey into the inner courtyard.

The tribesmen, upon seeing the prince's men, gave

a mighty roar and surged forward. They beat their hard leather shields with the blades of their scimitars.

The Elves redoubled their efforts and rained volley after volley of green shafts into the ranks of enemy archers manning the battlements.

An Urakian wearing a horned helm lunged at Kaden. The prince swung back and brought his shield around side on. He crashed it into the man's large gut. The soldier grunted and doubled. Kaden caught him under the chin with an uppercut that snapped back his head. He sidestepped and gutted him with his knife.

He spun to dispatch another who stood behind him. The man grabbed at his jugular, unable to believe the speed of the attack or the blood gushing from his ruined throat.

Rounding, he caught sight of Erik and Etan fighting back to back in the shadow of the north wall. Systematically, he fought his way toward them.

****

Across the courtyard, the newly promoted General Kraal stepped from the castle and surveyed the mêlée.

Donning his skulled helm, he signaled to a stocky warrior in the gate tower.

Lieutenant Castrin raised the drawbridge and lowered the portcullis, putting a stop to further entry into the castle. Or exit.

His orders completed, Kraal stepped out to engage the enemy. "Who wants to die this day?" He dragged a young Dorrachian from his horse, ramming a knife through the gap between the soldier's helm and breastplate puncturing his throat, then tossed the boy aside. Punching his fist into the face of another, he drove the blade of his short sword into the Elisian warrior's heart.

****

Tannith's steps faltered, as over the humming of the Cross came a terrible roar. She ran to the window and pushed back the shutters. Her eyes widened as she watched the portcullis drop, enclosing the rebel soldiers within the courtyard.

"Gods no!" The words were torn from her throat.

"What is it?" Ohma eased her out of the way to peer down into the walled courtyard.

"The gates—look at the gates. Our men are trapped. They are like calves to the slaughter."

Ohma stood silent, his gaze traveling over the battlements to the slope of an adjacent hill. "Yes. But that is not the worst of it."

She pushed in beside Ohma. Pouring into the valley, were thousands of foot soldiers. Behind them, scores of farmers, carrying crude implements of the field, pitchforks, picks, hoes, sickles, scythes, and shovels— anything they could use for weapons. Tools they knew well.

Tannith groaned, and Ohma patted her hand. "Erik or Kaden will find a way to reopen the gates," Ohma soothed, though deep in his heart, he held out little hope for the brave men below unless they could find the eye of Magus in time.

****

Hammer fumed. No gate would stand in his way! He had journeyed many leagues to fight this fight. He studied the lowered gate in disgust. Did they think this pitiful thing could stop Hammer Deathwielder and his army?

Shae had blood to spill and another legend to create.

239

The dwarf ordered his men to the slopes to fell trees for battering rams and to fetch ropes, grappling hooks, and scaling ladders from the wagons.

On the blood of his ancestors, no ironbound gate would defeat him!

****

Inside the inner courtyard, Phalae of the Blue Panther had found a kindred spirit in the form of the Swaithia, Demise. He grinned wickedly. "If we go now, we should be able to cut our way through to that ugly one in the skull helm. He has slain a score of men since I watched him slither from the castle."

"You keep him busy while I hack out his greasy throat."

Demise laughed and thrust his arm through his shield grip. "Let's do this. He has a face that won't be missed by his mother." Bringing his battle-axe around, he released a cry and leapt into the mêlée. "Death to the slayers of Tarlis! Death to the killers of children!"

"Today, you dung eaters die!" shouted Phalae behind, swinging his scimitar across an Urakian neck.

The front line of the Urakians slipped and slithered their way over bloody, rain-splattered cobblestones and sprawled bodies only to be cut down by the slashing blades of the resistance.

Breathing heavily, Kaden stood in the middle of the defenders. Radoch and Skylah, who had been separated from Erik when the battle began, stood at his side.

Time and again, the enemy swept forward, only to be turned back by the steadfast courage and sharp blades of the rebels.

****

Kraal, alone, was not surprised at the resolute

240

fighting of the resistance. He had been at the first battle against the Dorrachians. He knew the strength of his enemy, and grudgingly, he respected them for their purpose and determination.

However, he saw their strength failing, their losses were many. Without the reinforcements locked outside the castle walls, it would not be long before the leaders fell, their line broke, and they were crushed.

He read a battle like a game. There came a time when combat could be charted like a steady stream, its ebbs, and flows. That time was now. The rebel line was breaking, morale was dimming, and they were being beaten back.

Urakian voices rose in victory.

The rebels fought on doggedly, leaden-legged, and heavy-armed. Inch by inch, they were forced back toward the outer courtyard, toward the closed gates where their reinforcements battered for entry. The sound playing on their minds, eating into their confidence like a viper in the soul.

****

Erik saw what was happening and shouted to Etan. "I am going for the gates."

"No!" Etan ran in behind him, fighting with his back to Erik's. "It cannot be done!"

"I must at least try." Erik blocked a thrust to his chest. "Are you with me or not?" A warrior in a battered helm leapt forward. "After this one," he shouted. He parried a blow and reversed a cut, leaving the warrior's head hanging from his shoulders. "Now. Watch my back!"

Erik lunged toward the staircase leading to the ramparts.

"Jerak, to the battlements," roared Etan, sprinting in Erik's wake.

Jerak shouted the order. A volley of arrows flew into the mass of enemy archers at the top of the staircase, breaking into their ranks. The Elves notched and let loose again.

Death rained down on the Urakians and they fell back, opening a gap for Erik as he gained the ramparts. The sting of a sword blade licked at his thigh. He wiped the blood from the shallow wound and shouted to Etan to hurry. His blade whistled, swinging death at the head of his next attacker. The man fell screaming over the battlements. Erik ducked a sweeping battle-axe and plunged on. A two-handed swing drove his sword home across the neck of a long-haired warrior, and his head rolled as his body dropped.

Beside him, Etan leapt and twisted, cleaving and killing, his blade slick with rain and blood.

Two warriors ran at Erik. He blocked a knife thrust from the first and struck the man with the reverse stroke. His sword stuck in his opponent's armor, and a war hammer arched toward his head.

Etan parried the blow, lopping off the man's hand. The soldier fell back screaming.

"Take care, Dorrachian, next time you might not find yourself so lucky."

Erik flashed him a grin and raced on. The gatehouse loomed ahead, only twenty more paces. His dagger flew and thudded home between the bulging eyes of the gatekeeper. Lieutenant Castrin gasped and fell at Erik's feet, all life fading from his eyes.

Blood trickled from the cut in Erik's thigh and side, but he had reached his objective. He raised his broadsword and brought it down hard on the wrist-thick rope. After a second attempt, the rope split, the counterbalance dropped, and the portcullis rose.

A cheer went up from the men below the walls. Those starting up the grappling ropes and scaling ladders joined their companions in their chant. "Freedom! Freedom!"

The word broke over the courtyard and echoed around the valley as thousands swept through the gates into the courtyard, overrunning the enemy. They were still outnumbered, but with fresh men, they had the advantage.

Erik's heart raced as he ran back along the battlements. Men from the outside were also streaming over the walls. He spied Etan fighting twenty paces away, and with a grin, sprinted toward him. Together they would find Kaden and finish this!

Then he staggered. A burning sensation. He tried to right himself and looked down to see a red shaft protruding from under his ribs. Blood trickled over his fingers as his hand went to the arrow, and his legs slowly buckled. Dropping to his knees, he glanced up to see a warrior in a bear-skull helm clutching a longbow staring at him with a sneer on his ugly visage. Bright lights clouded Erik's eyes as the warrior turned and fled.

Etan caught him before he fell. He lowered him to lean against the battlement wall. "Easy, my lord." He snapped the arrow and dropped the broken piece to the ground.

Erik fought to grin. "That is the first time…you have called me that…now I know I am dying."

"Do not be a fool, of course you are not dying." Etan's voice was solemn, his face devoid of all emotion.

"Save your strength." He signaled to three Dorrachians to give them cover.

Erik stiffened as a new bout of pain stabbed into his vitals. "I did it…did I not? I opened the gates?"

****

"Yes, you did it. You saved us. The gates are open. These dogs shall soon bow before you." Etan's gaze fell to the red shaft jutting from between Erik's ribs. The young king's face was pale. There were rings beneath his golden eyes and a pale blue tinge about his lips. Signs he had seen too often. Etan looked up at a young Dorrachian soldier. "The one in the bearskin helm—see him dead."

"Consider it done, Captain." The man disappeared along the ramparts.

Erik's breath rattled in his throat. "Etan?"

"I am here Erik."

Erik clutched his arm. "Look after her…tell her…I loved her."

Etan found Erik's hand. "Tell her yourself, my friend, she comes even now as we speak."

The battle was drawn away from the two men with the opening of the gates, and the rebel warriors were storming into the castle grounds.

The three Dorrachians still stood with their shields locked in front of their king.

****

Skylah, from her position below in the courtyard, had seen Erik fall and her mind screamed. Erik. Not Erik! With reckless abandon, she slashed wildly at her opponent and dashed up the staircase through the enemy, pushing and slaying any who blocked her path. Her eyes met Etan's as she reached his side. The bleak look he gave her said it all. She dropped her short sword and sank to her knees beside Erik, seeing for the first time the shaft in his stomach, so close to his lungs. Too close.

Erik's eyes opened, straining to focus on Etan. "Find Kaden. I must see…my brother."

"I will go." The former Faerie made to rise, but Etan stopped her with a hand to her shoulder.

"No. Stay. He needs you."

When she met Etan's eyes, they held a wealth of pain. "May the gods be with you. Be careful."

He pushed to his feet, threw her a last look as if he were about to say something, then spun and sprinted along the ramparts.

"Skylah?" Erik croaked. His voice strained.

She swallowed the lump in her throat and forced a smile. "I am here, my love."

He coughed, and blood formed on his lips. She wiped it away.

Erik tried to focus on her face. "I am…sorry."

Rain blended with her tears as she took his hand, so cold, and brought it to her lips. "Why, my dearest? There is nothing to forgive. You saved us all. We have beaten them back."

Erik sagged and closed his eyes, the effort to keep upright becoming too great. "I wanted so much to see you my queen."

She slipped her arm beneath his shoulders and bowed her head, her lips close to his ear. "In my heart, I will always be your queen."

"Kiss me…let me taste your lips for a…"

His words trailed off as Skylah leaned forward, touching her lips gently to his. They tasted of blood and rain. "I love you," she whispered. "I will always love you." Tears slid down her cheeks, mingling with the rain.

He opened his eyes and gave a weak smile. "I know…you tried."

She made to speak again, to tell him she did love him, that he had to believe her, but Kaden ran toward them. She gave Erik into his care, and Etan helped her stand.

"Thank you." Kaden's eyes were dark with pain.

She cast Erik a last helpless glance as Etan led her along the battlements out of their hearing.

****

The Wolfhead Prince dropped to his knees and took his brother in his arms. "Erik, why?"

Erik coughed, and a tremor ran through his body. "I could not let you…have all the glory."

He ran a hand over his eyes. "I thought we had made it through together. One cursed arrow—if only I…"

His brother clutched his hand with a short bout of strength, and his voice reinforced. "No. I will not let you blame yourself for this also. I was the one who chose to open the gate. Not you. What is done cannot be undone." A cough rattled from his throat, and a dribble of blood escaped the side of his mouth. "Lean me against the battlement wall, and…my sword."

Kaden did as his brother bid and retrieved his sword from whence it had fallen and pressed it into his hand.

He slumped back against the stone battlement. "Promise me one thing."

He sat beside Erik, supporting him the best he could. "Anything."

The young king closed his eyes, each breath a greater pain. "Rule justly brother, and defeat Sernon."

Kaden's hand tightened over his brothers. " 'Tis already done."

"And…look after Skylah. She was to be my queen."

"Of course. You know I will. Stay." Tears brimmed his eyes." I need you. I cannot do this on my own."

"You can. You are stronger than you think." Erik relaxed, and a smile formed on his lips. "I can feel the sun on my face. Can you feel it, Kaden?"

He stilled. "No." He spoke slowly, his words heavy. "Just the rain."

Erik's eyes widened. He looked past Kaden and tried to rise. "Father, you have come to walk with me. You look…." The young king's voice softened, yet his words were clear. "Lend me your hand…Father. My strength has all but failed me."

Kaden let go of his other hand as his brother tried to raise it and looked behind him.

The three guards still stood blocking them from harm. When he looked back, he saw Erik's hand slip limply to his thigh and his head sag sideways against the wall.

He swallowed hard, trying to force down the lump in his throat, and hold back the tears that threatened to spill down his cheeks. He leaned forward to touch his lips gently to his brother's brow and close his golden eyes for a last time. Then, he leaned Erik back against the wall, pushed the arrow from his chest, and dropped it to the cold stone. "May the Gods of Elysium smile upon you, brother. You will walk into the Hall of our Ancestors, proud."

He rose and nodded to Skylah, and when he looked back, she was kneeling at Erik's side, holding his hand, speaking to him quietly words he would never hear. Tears trickled down her cheeks.

He turned and took Etan's arm, leading him from the

scene.

"Let her have her moment. Can you still fight?"

Etan's gaze slid back to Skylah and Erik. His hand tightened on his sword. "Try and stop me."

"Then let us be at it. I have a sorcerer to kill." Kaden took off at a sprint, racing halfway down the staircase. "Come to me you bitch-bred bastards and taste Dorrachian steel." He leapt over the side and drove his sword deep into the gut of an Urakian officer with the full weight of his body behind the blow, then dragged his sword clear and disappeared into a swirling sea of noise, blood slicked cobblestones, and lethal blades.

****

The young Elisian followed and vaulted onto the back of a giant with flowing white hair. The man momentarily stunned, spun, and slammed Etan to the ground. Winded, he watched in horror as a battle-axe rose above him.

Then the man faltered and dropped his axe. Etan rolled to the side, and the giant toppled to the ground to lie in the place he had occupied. He twisted and stared up into the face of a grinning, black bearded dwarf standing on the stone guardrail of the battlement stairs.

The giant's skull had been crushed by one powerful blow from the dwarf's giant hammer, "Come on, laddy, get up," he said with a grin offering his hand. "A battle is no place to rest. We have more skulls to crush!"

Etan took the dwarf's outstretched hand and came swiftly to his feet. "I do not know your name."

"I am Hammer Deathwielder, and you do now!" He held up his axe. "And this is Shae."

Etan could see the blood lust in the dwarf's eyes as he leapt down from the rail next to him. "Well met, dwarf, and you are a welcome sight indeed," he shouted over the din of the battle. "I will guard your back."

"As you wish, laddy," Hammer shouted back, ducking, and bringing his mighty battle hammer back into play. "But do not get in my way!"

****

Tannith and Ohma drew closer to the *Eye*, they knew because the Cross's song rang out increasingly louder.

They mounted the topmost step of the spiral staircase. The door of the tower room stood ajar. Light flickered from the gap around the edges and sounds of chanting emanated from within.

Tannith inched the door open with a sense of dread and peered into the dimly lit chamber. She knew soon she would be face to face with her nemesis.

Even with her night-sight, she was unable to penetrate the gloom at the far end of the room—as if an unnatural screen of darkness guarded those within.

She drew back, pulled her sword, and raised her foot to the door. It flew back on its hinges as she booted it inward.

Sernon's chanting stopped, the room brightened with an eldritch light as he raised his head. Her heart skipped a beat, and her short, sharp scream split the air. His was a face she had seen in the temple long ago. The face of her God.

A draught rushed from the corridor, extinguishing the candles, and plunging the chamber to darkness.

A flash of sheet lightning outside the window illuminated the room for several long heartbeats.

The Necromancer's face came back into focus as Magus's name split from her lips.

"No, my dear." Sernon mocked. "His brother." With a casual flick of his wrist, he relit the candles lining the ritual room and motioned to the black robed priests flanking him.

They charged in unison, the first coming from Tannith's left. She spun and brought her short sword around and across the neck of the priest. He died instantly, falling into a small brazier, scattering coals and ash across the floor.

Ducking to avoid a clumsy slash from the second man, she regained her balance and gave him a savage kick to the face. His hands flew up as she rammed her sword into his heart.

Ohma put paid to the third attacker with a hard crack from his rosewood staff, and the man crumpled.

Sernon watched the scene with casual interest as he leaned against the altar. He straightened. "Well done, my dear. You are more skilled than I thought. However, you have only served to delay the inevitable."

"I would not be so confident, Master of Darkness." Ohma spoke from the shadows. "Even now, your troops are beaten back. Your time is ending."

Sernon laughed into the silence. "Welcome, Ohma. I was expecting you sooner."

"I had more important matters to attend."

The sorcerer's face reddened as Ohma stepped into the light. "I see you still have your dry wit. But that is enough prattle. Did you bring the Cross?" His gaze went to Tannith's throat. "Ah, I see you have—and assembled as well."

"You will not have it." Tannith's hand curled tightly around the icon." I would rather die than allow you to touch it.

Sernon reached down and smoothly drew back a black sheet from the body lying on the altar. "And I had so hoped you would be reasonable."

"Father!" Tannith drew her sword and charged the sorcerer.

His hand swept up, and she hurtled through the air, aimed at a row of iron spikes jutting from the far wall, her sword dropping from her limp hand.

Ohma pointed his staff and a blue light of magick speared into her and she fell, sprawling and gasping, to the floor.

"Tut, tut." Sernon's smiled but his eyes were cold. "You cannot defeat me with a mere sword. I am all-powerful." He waited for her to regain her breath and come to her feet. "For this one infringement, I will forgive you. Do not provoke me again." He ran a hand through his dark hair. "I have watched you in my mirror of illusions. You are a woman of fire and steel, a woman of greatness. Join me. Be my bride and there shall be nothing that I will not give you."

A shiver of repulsion ran down her back, but she laughed mockingly. "Wed you? You are revolting and more insane than I thought. Never, would I marry you." She raised her chin, and her voice rang out cold. "Release my father at once."

A tall, dark figure filled the doorway—a bloodied warrior, with eyes of green ice and a voice of cold iron. "Do as she says."

Sernon spun. "Ah, so Prince Kaden, you have arrived at last. This gets better and better. You are in time for the ritual."

"You die now!" roared Kaden, his dagger flying from his hand.

As Sernon pointed, the blade stopped in mid-flight and transformed to a toad to drop and hop across the black marble floor.

Kaden rushed at Sernon, but he threw out his hand and the prince's feet stuck to the ground. Rapping out unintelligible words, he conjured flames from the floor to encircle the Dorrachian Prince. Steam hissed from Kaden's rain-drenched clothes, and fire licked at his flesh as the circle tightened.

"Stop!" Tannith grabbed a wolf skin from the floor to beat out the flames, but the magickle fire would not die. Tears of frustration filled her eyes. "Stop this. Stop it now!"

"Let the boy go," demanded Ohma. "He is of no consequence. You want the Cross? Here take it!" He snatched the still humming icon from Tannith's throat and tossed it at the sorcerer.

Sernon caught it one handed, and with the other, vanquished the flames.

"No!" Tannith rounded on Ohma. "Do you realize what you have done? You have destroyed our one hope of stopping him."

Ohma made to touch her arm, but she pulled back.

" 'Twas the only way…" he trailed off.

"I would rather be dead," Kaden said, wiping the sweat from his brow as he threw Sernon a deadly look, "than sacrifice the Cross to him."

The sorcerer grinned. "I shall accommodate you soon enough. However, first the ritual must be completed." Sernon looked from one to the other. "I see you have supplied the main ingredient." He pointed to the floor. "Feel free to stay."

Their feet stuck solid to the black marble floor, and

Sernon's harsh laugh rang out, reverberating from the stone walls, and he turned, dragging the ebony sheet from Ephraen's body, and proceeded to lay the Cross over the old king's heart.

"You had this planned all along," Ohma accused.

Sernon's lip curled. "Is it not grand when a plan comes together?" A sardonic smile curved his lips as he drew his dagger and brought it down hard on the king's ring finger, severing it from his hand. He then dropped the bloody appendage into a bowl of glowing green ingredients on an onyx pedestal beside him.

Bile rose in Tannith's throat, and she forced it down and looked away. This could not be happening—to find her father, only to have him snatched from her in such an evil way. And her, helpless to come to his aid. She scanned the room—there must be a way.

Sernon lifted the silver bowl in supplication to the dark god, Arahmin. Rain fell upon his upraised face, plastering his ebony hair to his scalp. Lightning illuminated his pale features and red-rimmed eyes as arcane words trickled from his tongue.

"Bara'k, Halagraf, Narva, Del'ramok."

The three friends stood, looking on in spellbound horror.

To Tannith, Sernon appeared the embodiment of all her nightmares, and like in a nightmare, she was unable to act. Drenching rain plastered his robes to his body, running in small rivulets down his face. Nevertheless, he was oblivious to her stare. Every person in the room seemed caught up in a sense of suspended time where there was no reality.

All except one.

"Wait!"

Sernon surfaced from his trance, a deadly white light in his eyes. He focused on Ohma. "You dare interrupt me? I could turn you to dust with a snap of my fingers."

Ohma straightened to his full height and pulled his royal blue cloak around his bony shoulders. "Perhaps, but what would that achieve? Are you really the most powerful mage that ever lived? If you destroy the Cross, you will never know."

A harsh laugh escaped Sernon. "Of course, *I* am the most powerful! Who could be *more* so? Surely not you?" he scoffed.

"Did not your brother defeat you in battle? Did not Magus send you to the Void and your body to the depths of an icy lake?"

Fleetingly, fear flickered in Sernon's eyes, only to be replaced by a mask of arrogance. "I was tricked—I had him beaten."

Ohma raised a snowy brow. "Did you?"

"That is the past, this is now." Sernon's tone was cold, flat. "Magus is dead."

"With the Cross, you can evoke his spirit. Breathe life back into his body. You can have another chance. Only then will you know if you are greater, know whether you can *really* defeat him. If you are the true *Master Sorcerer*."

For what seemed an eternity, Sernon's pale, death-like eyes studied Ohma as if judging his intent.

Quickly, he bent and plucked the Eye of Magus from the Dragon's claw at the head of his rosewood staff leaning against the altar.

With careful deliberateness, he fitted the stone to its rightful place at the center of the Cross.

****

Multicolored lights streamed from the faceted stone as the Cross vibrated. Its humming rose to a crescendo that resonated into the watchers' heads. The room filled with white light. The rain stopped and a brilliant beam of sunlight streamed through the opening in the roof. On that beam, seeming to float on naught but the light itself, came the shadowy image of a man.

As the image reached the floor it manifested into a tall figure with white flowing robes. His strong, clean jaw, dark hair, and features matched those of Sernon exactly, except for his golden eyes, glowing now with a strange inner fervor.

"You have not changed at all, brother," Sernon announced, his voice strained. "Always, the grand entrance."

Magus smiled magnanimously. "You, on the other hand, brother, are looking decidedly haggard." He raised a dark brow. "Have you been ill?"

Sernon's red-rimmed eyes narrowed. For some uncanny reason, he felt unnerved by Magus's glib reply. He seemed to have grown in stature and exuded a confidence he had never before felt in his presence. "What rules will apply?" he snarled. "The same as before?"

"No!" Magus roared. "None!" Lightning flashed from his eyes, striking into Sernon's chest, hurling him across the black marble floor.

Singed and winded, Sernon's fingers flew open, and the Cross dropped to skid along the ground.

Without giving pause, Magus clutched the neck of Sernon's robe and grasped his leg, slamming him into the steel spikes on the back wall.

Pain like a thousand fires tore into his back and

buttocks and bit into his thighs. He screamed. "You have killed me."

"No, you will not die so easily. You will suffer for the anguish you have caused my people." Magus's jaw hardened. "I have dealt with Dannock-Shae in the Void. There are worse things than death."

Magus plucked him from the wall and dropped him face down on the marble floor.

A grisly rattle escaped his throat. With three words from Magus, his bloodied wounds healed over, but agony like a beast still raged through his insides.

Even as he lay crumpled at his brother's feet, he knew he would not surrender. The small respite was all he needed. He groaned, rolled onto his elbow, and pushed out his hand. Flames sprang from his fingertips aimed at Magus.

His brother parried with a blast of freezing air that toppled a heavy stone column. He made to dodge it but was trapped as the column fell across his chest—pain tenfold than before seared his body. He attempted to focus, but his eyes blurred. He threw out a hasty command, summoning his staff from beside the altar. But Magus intercepted it and transformed the rosewood staff to a writhing serpent complete with wings and fangs. It reared its head at its Master. Sernon punched out his fist, and the stave converted to dust.

"Is that the best you can do?" The god gestured to the pillar of stone.

The pillar vanished, and Sernon flew with the flick of his brother's wrist to slam into the ornate ceiling, floor, and walls.

Then he released the spell, allowing Sernon to drop to the floor like a crushed and broken doll, all breath knocked from his lungs.

Summoning his strength, he willed his mind to heal his wretched body, but Magus would have none of it.

"No, brother. Allow me." With painstaking slowness, he used his magick to snap Sernon's bones back into place, dragging, stitching, and gathering each small segment of mutilated tissue and sinew.

Every small act tortured him to the fullest, exacting payment for his evil deeds. Finally, the mending was complete and outwardly he seemed healed, but claws of torturous pain still worked at his insides.

He glared up into his brother's handsome visage, and anger burned in his gut like fire at the humiliation he had suffered in the presence of his enemies. He turned his head to peer at Ohma, the old charlatan, so pure, even now he carried sympathy in his eyes. Then there was Kaden of the despised Wolfhead, and Tannith, Princess of Dragonbane…another detested name. How their ancestors would laugh if they could see him now.

With a curse, he closed his eyes, blocking out the look of triumph and pity in theirs. His strength returned with the retaliation he planned. He had not come so far, so close to seeing his dreams fulfilled to have them snatched away so easily. His milksop brother would not defeat him. He would not allow it!

He rolled and shouted a command. A marble dragon in a far corner grew scales and reared to life. It opened its maw and fire rained down, searing hot and bright on Magus's head.

The god flung up his hands and the flames reversed to flash back at him. Crying out, Sernon ceased his fiery spell. His hands burned as he clutched his face, great hunks of flesh clinging to his fingers.

Magus remained unscathed, and with casual mastery, exploded Sernon's beast to ash, then with a casual flick of his wrist, drained the searing agony from his ruined face.

"The game is over, brother. 'Tis long past time we finished this." Magus bent to pick up the Cross and place it around his neck.

"No!" He lunged, threw Magus to the floor, and straddled his body, raining blow after blow down into his face. He ripped at the Cross, but it slid from his burned fingers, scudding across the marble floor. He scampered after it.

Magus yanked him back by the hair and thrust a hard right into his jaw.

Stunned momentarily, he quickly recovered and clutched Magus's throat. His fingers closed like talons about his brother's larynx, but his grip faltered because of the pain in his hands.

He reeled as a blow struck the side on his head and Magus flipped him onto his back. Together they rolled across the hard, shiny floor—back and forth, each man battling for supremacy, each giving no quarter, both trying to gain the upper hand.

Magus's punches powered into his head, his jaw, then his eye.

"Cease." Sernon struggled for breath.

His brother bent over to retrieve the Cross and came to his feet looking down on him.

Sernon watched his twin through narrowed eyes, and his fear rose. He raised his hand. "Magus, we are brothers. You are a god—all-powerful. Grant mercy. Do not send me into oblivion. I beg you on our mother's grave. I swear to obey you in all matters."

Magus shook his head as if reading the lie in his mind. "We may be of the same blood, but you ceased to be my brother the day you donned the black robes. You are a blight on all sorcerers, a blight on the name of Asomos, a plague that will soon be rectified. There will be no mercy for you, brother."

He raised the Cross, but still, he did not release its power. "You could never have won, you know that. For the stone you and all others thought the Eye of Magus was never my eye alone. The jewel was placed in my statue by the Gods of Creation." He lifted the Cross to the light. "The stone at the heart of this Cross is the Eye of the Gods. The Gods have been watching you. And you have been judged!"

A brilliant light broke from the jewel, striking Sernon's chest and encompassing his body. He threw up his hands and screamed, trying to shield himself from the searing heat. He had known pain before but nothing like this. This was infinite, gut-wrenching. Agony like a thousand fires from the Abyss, tearing through every fiber, every membrane of his body, ripping, clawing, and gouging at his entrails—burning into his head—his mind.

Black, hideous creatures sprang from a dark cloud that had formed in a top corner of the room. Screaming in dissent, they clutched at him with icy talons.

He raised his arms to ward them off.

Then the beasts swooped again, gripped his arms, and with a last piercing scream, dredged up from his soul, disappeared into the shadows.

****

Tannith stared, numb with disbelief, at the smoldering pile of white ash on the flagstone floor…all that remained of Sernon.

All these months of trials and hardships, all that time of living in fear of this one man. Now he was no more, his life snuffed out like the frail flame of a candle—life so fragile, death so profound.

Slowly, she dragged her gaze from the place where the sorcerer had lain and made her way to her father. At the death of the sorcerer, Ephraen had regained consciousness. She removed his gag, then, pulling her hunting knife from her leg sheath, sliced his bonds and helped him sit. He appeared so frail. The blood loss from his severed finger probably contributing to his weakness. She pulled a scrap of linen from her waistband and bound his hand.

She looked at him, then smiled. His milk-white eyes blinked and tried to focus.

It was then she realized with horror her father was blind. She ran her fingers gently down his scarred cheek, and he flinched. "Father, 'tis I, Tannith."

"Daughter?" The one word held a sob. "How can this be?" His two hands covered hers.

"The story is long Father. Rest now." She put her arm around his shoulders and eased him back onto the altar. He seemed so frail. It was hard to reconcile that he was the same strong man he had been.

Tannith beseeched Magus. "Please, my lord, can you not help him?"

The god glided across the floor and laid his cool hand on the king's brow.

The old man groaned. His eyes fluttered open, but this time they focused on his daughter, violet, bright, and full of life.

Magus touched the king's cheek and the burned

flesh healed, then he placed his hand over his fathers and a new finger appeared.

Shakily, Ephraen pushed his legs over the edge of the altar and hugged Tannith to his chest, tears of joy staining his weathered cheeks.

****

Ohma joined Magus and drew him aside. "So, it is finally over."

"Aye, Sernon has gone, and his soul vanquished into the Seventh Level of the Hell Pit. From which there is no escape, ever. He will never rise again." Magus took the Cross from around his neck, lifted Ohma's wrinkled hand, and placed it in his palm. "I am entrusting the Cross to you, my friend. Use it wisely. Help my people restore Tarlis to the greatness it once was. And when the time comes, pass it to your successor."

"But how will I know—"

Magus stopped him with a raised hand. "You must choose but be careful. She must be pure of heart and body when she accepts the Cross, or it will destroy her."

Ohma arched a snowy brow. "She?"

Magus smiled. "Your successor will be female. That is all I can tell you."

"But when—"

"When the time is right. In many summers to come."

"But, my lord, I had expected to travel to Elysium with you. I am old—I am tired."

Magus shook his head and gave Ohma a sad smile. "I am sorry, my friend. One day you will stand beside me in the place of our faith, but your time is not now. You still have much to accomplish before you journey that path. These people need you, and I need you to help them."

261

Ohma sighed, unable to answer. How could he be expected to carry so great a burden? He was not worthy.

"If I did not think you up to the task, I would not ask it." Magus had read his mind. "Take heart, old friend, for you are stronger and more worthy than you think. Whom else could I depend upon to see the chore completed properly?"

"Who else, indeed?" Ohma replied wearily. He nodded and gave Magus a half smile as the god's image faded.

The elderly man moved to the window to stand beside Kaden. "You must speak to your people and end this slaughter. It is useless to fight now that Sernon is dead. The Urakians must be made to surrender."

"I know, but how do you hold back the tide?"

"With the help of the Cross, I can blot out the sun. If they cannot see, they cannot fight."

"Then do it, for I would have no more of my men die for a cause already won."

Ohma raised the Cross to the weeping sky. The rain stopped and the sky lay flat and gray above their heads. Ohma spoke, and a darkness blacker than night descended over the land.

Shouts rang out from the courtyard, then no sound at all as the battle ceased.

Kaden called down to the grounds below. "Urakians, this is Prince Kaden of the resistance. Sernon is dead! Lay down your arms, and I shall be merciful!"

There was silence, then murmurs of dissent.

One by one, Kaden heard the distinct sound of iron and steel hitting earth and cobblestone. Realizing they were victorious, the rebel army let out a tremendous roar.

With a wrinkled smile, Ohma reversed the spell.

The sky brightened, and the sun burst forth, filling the courtyard with light.

"Etan! Radoch! Have the weapons collected and the prisoners assembled in the inner courtyard. I will meet you there," shouted Kaden.

They waved at him, and he turned back to Ohma. "Where is Magus? Will he not speak to his people?"

Ohma shook his head. "His time here has been and gone. The people have no more need of him. It is your time for glory now." He placed both hands on Kaden's shoulder. "It is you who must lead these people. We have won the battle, but there is still much to be set to rights. The people must have someone to look up to, someone to follow. This is your time Kaden. This is what the prophecy foretold."

Kaden stepped back, and Ohma's hand dropped to his side. He stared at him slowly, shaking his head.

Ohma cringed, so lethal was the look on the young Prince's face. In his cold green eyes. "You..." He pointed at Ohma. "You knew my brother would die. You knew all along," he accused.

"Not all along, no, but for some time, yes."

"You could have told me—warned him. We could have—"

"There was nothing I could do."

"Karnak said the pathways could be changed."

"Not this one, it was ordained in the stars. It had to be this way—"

"For me to lead," finished Kaden lamely.

Ohma nodded. "You cannot know how sorry I am.

"Sorry? Sorry about what?" asked Tannith, moving to join them. She smiled at the men and linked her arm through Kaden's. "So where is Erik? I thought he would be here by now. I could not see him in the courtyard. He will be king now, will he not?" she asked looking up into Kaden's eyes.

****

Ohma drew back. "You will wish to speak alone."

He nodded at Kaden, and Tannith noted his bleak expression.

"You must be pleased." She hesitated at his silence. "Erik has Wolveryne Castle restored."

"My brother is dead," he replied flatly, staring at a spot over her head. "He will never sit on the Wolfhead throne or be crowned king of Glen-Dorrach. He gave his life to open the gates."

Tears sprang to Tannith's eyes. Her hand found his. "I am so sorry. I do not know what to say. I know you loved him very much." She chose her words carefully. "Erik was a good man. He will not be forgotten."

"No, he will not." Kaden brought her into his arms and rested his chin on the top of her head for several moments, then he pushed her to arm's length and straightened. "Come." He took her hand. "It is time to face our people and make this land whole again."

****

Tannith and Kaden stepped onto the landing overlooking the crowded inner courtyard. The wounded and dead had been cleared or taken to safety, and the Urakian soldiers waited on bended knees to hear their fate. Men of every race flanked them, weapons held in readiness.

Radoch climbed the steps and drew his sword. He raised it into the air, and his voice boomed out over the people. "Hail the new king. Hail Kaden of Glen-Dorrach!"

Cheers rose long and loud from the courtyard.

Kaden raised a hand to settle the noise, at the same time searching the ranks of the Elisians until he found the one, he sought. "Captain Etanandril Jarrisendel, I call you to my side. This is your victory too!"

The fair-haired Elisian reddened and took the steps two at a time to the applause of his troops. He stood beside Kaden, cheers and clapping reaching a thunderous roar.

Kaden held up his father's broadsword, and the noise softened and finally ceased. There was silence as all waited for the new King of the Wolfhead to speak.

"People of Tarlis, today is a proud day for us. Today, we conquered an army we thought invincible. Today, we stood as brothers, shoulder to shoulder, and fought for freedom from a man who would have seen you on your knees as slaves. This day will burn in the hearts and minds of our people for all time. Let us always stand together as one!"

The cry from the ocean of faces below sounded their approval.

"And let us remember another king, my brother, Erik. He came to power in a time of peril. He had no chance to take his rightful place among you but loved his people no less. Many may not know it, but he gave up his life today to open the gate. Without him, we would have no victory."

Another roar went up, louder than the last. Chanting Erik's name. He waited for the cheers to subside. Some of the soldiers were weeping openly.

"By the end of today, an alliance will be drawn up between all creed and race." He looked to Ephraen who moved from the shadows to the left of his daughter.

The Elisian King nodded.

Kaden's voice rang out. "If any of our brothers should be in need, they have only to send word and the army of Glen-Dorrach and Ellenroh will ride to their aid. What do you say, people of Tarlis? Shall it be so?" He punched his arm into the air.

Cries of agreement started softly and grew to a crescendo, echoing out over the valley.

Kaden let go the breath he held, and the tension drained from his body. Then he tensed again as he looked down at the prisoners on their knees in the courtyard.

What to do with several thousand Urakians? How easy it would be to have them put to the sword? However, it was not an act he would like to be remembered for on his first day as king. He ran a hand over the back of his neck. What would Erik have done?

He stared out over the castle walls. The sun was setting, signaling the end of the day. Crimson and black filled the sky—the color of blood and death. On the ramparts, a white tiger stood watching him. The large cat raised its paw and roared, then turned and padded along the battlement to vanish.

Kaden nodded and brushed a hand across his eyes. "Thank you, brother," he whispered, knowing Erik would never hear him. He straightened and cast a last lingering look at the battlements, then searched the ranks of the prisoners. There had been too much slaughter and bloodshed already. Let his reign be the start of a new age. Let *his* be a rule of honor and mercy.

He strode down the steps to the first line of Urakians. A man in a skulled-helm knelt at his feet. His side oozed blood, and there was a shallow cut across his throat.

"Remove your helm," he demanded. "I would see your face."

The warrior spat on the stone at Kaden's feet. "I will not die on my knees," he growled.

A Dorrachian stepped forward and knocked the helm from his head.

Kaden ignored the slight and stared into the ebony eyes of the man before him. "What is your name soldier?"

"Kraal." He grunted, and his lip curled. "General Kraal."

"Do you lead these people, Kraal?"

"Aye. If they have no one else."

Kaden smiled thinly and crossed his arms over his chest. "You shall see your people exiled to Kragg Island, which will henceforth be known as a penal colony. There, they will remain for all their days. Glen-Dorrach troops will man the castle. Any Urakian caught trying to escape will be hung without trial. Your people will not bear arms. They are to have no tools in their possession made from steel or iron. The penalty for this is also death. Is all that clear?"

Kraal's lip curled, and his eyes darkened.

"They are to farm the land," continued Kaden, maintaining his hard expression. "Seed, wooden tools, and livestock will be provided. Each season, they will pay a quarter of their harvest to the Kingdom of Glen-Dorrach in taxes, which in turn will be distributed among the needy."

Kraal remained silent, hate etched clearly into his harsh features and every line of his taut body. He bent and spat on Kaden's boots.

The king drew his dagger and the tip bit into the big

man's throat, drawing a trickle of blood. "Is that clear?"

****

Kraal knew all he had to do was to fall forward and his humiliation would be at an end, but he had never been that brave. "Aye…I hear you."

"Louder!"

"Aye…milord," he growled, pulling back from the knife.

"Then rise and join your men."

Kraal watched furtively as the new king turned and strode toward the stairs. He slipped a small steel spike from the confines of his heavy leather battle coat, and slowly eased to his feet. Drawing back his arm, he took quick aim, but the spike never left his hand, instead, it dropped from his nerveless fingers and clattered to the cobblestones, excruciating pain ripping through his innards.

He stared down in disbelief at the pearl-handled throwing knife jutting from between his ribs. Unable to stop himself, his legs buckled, and he sagged to his knees beside the spike.

A soldier bent to retrieve the weapon, and with a nod from his king, moved aside to make way for a lone figure.

A shudder ran through Kraal's body, and he stared up into the face of a woman with hair the same hue as the crimson sunset. Was she the angel of death come to claim him? It hurt to breathe, and he gasped for another ragged breath and collapsed back on the cobblestones.

The woman's brilliant green eyes met his as he struggled to focus.

"Who are you?" he rasped.

She ignored his question and dropped to one knee,

twisting the dagger, driving it deeper between his ribs. "This is for Erik, late king of Tarlis, who was to be my husband." She pushed the dagger a little deeper. "And this is for the Fae people of Sabiah. If only your agony could be tenfold." With a final thrust, she drove the dagger home.

Kraal gasped and blood dribbled from his mouth. Comprehension dawned as black-winged chariots filled his sight, and his life force flowed from his body.

****

Skylah, who had been staring down at Kraal with a sense of pain and bitter satisfaction, looked up as Etan offered his hand. For a moment, she hesitated, looking into the sun, not able to see his face, then she took it. He drew her to her feet, and she went into his arms.

" 'Tis done," she said. "My people and Erik have been avenged."

He rested his chin on her head. "Yes, it is over. Now you can rest." His face mirrored his pain as he looked wistfully over her head, knowing their embrace was but for a heartbeat only.

It would be a long time before she would accept anything from him other than friendship. It would be a long time before he would bring himself to offer more.

Erik's death had touched them more profoundly than he would ever have envisioned.

****

At dawn two days later, on the shore of Tranquil Bay in the shadow of Wolveryne Castle, Kaden stood beside Tannith. Surrounded by the armies of Tarlis, they watched Erik's body float out to sea.

The young king was laid to rest on a wooden raft piled high around the edges with kindling drizzled with

269

fragrant oils and flowers. With the signal given by Kaden, the raft was set alight by a well-aimed fire arrow from Jerak, and the craft glided across the water toward the golden rays of a new sun and the gates of Elysium.

Chapter Nineteen

A day later, Kaden and an escort of men rode behind a column heading for Ellenroh.

Etan was at his side. "Why not ride up front with Tannith? Ephraen would be pleased to have you. You *are* a king now."

Kaden shook his head. "I would feel out of place. Besides, I am certain Tannith would appreciate time alone with her father."

Etan laughed. "I think you are afraid of him. Have you asked for her hand yet?"

"No. And, I am afraid of no man. Why are *you* not with your king?"

The fair-haired Elisian shrugged. "Perhaps I have gotten used to roughing it. I no longer have the stomach for the fanfare. Besides, I would miss your ugly visage."

Kaden laughed, and the two rode the next half a league in companionable silence. The azure sky held no trace of rain from the day before. Refugees lined the roads, returning from whatever haven they sought during the long months of war.

Etan spoke first, breaking the quiet. "Do you think the Urakians will cause more trouble?"

"I left orders with Radoch to round up the troublemakers and deal with them accordingly. We will not be hearing anything from the people of Urak for quite some time, if ever. They will be busy settling on Kragg."

"Is it as bad as they say?"

"Worse. Barren mountains and desert, but they will survive. There are some small forms of wildlife, and I believe there is one corner of the Island which is quite habitable during winter."

"And Ohma, where is he? The old rascal; I have not seen him since the feast two days ago."

"He travels with a company of Dorrachians to release the Mystic Warriors from their enchantment, and free the slaves from the mines. With the power of the Cross, he should have little opposition. Slavery has been outlawed, and never again will the people of Glen-Dorrach be yoked; nor anywhere else in this realm, if I have my say."

Respect entered Etan's eyes as he glanced across at the former prince. "You are a fine man, Kaden of Glen-Dorrach, and will be a good king." He shook his head. "I do not know why I disliked you so."

"I do." He grinned. "She is riding up front, with her father."

Etan nodded and smiled. "Women have a way of turning a man daft." His gaze alighted on a young red-haired woman riding ahead of him.

****

It took thirty days to reach Jahl and the green borders of Ellenroh. They crossed the Tarlis River and camped overnight in Druh Forest. Then, after leaving Jerak and his men at dawn, they proceeded on through the Living Forest. The cavalcade crossed the Blue Grass Plains, arriving at Dragonbane Castle at midday on the forty-fifth day.

On arrival, Kaden was kept busy with the signing of the treaty and seeing his escort fed and quartered. During their journey, he and Tannith had scarcely had a private moment together and managed to catch only short snatches of conversation. Nevertheless, he had promised on arrival at the castle that he would speak to her father concerning their marriage. However, things had not been as simple as presumed. It was as if the whole of the kingdom conspired to keep them apart.

Ephraen was avoiding him.

The only time he saw Tannith or the king was at supper when she was seated beside her father across from him at a long trestle. Several times, she cast him a helpless glance, only to be caught up in another conversation by one of her kinsmen.

Although Kaden had always prided himself on a certain amount of forbearance when it came to matters of State, his patience was worn thin by the end of the second week. His attempts to meet with Ephraen on a personal level, to ask for Tannith's hand, were being met with excuses.

Ohma, who arrived three days previous by Dragon, cautioned tolerance, but Kaden had no patience left.

Finally, after cornering the king in his garden late the day before, he was informed, in no uncertain terms, the matter was out of Ephraen's hands and would have to be settled by the Council of Elders. Kaden would be called before the Council at dawn, and there, he would have a chance to present his suit.

Matters had not gone in his favor.

So here he was, climbing the steps to the battlements, faced with the hardest task he had ever had to undertake in his twenty-six summers of life. He would rather face the terror of the Glaisling again than tell Tannith he was leaving Ellenroh without her.

The Council had given him no choice. The pompous old windbags treated every one of his arguments with contempt. *An Elisian could not marry out of their race and that was final. No, there was no exception to the law. There was only one law and it stood for all the people, princess or not. They were incredibly grateful to the King of Glen-Dorrach for all he had done to aid them, but no, he could not marry their princess.*

Well, they would not stop him. He would bring the whole of the Glen-Dorrach nation down on their heads. If they would not give her freely, he would take her! She was his wife by Dorrachian law.

****

Tannith heard him approach. It had been a day and a half since she had last seen him. She scanned his face. His eyes were red-rimmed, his usually sleek black hair tousled like he had run his fingers through it numerous times, and black stubble covered his jaw. His scar stood out in white relief on his tanned cheek. He looked bone-weary. Yet, to her, he would always be the most handsome of men.

She strode toward him, her hands outstretched. "I was afraid something had happened. It seems everyone in this castle is contriving to keep us apart. We have barely been alone since the battle."

****

Kaden nodded and searched her lovely face, unable to wrap his tongue around the words he knew must come.

She frowned. "Have you spoken with the Council? When are we to be wed?"

He took her gently by the shoulders. "You must be brave."

She tensed and laughed lightly. "Brave? I do not

274

understand. I can handle anything as long as I am with you."

"I am leaving."

"Leaving?" She looked into his clear, green eyes and frowned. "How can you leave? We are to be married."

"There will be no marriage." He shifted uncomfortably.

"What are you saying? Of course, there will be a marriage. You love me." Again, she frowned. "Or was that a lie?"

"Do not ever think that." His arms closed around her. "You are my heart."

"What can I think?" She pulled away. "When you say you are leaving me?"

"Permission was denied."

She shook her head. "I do not understand. How can they deny us? We are handfasted. Already joined in the Dorrachian tradition."

Kaden brought her back into his embrace. "I told them. They said it was a pagan ritual and had no bearing. They are convinced you were under duress and knew not what you were doing, convinced I led you astray, coerced you, and I am lucky to be leaving here with my head."

Tannith pulled back to look at him. Her eyes flashed a brilliant purple. "They said that? Why, those ungrateful sons of…Did Etan and Ohma not speak on our behalf?"

"They spoke, but the Council would not hear. They are a pack of old dotards, their heads buried in ancient Elven tradition. They have dreams of turning back time and making Elisians into Elves again. It cannot be done. It would take thousands of summers of selective breeding, and then it still might not be possible."

Tannith threw her arms about his neck. "I will not let you leave. I will speak to my father. He will see it my way. You saved them. You led the army that conquered Sernon. Do they not know that? You are honored among my people—or should be."

Kaden sighed and shrugged and drew her hands from his neck and held them in his own. "Ephraen will not break the laws of his people for me or for you."

"Then I am coming with you. I am nothing without you. You are my strength."

His arms closed around her again, and her heart beat frantically against his. How could he let her go? "You are wrong. You are strong. You had to be to go through everything you did on our quest." He kissed the top of her head then pressed his forehead to hers. "Your Council will never allow it. Your father's men would be on us before we passed through the gates." He pushed her to arm's length. "I will be back."

"What…what do you mean?"

"They will not keep me from you. I am riding for Glen-Dorrach, and I am bringing back my army."

Her eyes filled with tears. "You are my life," she whispered. "What if something should happen to you?"

"Trust me." His hands tightened on her arms. "And do not make this any harder. In my soul, you are my woman, my wife, my life. I *will* be back." He touched his lips gently to her eyelids. "Now wipe your tears and give me a kiss to remember always."

He dragged her into his arms, and his lips came down over hers hungrily, telling of his love, his desperation, drawing from her the strength to leave.

****

Tannith held him close, forcing a brave façade, and

fought against the ache in her heart. She was unable to form the words lodged in her throat, words begging him to stay.

He gave her one last look as if imprinting her image in his mind, then turned and strode from the battlements.

She watched and listened with a plummeting heart as his footsteps rang back on the ancient stone, signaling the sound of finality.

She struggled to regain her composure, but all she could think of was Kaden, and how empty her life would be without him. A sob escaped her lips. He was gone. As simply as he had entered her life, he had left it. From the balcony of the tower room, she watched him cross the drawbridge and make his way along the road to disappear over the rise. A lonely figure at the head of his men.

Shivers racked her body, and tears fell as she wrapped protective arms around her waist.

Her father had rewarded him with an Elisian thoroughbred the same coloring as Phoenix, all the better to take him from her.

Sometime later, Etan found her still standing in the cold wind, staring at the horizon.

"Why did you let him leave?" He removed his fur-lined cloak and spread it around her rigid shoulders.

She shook her head unable to answer, the lump in her throat too great.

He fastened the golden clip of the cloak and looked into her eyes. "I once let someone go, who I loved very much. If I had that time again, I would trade my very soul to keep her."

She glanced away and scrubbed at her tears. "What choice did I have?"

"There are always choices, Tannith. You taught me that. Had I taken a different path, I would now have the woman I love in my arms. Instead, she is locked in her room mourning another man whose child she carries."

Tannith pulled back and turned to look down at the drawbridge, awash in her own misery. "Skylah is with child?"

"She is." He brought her around to face him. "Do you know your father intends for you and I to marry?"

Tannith shook her head. Uncomprehending. She opened her mouth to speak, closed it, and tried again. "You cannot be serious?"

"Very. I just came from his study. He has it all planned, right down to the three days of feasting."

"No." She backed away. "He cannot do this. First, he sends the man I love from my side, then he expects me to go straight into the arms of another. He must be a fool. All those months in Sernon's dungeon has befuddled his wits."

"Do not tell me, tell him." Etan folded his arms across his chest. "Do you think I want this after everything that has happened? But I am honor bound. If it was not for your father taking me in when my own father died…" He stared into the distant trees. "What I cannot understand is what went so wrong. What about the prophecy? Surely things were not meant to be like this."

She frowned. "What has the prophecy to do with this?"

"Did it not foretell of two kingdoms ruling as one?"
"When the land is without hope,

When evil and despair cover the two great kingdoms,

The four corners of the Cross must be joined by the chosen Queen of Tarlis.

For only then, can the Eye of Magus shine,
And bring about the downfall of the Dark One.
And the land be cleansed of evil,
Healed by the joining of the two."

A half laugh escaped her throat, and she shook her head. "How did you remember?"

"Because it was important to *you*." He met her eyes, his as clear as a summer's day. "How else are the two kingdoms to be joined as one if you do not marry Kaden? Did you learn nothing from what we went through? We should fight for what we believe in." He smiled sadly. "A tiny Faerie once taught me that."

Tannith remained silent, contemplating her friend's words, then nodded. "You are right. My father will not keep me from Kaden's side." She reached up and brushed a kiss across Etan's cheek, then raced for the door.

"Good luck," he called after her, his voice trailing off as she disappeared down the stairwell.

****

She burst into her father's study unannounced.

Upon seeing his daughter, Ephraen leaned forward in his chair, poured a goblet of wine, and held it out to her.

She accepted it absently.

"I was going to send for you." He started to rise.

"No, Father." She set the goblet on the table beside him and pushed him firmly back into his seat. "I will do the talking." She folded her arms across her chest. "Who gave the Council the right to deny Kaden my hand? Who gave *you* the right to say whom I will marry? I think, after all I have been through, I have earned the right to that choice."

Her father made to rise. "Tannith, I—"

"No." She cut him off. "Kaden raised a force to defeat the mightiest enemy to ever assemble on Tarlis. After seeing his family slaughtered, he guided an inexperienced princess on a quest to save a nation. He loved me as no man will ever love me. And you, Father, sent him away." She breathed deeply. "I hope this is a proud day for you. For it is one I will remember always."

She picked up her goblet and flung it into the blazing hearth, and the fire hissed and danced in the grate. She turned back. "Kaden earned the right to my hand. He is the bravest man I have ever known. And by the gods, I shall wed him with or without your blessing. He will return with his army and when he does," she straightened and met his violet eyes, "I will be leaving with him for Glen-Dorrach. And—" She took a breath. "As for me being wed to Etan…I—"

Ephraen leaned back in his red velvet chair and clapped his hands. "Fine speech, daughter—worthy of a future queen—however, totally unnecessary."

She frowned. "Unnecess—"

He raised a hand. "Sit." His words were calm, but their softness cut through her anger. "A man cannot get a word in edgeways. If you had not interrupted me when you first entered, you would be halfway to catching your young king by now."

Disbelief warred with hope. "What do you mean, interrupted?"

He glanced past her to the open door, and she rounded to see Ohma step through the archway, his wrinkled face holding a smile. "My lady, how nice to see you again."

"Ohma has been using his powers to allow his mind to float free." Ephraen moved to greet the Mage. "He has been searching the words of every ancient script and tome of Law he has been able to get his wrinkled hands on since arriving." The old king smiled sinking back into his chair. "A thousand summers of ancient chronicles to be precise." Her father's deep violet eyes gleamed.

"Nowhere can a *written* law be found stating an Elisian cannot marry out of their race. I had been trying to stall your young man until Ohma could complete his search, but he was determined to have his answer. I had to allow him to face the Council." He watched Ohma straighten his robes out behind him and settle into the seat opposite.

"Your Druid friend has, only a short time ago, found that which we sought." He smiled. "No answer at all. Now if the Council decides to object to my decision, there will be nothing they can use to support their claim. The books are empty of any law stating you cannot marry out of your race."

"But Etan said—"

"A ruse only." Her father cut her off and settled back into his seat. "I had to know how much you really cared for this young man. I had to be certain." He threw her a pleading look. "Can you forgive an old man? Or two?" He glanced at Ohma.

Tannith fought a gamut of perplexing emotions, anger, surprise, then…hope. "Of course, I can forgive you. But what does this mean?" Her heart stilled.

"Are you daft, child? You are able to marry who you will. It was an old Elisian custom that had been adhered to throughout the generations to stop our bloodline from being diluted further, but it was never made law. Customs can be changed or broken, laws cannot. I will speak to the Council. Now you best be off, should you wish to catch your king before sundown."

Tannith released the breath she was holding. She leaned forward to grasp her father's cheeks between two hands, and kissed him soundly on the forehead, then did the same to Ohma.

"You devious old men." She smiled. "I love you—I love you both."

Ohma chuckled. His dark gray eyes alight with merriment.

Tannith grinned and spun on her heel to dash from the room. Laughter from the two old men followed her down the staircase and across the foyer out the castle doors. There she drew to a halt as she spied Etan holding Phoenix.

The stallion was saddled and whinnied and stamped impatiently.

Etan pushed the reins into her hand. "I thought you might need him."

She leaned up and placed a kiss on her friend's cheek, then leapt down the steps to her horse, and threw herself upon his back. Slapping the reins lightly to his neck, the black horse bolted through the courtyard and out the castle gates.

Once over the rise, she turned her horse from the road and cut across the open fields. Sensing her urgency, the great stallion's hooves barely touched earth. It was as if he and the wind were one.

Through the village and down the Itana Pass, woman and horse moved in unison. They broke onto the Blue Grass Plains, Phoenix's powerful strides eating up the miles as the Gods of Creation splashed orange and gold across the heavens.

Tannith veered toward the river and spied Kaden's men camped at the edge of the Living Forest. She drew Phoenix to a rearing halt, slipped to the ground and tossed a young Elisian soldier the reins. "Kaden? Where is he?"

"My lady, what—"

"The king, where is he?" She cut across his speech.

"By the river." He pointed. "He wanted to be alone."

She turned and ran toward the nearby rise.

"He does not want to see anyone," the young man shouted.

"He will see me," she called over her shoulder.

****

Tannith found Kaden sitting on the riverbank, knees bent, his midnight hair falling forward around his face as he stared blankly into the water.

"Leave my supper, Yole, and go. I have no wish for company."

"Shall I also leave, my lord?"

Kaden swung. "Tannith—"

She dropped to her knees and touched a finger to his lips. "Hush. It is all over. It was a mistake."

He dragged her into his arms with a frown. "What are you talking about? What mistake? What are you doing here?"

"We can marry. There was never a law forbidding it. All this time, it was a folklore which my people had adopted, forbidding intermarriage, but it was never decreed a real law. Ohma found the truth. He has been searching ancient books and scrolls of Elisian Law for days." Tannith smiled shyly and looked away. "My

283

father gives his blessing."

Kaden smoothed her hair back from her face. "Had he not, it would have made no difference. You know that?"

She smiled, her arms encircling his neck. "That is why I love you. You are so stubborn."

He stood and brought her to her feet and swept her up hard against his chest. His mouth coming down over hers to seal a pact that would be stronger than life itself— a love that would stretch through the mists of time and follow them both into the Ever-after.

****

From his vantage point beneath a craggy oak on the next hill, an old man in indigo robes and a face like worn parchment watched two lovers embrace and sink beneath a willow.

Contented, he turned away, and from the deep confines of his cloak, he pulled a page torn from a tome of Elisian Law. Tearing it into tiny pieces, he scattered it to the breeze to be swept away.

"So, in the end, there will also be a beginning," he murmured to the wind, and a white crow cawed in the tree overhead.

Epilogue

Tannith and Kaden were married at Wolveryne Castle in the proper Dorrachian tradition, eight days and eight nights of merriment and feasting. They stayed to rule the Kingdom of Glen-Dorrach.

In the clearing that overlooked the Tinsliegh Valley, Kaden erected a monument in commemoration of his parents and young sister. Beside it stood another, for those who had lost their lives in the battle at Wolveryne Castle, and in between, a large statue of a white tiger in memory of Erik, the young king who never had a chance to rule.

A year later King Ephraen's heart failed him, leaving Tannith and Kaden the undisputed rulers of Tarlis. They moved their court to Dragonbane Castle.

Kaden and Tannith's rule was a popular and prosperous one. She bore him a son and two daughters.

Kaden bestowed the title of Regent on Etan, until such a time as Erik's son would come of age.

For two summers, Etan ruled the province of Glen-Dorrach alone. Then, one day, he saddled his horse and made the long journey to Dragonbane Castle. There, he asked Skylah, The Lady of Sabiah, to be his wife.

She accepted.

A word about the author…

Julie A. D'Arcy grew up reading the likes of Lord of the Rings, Once and Future King, and every fairy-tale she could get her hands on. Later on, falling in love with the works of David Gemmell, Terry Brooks, and Johanna Lindsey.

Her love of both the Fantasy and the Romance genres prompted her to try her hand at writing her own novel.

She began writing her first novel in 1995 and had her first book published in 1999 and went on to win the 1999 Dorothy Parker RIO Award for Women's fantasy fiction. The same novel was also runner up in the Australian RWA Ruby Award, 1999, and several other U.S.A awards.

Julie A. D'Arcy has written eight full-length novels, four novellas, and has just completed another Fantasy novel, a sequel to her two-book, Dark Fantasy series, The Cross of Tarlis: The Awakening, and The Cross of Tarlis: The Reckoning.

Julie lives in rural Victoria, Australia with her spoiled Oriental cat, Keila.

She has a Diploma of Art and Design and for many years ran a prosperous Fantasy Pottery business as well as writing. She has a love of travel and has visited the UK, Asia, many European countries, and hopes to one day visit the U.S.A.

Blog: https://authorjuliedarcy.com/
Website: https://juliedarcyauthor.com

CPSIA information can be obtained
at www.ICGtesting.com
Printed in the USA
BVHW091515200922
647492BV00011B/747

9 781509 243051